Night Before August

Night Before August

by

Ron Peters

A Dun Wheeling novel

ISBN 1-58961-205-1

Published by PageFree Publishing, Inc.
733 Howard Street
Otsego, MI 49078
www.pagefreepublishing.com

Dedication

In loving memory of

my parents,

George and Evelyn Peters,

and our children's adopted grandparents,

Harold and Mary Power.

ACKNOWLEDGEMENTS

TWO very special people have made significant contributions to this work and deserve particular recognition: Jennifer Nielsen and Tom Horner. Their online critiques, comments, suggestions, and encouragement have distinctly shaped this novel. Thanks so much, critters. You guys are great.

A special thanks to Nancy Civale for her review and reality check.

And to Sharon and Julie, wife and daughter, for their honest feedback and belief that I may one day become a serious author.

Guilt is nature's reminder that you've screwed up.
—Dun Wheeling

—

CHAPTER 1

THE remote hunting camp was the only place he knew to hide. His identity was compromised—they were trying to kill him again.

This time there was a warning. When he'd returned to his apartment, something had been out of place. He couldn't put his finger on it. He just knew. Knew enough to pack and flee.

There'd been no warning the first time. A sudden explosion of glass as the bullet shattered the window and lodged itself in the chair, an inch from his head.

Now he was on the run again. How many times could he do this? How many times before their threats became lethal?

Alex struggled to keep the nose of the canoe pointed parallel to the shoreline, but a stiff breeze blowing from the northwest fought him all the way. Shifting more to the mid-section of the canoe, he hoped to relieve the strain and tension on his neck and back muscles that were beginning to ache from the effort.

The July moon offered little illumination as it cowered behind the coal-black clouds that rose in the sky like huge, angry fists. If he remembered its description correctly, the lake wasn't very deep, and tonight its molten-black surface concealed anything hidden beneath. He was torn between staying close to shore for safety and far enough out to avoid any submerged boulders and logs. With no light and the wind whipping the water into frothy whitecaps, he might as well have been blind.

Alex pushed on, tempted to raise his voice to the sky and scream out his frustrations, but he knew there'd be no answer. Not tonight.

The soulful cry of the loon echoed across the darkened waters, as though searching for something no longer there. His eyes scanned the lake, looking for the loon, but neither sight nor sound revealed its location. Perhaps they had that in common.

His body tensed as the canoe bottom scraped across something under the water, then relaxed somewhat as the fragile craft floated free. Alex looked up. There, in front of him, some fifty yards ahead, was the shrouded outline of a wooden structure. Maybe this was his answer, after all.

As he got closer to the shoreline, the tall pines that guarded the lake acted as a buffer to the wind and allowed the angry waters to calm somewhat. He was there. The small hunting camp his boyhood friend had described to him so many times. A wooden, one-room hunting and fishing camp with bunks and a wood stove. But not much else. Oh, yes, he almost forgot. The outhouse. He laughed at the thought, but quickly choked it off as he looked over his shoulder.

But here, he'd be safe for a while. If he were careful.

In spite of his relief, he shivered—not that he was all that cold, he just wasn't used to being the prey.

CHAPTER 2

THE sharp crack of a breaking twig invaded Alex's senses. He'd been lying on one of the bunks in the camp, half-asleep, desperately wanting to escape the reality of his situation, but not daring to close his eyes. He struggled to fight off the beckoning blanket of sleep.

Alex half-rose and leaned on one elbow. Maybe it was an animal foraging in the night. He hoped that was true, but the shuffle of dry leaves erased that wish and brought him to full alert.

He sat on the edge of the bed and slowly turned his head from side to side, like a radar dish trying to find the source of a weak signal. Still fully clothed and ready to go if necessary, he considered crawling over toward the front windows, but quickly put that aside.

A faint whisper, maybe the wind wrestling with the pines, maybe not. Alex now had to assume they had found him, and he didn't have time to figure out how. They were there to kill him.

He eased off the bunk and crawled on hands and knees to the back door. As he opened it, inch-by-inch, he inhaled, expecting the hinges to squeak. He was lucky, not a sound. The woods behind the cabin looked like they were immersed in a tar pit; he could barely make out the nearest tree. Thankful he hadn't lighted the oil lamp and ruined his night vision, he slipped out the back door. In a low crouch, he ran for the nearest clump of wild raspberry bushes at the edge of the forest, where the aisles between the white pines began.

He needed help. But who? He couldn't trust his handler, not after this. He had the name of an agent, but could he trust him? He'd never know unless he got away.

Another twig snapped, and then another. The jarring noise carried like a whip crack in the still night air. Whoever they were, they were right outside the front of the cabin. He didn't have much time. Still in a crouch, he ran to a large pine tree and stopped. Using it for cover, he looked back at the cabin.

Oh, Jesus! He'd left the back door of the cabin open. They would know he'd left that way and would be on him in no time. His first impulse was to flee, abandon all attempts at stealth, and hope to outrun them. But they had guns, and you can't outrun what's in them.

Forcing deep breaths into his lungs, he turned and stayed in a low crouch as he made his way deeper into the forest. The veiled moon was his friend, for it hid his escape route. But it also was his enemy—he was already running into branches and stumbling over roots and rocks.

He didn't care. His need to survive was strong. Even stronger than his need for justice against those that were doing this to him. He wished for a gun, a knife, any weapon, while realizing they would be useless in his hands against professional killers.

Still maintaining caution, he increased his pace through the bushes and low tree branches. They grabbed at him, tried to capture him, but he forced his way through as they tore at his clothes and ripped long cuts in his skin. He wiped his hand along his arm, and felt the wet, sticky blood. No matter. His injuries were not life threatening—his pursuers were.

Alex stopped to listen. Not a sound. Maybe they hadn't found his trail. Maybe they'd found the camp empty and assumed he'd left earlier. He still decided to keep working away from the camp, to get into the woods as far as he could, find a place to hide and hole up for the night.

As he turned to continue, a grouse exploded into the air right in front of him, its wings beating frantically against the air to gain altitude. Alex's body recoiled, then froze. He gulped huge drafts of air as his heart started again, and he could feel the strong surges in his temples as it worked to catch up.

A dead branch exploded just behind his head. Another branch on his left shattered and swung on its bark hinge. His panicked mind now registered the soft popping sounds of the silenced weapons. They were close behind.

All need for caution abandoned, Alex urged his body forward to breakneck speed. Twisting, turning, leaping over small gullies, hurdling fallen logs, careening off unyielding tree trunks, he ran on without looking back.

A narrow trail branched off to his right, but he ran straight ahead, hoping to confuse his pursuers. The pine trees were thinner here, but the wild berry bushes more dense than ever. He pushed on, like a lunatic in a giant maze, stopping for nothing, running until he thought his lungs would burst.

Ahead he heard the gurgling of a small stream. Reaching a small rise, he looked down and saw it. The stream was shallow, but the water was racing by as if it were also being pursued.

Alex rushed down the hill and skidded to a stop just short of the water's edge. The stream looked to be about ten feet wide. He climbed part way back up the hill, turned, and without hesitation ran down the slope like an Olympian going for the long jump of his life. Launching himself from the bank, he sailed over the stream and prayed for soft dirt on the other side.

It happened too fast for him to be disappointed. No soft dirt awaited him. The other side of the stream was strewn with large sloping boulders partially covered with moist green moss. Seeing the moss, the thought that he must be traveling north flashed through his mind just before his feet slammed into the boulders and instantly lost traction. The impact jarred his whole body, the pain shooting up his legs like sharp spears. The steep upslope of the boulders stopped his forward momentum, but he couldn't hold his balance and slipped backwards towards the cold water. He tried to twist his body in midair, but to no avail. He landed on the back of his shoulders, and his head snapped back into a granite-veined rock.

As his body slid into the waiting stream, his last thought was that he was no longer heading north.

CHAPTER 3

THE shrill ring of the office phone startled Lucy Cannon. She jerked her head around and banged it on the underside of the desk drawer. "Damn!"

Climbing out from under the desk, where she had been trying to arrange the tangled mess of computer and phone cords, she picked up the phone as she rubbed the bruise on the back of her head.

"Wheeling Associates," she announced in her most professional voice. She cradled the phone on her left ear while she searched for a pen and something to write on.

Her desk was in complete disarray, in spite of this being the third day in the new office. Most of that time had been spent arranging the new furniture, hanging what few pictures they had, placing the potted plants she had bought with her own money, and getting Dun's office in shape. Now, she was finally getting around to her desk. With her luck, the phone rings.

"Good morning. I need to speak to Dun Wheeling."

"May I tell him who's calling?"

"Agent Harrison of the FBI."

"Er…excuse me?"

"The FBI, ma'am."

"Oh…just a moment, sir."

She tried to put the call on hold and stabbed at the intercom button, missing it slightly. "Damn!"

"What?"

"Oops…not you, sir. I hit the wrong button. Hang on."

Lucy pressed the hold again, smoothed out her dress, put on her glasses, and found the intercom button. She wasn't used to the new phone system, and neither she nor Dun had expected any calls this early in the game.

As she pressed the intercom, she reached behind her for her office chair, pulling it closer so she could sit. Unfortunately, she didn't pull it close enough, for as she eased into the chair she settled on the front edge. Now aligned in the proper position, the chair castors rolled backward, leaving nothing but air between Lucy and the floor. She hit the thin layer of carpet that covered the concrete floor with a thump, toppled backward, and came to rest with her feet higher than the desk and the phone cord in a tangled mess around her legs.

"Double Damn!"

Dun heard the commotion through the intercom. "What's going on out there? Sounds like a one-woman demolition team. Are you all right?"

Lucy caught her breath, untangled the phone cord, and pulled herself to her feet. "Of course. Everything's fine." She decided to wait until she transferred the call to Dun before trying to untangle herself further. She didn't want him to think she was a complete bumbling idiot.

"Could have fooled me. What's up?"

* * *

Dun Wheeling was sitting at his desk, working on a plan to promote his newly opened PI agency, which consisted of a small three-room office in a leased one-story building in the not-so-nice outskirts of Alexandria, Virginia.

Lucy's voice rasped and warbled through the intercom line. "There's a man on the phone wanting to speak to you. He says he's from the FBI."

Dun made a mental note to call the phone company and have the intercom line checked. "The FBI? You're kidding. We haven't been in business long enough to get in trouble. And it can't be one of those damn collection attorneys, all my debts are paid. Are you sure he said FBI?"

"Sure as my name is Lucy Podunkis."

"That's reassuring, Mrs. Cannon."

"Do you want to speak to him?"

"Sure, I'll take it from here." He switched over to the incoming line and released the hold. "Dun Wheeling."

"This is Knott Harrison of the FBI."

He paused. "OK. I'll play your game. If you're not Harrison, who are you?"

"I'm—"

"Wait a minute! Knott Harrison? The one I graduated with?" Dun's brain was just kicking into gear after his second cup of coffee.

"You got it, buddy."

"For God's sake, how the hell are you? Been…what…fifteen years?"

"Yep, 'bout that. Missed seein' your ugly mug. Missed your wiseass cracks even more."

Dun smiled. "Ass cracks? Yep, that's you."

"Funny. Got yourself set up in a new fancy office, I hear."

"New, yes. Fancy, no. But how did you know that? I just hung out my shingle yesterday."

"I work for the FBI. Remember?"

"C'mon, Knott. You're kidding."

"Nope. I'm not. When have you and I ever kidded each other?" Knott chuckled, then continued. "I just finished reading the file about how you handled that kidnapping case in Jacksonville. Nice work."

Dun sat up in his chair. Knott wasn't kidding. He must work for the FBI, otherwise how would he know about that case?

"Thanks, but a lot of luck, really." His eyes briefly went unfocused as the painful reminder of the outcome of that incident brought moisture to them.

"Not from what I see. Reading between the lines, it looks like you outsmarted our local boys down there."

"I think I may have outsmarted myself on that one."

"What? How's that?"

"A long story, Knott. For another time…"

"OK. Anyway, when I got the file and saw your name, I couldn't believe it. Here we are, almost working side by side for years, and not knowing it."

"Sounds like a lunch invitation."

"It is. How 'bout Joe Theisman's? Right near you."

Dun's face drew into a thin smile. He felt quivers in his stomach whenever he thought of his experience hugging the porcelain pony in the restroom at Theisman's. And that's where he had first met Sally Olivia's pompous brother, Aaron Suttle Sawgrass.

"Ah…let's try someplace else."

CHAPTER 4

SIDNEY sat at the bar, cradling the cold beer between his palms. It felt good. The weather was so damn hot in Washington in July. He couldn't believe it. Just moved here two months ago and the hottest heat wave in years hits. Unreal.

He was beginning to have doubts about taking the job with the FBI. The pay wasn't so great, his lousy apartment was more than he could afford, the traffic sucked, and the heat was miserable. His apartment air conditioner couldn't keep up with it, and sounded like a dying donkey sucking air through its ass.

Here he was, over one thousand miles from home, with a new job in a new location, and nobody knew he was the greatest programmer in the country. His boss was a complete idiot, didn't know an IP address from a bit bucket.

"Another beer, Sid?" The bartender wiped the bar in front of Sidney with a damp towel and then threw it over his shoulder.

"Sidney. It's Sidney."

"Oh. Sorry, Sidney. No offense, buddy."

"Sure. Yeah, bring me another. This one's almost dead."

"Comin' atcha, Sidney." The bartender moved to the beer locker and pulled out a popular brand of bottled draft beer. With a quick flick of his wrist, he popped the cap and put the bottle on the bar in front of Sidney.

"There ya' go, Sidney. That'll cool your insides."

"Maybe I should pour it in my air conditioner."

The bartender laughed, then moved to the other end of the bar to serve a new customer.

* * *

A blonde sitting at a nearby table with her girlfriend scanned the room and stopped when she saw the geek at the bar. She whispered something to her companion and they both laughed.

"I used to know a guy that looked like him," the blonde said, but her companion just nodded her head and continued to stare at the ice in her drink.

Returning her gaze toward the bar, the blonde took in the geek's features, while trying to remember the name of the guy he looked like.

Tall, gangly, fingers tap-tap-tapping on the bar. He was either nervous or had lots of excess energy, she guessed.

His pale freckled skin told her he was new to the area. No one was that pale, even if he stayed inside all the time and had red hair, which he didn't. Or maybe he came down from Alaska, or worked nights and slept all day.

His chicken lips framed a mouth that was too wide, and his squat bob of a nose seemed stuck on his face slightly off-center. Close-cropped light brown hair cemented the geek look.

She smiled. Only a face a mother could love. *God, I'll die if I ever have kids that look like that.*

The one redeeming value was his eyes. Large brown globes flashing intelligence, curiosity, and…what? Smugness? What'd he have to be smug about?

She couldn't remember that guy's name. Her scan moved on.

* * *

Sidney had noticed the blonde looking at him. He guessed she and her friend were here looking for excitement. Maybe if she knew he worked for the FBI, her glance might have lingered longer.

He admitted that the lure of working for the FBI got the better of him. Images of carrying a badge, wearing a shoulder holster, and people awed when he told them whom he worked for were naïve—he knew that. It was just another dull job, in a dirty old office, and a boss and colleagues who didn't appreciate his talents.

Sidney was a mainframe programmer. The only positive aspect of his work was receiving a Top Secret clearance. For what? A clunky system that was older than Einstein? A third-grade hacker could bust it in five minutes!

His job was to improve the security of the system and protect the sensitive information it contained. He had access to almost everything: Files, field reports, memos, analysis, planning documents, email accounts—everything except finances and personnel records. They were in another system in a different location. No big deal, he hated that stuff anyway.

The most interesting area was where the records for the Witness Protection Program were stored. They were supposedly double secured, with passwords that changed every thirty days. Big deal. You could drive a trailer truck through that security.

Out of the corner of his eye, Sidney noticed a young gal sitting next to him. Where'd she come from? He hadn't seen her sit down. Not bad. About his age, maybe a bit older. Nice figure. He tried to scope her out without looking at her, but turned away when she glanced his way.

"Hi," she said. "I've seen you here before. Live around here?"

Sidney cleared his throat and choked out something that sounded like "Hi."

"I'm Gloria. Live just around the corner. Came here to get out of the heat. You?"

"Ah…I'm Sidney. Live close by too." He half-turned toward her.

"Boy, isn't this heat something? I can't stand it. Moved here a week ago and haven't stopped sweating yet."

"Yeah, me too."

"Moved here, or sweating?"

Sidney laughed. She was sharp. "Both. My AC isn't working right." He was trying to act cool and not look at her, but his heart was beginning to accelerate some. Stay loose, he told himself. Women like men who aren't too anxious.

"Nothing works right in this heat! Even me." Sidney thought he saw a brief wink after that statement, but he wasn't sure.

He turned fully toward Gloria and smiled. She was not a great looker, but fairly pretty. She wore her clothes too tight, but that's okay. He liked that, made her exciting. She also seemed easy to talk to. That helped—he wasn't.

"Yeah. Me too. Uh, just hanging out here for a while."

"For a while?"

"Um, yeah, until my place cools down. Probably won't happen until Midnight. Can't sleep when it's hot."

"Gee, Sid, that's too bad. I just came in for a cold beer, then heading home to watch the special on ABC."

"Yeah... was gonna' watch that too. Not in this heat."

"Man, that's tough. Place really hot, huh?"

"Yeah, uh, like a steam bath."

"God, don't even mention that. Just thinking about it makes me sweat even more." She rubbed her hands over her shoulders and then down the sides of her dress. He followed her hands as they slid down her thighs and over her knees.

"OK." He didn't know what else to say. He turned away, hoping she hadn't noticed him staring.

"Don't take this wrong, but if I were you I'd be sleeping buck naked in that kind of heat. Least my nightie wouldn't be glued to my body."

The image of that made Sidney even more nervous. He took a sip of his beer to get his courage up. "Might try that. No one there but me. Who'd see?"

"Not me," she said with a soft giggle. "I can only imagine it."

"Yeah. Well, guess I'll go. Take a walk down by the river. See if I can find some cooler air."

"Won't find anything cooler than here. Brutal out there."

"Guess so. Wish they had a TV here."

"Well, ah...don't take this wrong, but you're welcome to watch it at my place. Long as you promise to behave yourself. I don't need any funny business."

"Ah, thanks, but guess not. You don't even know me. Don't want to put you out."

"You seem harmless enough to me. And I promise not to bite. I'd love the company; don't know anyone here yet. C'mon."

"Well..."

"Sure. I like talking to you. Maybe we could be friends. Whatdaya' say?"

"Yeah. Guess so. I don't have anyone to talk to either."

"Great. Let's stop by the sub shop around the corner and get a couple of roast beefs to snack on. Got a couple of beers in the fridge to wash them down. I get the couch. You get the floor. When it's over, you scoot. OK?"

"Yeah. No problem. Ah...thanks, Gloria."

"Oh, my pleasure, Sid." With a big smile, she hopped off the stool, took Sidney's arm, and led him toward the door.

He hadn't even noticed she called him "Sid."

CHAPTER 5

"KNOTT Harrison, you old duff." Dun extended his hand, thought better of it, and gave his friend a bear hug.

"Hey, Dun, you're lookin' good. For an old fart, that is." Knott was a big man, with a ruddy complexion that matched his flaming red hair. A few inches taller than Dun, wider across the shoulders, and several pounds heavier, his size and hair gave the word 'conspicuous' new meaning. While most men in the FBI avoided anything conspicuous, not having the 'FBI look' was an advantage for Knott in many situations.

Dun and Knott had been the tallest guys in their high school class, and that had formed the initial bond for their friendship. That and their sometimes-wacky sense of humor.

"Put on a few pounds since I last saw you," Dun said, picking up where they had left off years ago.

"And you seem a freckle shorter. Maybe gravity pushing you down as you age, causing you to bulge a little at the equator?" Knott laughed. They were back at it.

"Seriously, Knott, it's great to see you. Thought of you often, but never found out where you'd disappeared to."

"Well . . . can't really say. Did some spook stuff overseas for a while, then ended up with the FBI. You?"

"The only spook stuff I've done is to scare myself in the mirror in the morning. Dropped out of law school and became a PI."

"Really? Why'd you want to do a dumb thing like that?"

Dun scratched his chin. "Well, I went on to law school because of some misguided notion of protecting the rights of the poor and downtrodden. All I found were classmates who couldn't wait to graduate and start billing customers for their time. The big bet on campus was in which year of practice they would hit the million billing mark.

"Yeah, that sounds typical."

"So," Dun continued, "after my third year I left. Couldn't stomach those jerks. All I took with me were several large student loans that were hard to repay at non-lawyer wages. Went from there to using my limited law knowledge in working for local law firms, gathering information they needed for their cases. But, I quickly found that making a good living as a contract investigator had a limited future."

"Now you've got your own PI agency. Wheeling Investigations?"

"Yep. My dream. All I have to do is make it work."

"Speaking of that, where did you get that assistant?"

"Lucy? She's great."

Knott smiled. "Well, she must be hot, since she doesn't seem to have any other talents."

"Hot?" Dun laughed and slapped the table. "Hot? She's old enough to be my mother, you moron. She was the central secretary when I rented the shared office space in my other location. Maybe a mite unpredictable, but fierce as a female lion protecting her cubs, loyal as an eunuch guarding his harem, dependable as a—"

"Okay, I get the picture."

"Not really. Her husband took off to the Bahamas with his Barbie doll look-alike. Left her holding the bag without a penny. After working with her for a couple of years, I jumped at the chance to take her with me when I opened the new agency. I'd bet my life on that woman."

"Let's hope you never have to. But a PI? God, how could you? What happened, you couldn't make it in the FBI?"

Dun was aware that the FBI considered PI's as wannabe Feds, but he also knew Knott's style of barbed humor and came right back. "Well, you're right. I wanted to. But I was finally turned down by the FBI because I was too intelligent, left handed, and good looking."

"Man, if BS were money, you'd be rich. OK, but before we get into all that, let's grab a booth. I'm so hungry I could eat the ass out of a skunk."

"Only at a separate table." Dun laughed, grabbed Knott by the arm, and steered him toward a booth in a quiet corner of the restaurant.

After they ordered, they caught up on the years since graduation.

"So, no ring on your finger. Any women in your life?"

Knott paused and looked out the window before responding. "Just one. Was married for a short time, but my occupation at the time wasn't conducive to Cape Cod cottages with white picket fences. Long, unexplained absences didn't help much, either."

"Sorry. I didn't realize…" Dun punched his own leg under the table.

"No problem. My fault. After all this time, guess I'm still not over it."

"Yeah, really sorry. Let me stand up and bend over so you can kick me."

"No need, Dun. You didn't know. How about you?"

Dun inhaled. "Something similar, except we weren't married."

"Sally Olivia?"

"Jesus! How the hell do you know that?" Dun sat up straight and put both hands on the table, his knuckles turning white from squeezing the edge.

"Now I'm sorry. My turn to apologize. It was all in the file I just read. How's she doing?"

Dun slumped back into the booth. "Not too well. She's . . . ah…"

Just then, the waitress brought their order. "Two cheeseburgers for you, sir. With fries and a Coke. And, the grilled chicken salad for you sir. And a Coke. Anything else?"

"That's fine. We're all set. Thanks." Dun picked up his fork and started to attack his chicken.

As they ate, Dun and Knott continued to review old times. They had been quite a pair in high school, with a reputation for quick wit mixed with sometimes-obnoxious humor.

"Speaking of skunks, remember when you put that skunk in the high school ventilation system? The girls were screaming and some kids were out puking on the front steps. How'd you ever get that skunk in there without getting sprayed?"

Knott got this huge look of innocence on his face. "Moi?"

"Yeah, you. I know you did it."

"Okay, I'll fess up. I found a baby skunk in the woods just behind the school. Really cute, looked like it had lost its mother. I carried it up to the ventilation screen, opened it, and put the little guy in there. Then I closed the screen and poked at it with a long stick until it got mad and began exuding that wonderful odor."

Dun bent over with laughter. "I knew it. If they'd ever caught you, you'd still be in jail."

"Well, don't tell my present employer. They think I was a model citizen growing up." Knott pointed a finger at Dun. "And, what about you, Mr. Clean? How 'bout that time you were stealing pumpkins on Halloween night and bowling them down that long hill at cars coming up. Talk about a delinquent."

"You ought to know, you were there helping me."

"Oh, yeah…guess you're right. Well then, what about when you put that bag of fresh dog shit on that grumpy guy's front porch? You lit it on fire, rang the doorbell, and split."

Dun now had tears in his eyes. "Jeeze, I'd forgotten about that. He sure was pissed."

"And I bet his shoes smelled real nice after stamping out the fire."

Dun choked with laughter, but managed to spit out, "Oh yeah, grilled dog shit really does a number…" He couldn't finish.

The swapping of war stories went on until the waitress returned to the table and looked at Knott.

"Are you done, sir?"

"No, I'm Knott. He's Dun."

The waitress turned toward Dun and started to remove his plate.

"Hey! I'm not finished yet," Dun said as he retrieved his plate from her hands.

"Oh, I'm sorry, sir. I thought he said you were done."

"I am." Dun plunged his fork into the chicken salad and hefted a large mouthful.

The waitress paused for a moment, then started to turn away.

"Miss?" Knott said. "I'm finished."

The waitress turned around and gave Knott a quizzical look. "But, sir, you just said you weren't done."

"Right. I'm Knott. He's Dun."

"I must be losing my mind. Please excuse me for a moment." Without another word, the waitress turned and walked briskly toward the kitchen.

They waited for a moment, and then burst into laughter. "Man, we're still cookin'," Knott said, tears running from his eyes.

"Yep. Never fails, after all these years," Dun said, half-choking on his salad. They both reached across the table and gave a high five.

"We'd better give that poor woman a healthy tip."

"The best tip we could give her is to never wait on us again." Dun sat down, pushed his plate back, and folded his napkin on the table.

Still laughing, Knott continued where they had left off in the conversation. "Seems like our banter still works, but neither of us has had much luck on the women side."

"That's for sure." As Dun wiped his eyes, the smile erased from his face.

"Want to talk about it?"

"Not really. I'll work it out." Dun put the napkin back in his lap.

"OK. Let's skip over the women for a while. Besides, I've got some questions I need to ask."

Dun looked up. *Questions?*

CHAPTER 6

DUN scratched the little scar on his chin. *Questions? Oh yeah, I've got one big one. Like, what am I doing in this profession?*

His father wanted him to be a lawyer, or at least be in some profession where he had security and didn't have to make up everything as he went along. He tried that, and it didn't work. Law interested him. Lawyers didn't.

He was good with details and planning, and then again, he wasn't. Sometimes he would plan something to death; other times he'd rather wing it as he went along. Being left-handed and right-brained got complicated at times.

Yes, he was inexperienced, so of course he had to improvise. Nothing better than on-the-job training, as long as you weren't killed doing it. At least his instincts had kept him alive so far.

He vowed never to turn into the rough, casehardened gumshoe that always solved the case and got the woman. Well, maybe the woman part was okay. And solving cases did bring home the bacon. But, still, the gumshoe status—no way.

His mind lapsed back to when he had rescued Sally Olivia Sawgrass from the kidnappers in Jacksonville. That he found her was a bit of luck, he had to admit, although persistence also played a major role in his investigation.

But then, like John Wayne with a pistol drawn, he barged into the motel room where they were holding her and promptly got his brains scrambled by an old wooden chair. The real luck was that the abductors panicked and ran, leaving him the hero—with a new crease in his head.

That began his relationship with Sally Olivia. Then he broke the most sacred rule of his profession—don't get involved with a client. Oh, he got involved all right. But now she was gone again, and he didn't have a clue where she was or whether she was okay.

His luck with women usually turned into disaster.

Dun remembered one painful incident a few years earlier that now brought a smile to his face.

As Dun walked into the men's section of the local department store, he saw an attractive young saleswoman look up at him. *Wow! Now this could make my day!*

She was a knockout for her age, which he guessed to be about five or so years beyond his thirty-five years. Shoulder-length light brown hair, scooped behind each ear, and a face that could launch maybe not a thousand ships, but close to it. She was wearing a conservative, brightly colored blouse and a matching skirt—both beautifully tailored to accent her full figure. He surmised she must be a model working part-time between jobs.

She moved out from behind the counter and approached him. "May I help you, sir?"

Before Dun could kick his brain in gear, he muttered, "No thanks." He normally liked to browse by himself and not be flanked with pesky salespeople. Now, looking at her, he quickly changed his mind and tried to recover.

"Well, actually, I do need some new clothes." *Boy, that was a stupid response, Dun. Way to go. Strike one.*

She smiled as though that was actually an astute comment. "Are you looking for any particular items, sir? Sports jackets? Slacks? Let's see, I'd guess you to be about six-two, a little over two hundred pounds. Perhaps something in the tans to go with your sandy-colored hair? Definitely a blue shirt to bring out those dark hazel eyes."

Dun stared at her. He hadn't heard a thing she had said. Those two swimming pools she called eyes were inviting him to take a plunge. *Maybe she's not five years older than he was, definitely closer to his age. But then, hard to tell. And who cares?*

"Sir?"

"Oh, sorry. Yeah, about right. It's been a while since I've bought anything new. Too busy, I guess. By the way, didn't they used to have men working in this department?"

"Normally, yes. But we're short handed today, so guess you're stuck with me." The smile was gone, and the look on her face was a cross between disappointment and disgust.

Strike two.

"I'm sorry, Miss. That was stupid of me. I don't like shopping much."

"Perhaps you'd be more comfortable if I found a salesman to wait on you—"

"No! Not at all. In fact, I think a mature woman's viewpoint would be helpful." Just as those words escaped his lips, he knew he was in trouble.

"I'll call someone else."

God, I didn't mean 'mature' that way. Strike three. You're out.

"Look, I do apologize, Miss. Please forgive my stupid remarks. My brain and my mouth don't seem to be connected today. I'm very sorry. Please, I would appreciate your help."

"Certainly, sir. What would you like to see?" The iciness of her tone would freeze the fires in Hell.

Not knowing what else to say, he asked to look at dress shirts. "I prefer broadcloth, button downs."

"Button down shirts are not much in style these days," the saleswoman said, her expression broadcasting that she wasn't sure why she was trying to be helpful to this unsophisticated Neanderthal.

"I'm sure that's true," he said, smiling, "but I like the classic look. It also gives me a place–the collar button–to hang my sunglasses."

Without commenting, the saleswoman scooped her hair behind her ear and steered Dun toward the section where his style of shirts were located. "You can look through these, sir. I'll be over by the cash register if you need me." She turned and walked away.

He had not only struck out, he'd been thrown out of the ballpark.

Dun selected two shirts, one blue striped, and one a light blue, careful not to pick any with the manufacturer's name or logo displayed over the pocket—he disliked being caught up in the latest trends. Besides, someone had to take a stand against being a walking billboard.

He then ambled over to the belt section and fingered through two racks of belts. Not finding what he wanted, he searched for the saleswoman. She was across the aisle in the ladies underwear department.

Crossing over and passing through the bra and panties section, Dun approached her and asked for help in finding a belt.

"Garter?"

Dun's abrupt laugh turned the heads of several women nearby. "I deserved that," he said, still laughing.

The glacier surrounding her started to melt, her eyes twinkled, and she offered a slight smile. "I guess it's my turn to apologize. That was not very professional of me." Her face showed a slight flush.

"Not at all. I had it coming. I'll wait across the isle until you have a moment. I know you're busy. Take your time." He walked back to the men's department, still chuckling to himself.

Before long, the saleswoman returned, saying, "I appreciate your patience, sir. I'm afraid I have to cover two sections today."

"First, please drop the 'sir' bit. I'm not that old. Second, I admire your quick wit. And, as I said, I more than had it coming. Third, let's shake and start over." Dun extended his hand. *Maybe this will get me back in the ballgame.*

The saleswoman hesitated, then took his hand. Her face blossomed into a wonderful smile. "Deal," she said.

Her hand was firm, but soft. And warm, so warm. He didn't want to let go. He looked into her brown satin eyes for an embarrassing period of time. Finally, and with great reluctance, he released her hand.

At the same moment, the two new shirts, each wrapped in a shiny and slippery plastic bag, tumbled from his grasp. Dun instinctively tried to grab the bags as they spiraled downward, but the slippery plastic covers made them impossible to catch. They hit the floor and slid in opposite directions.

Dun and the saleswoman bent over at the same time to retrieve the new shirts. Their closeness and timing guaranteed that they would bump heads on the way down. Dun's weight also guaranteed he would win the collision contest.

The poor saleswoman was sent sprawling backward, her back hitting the wall behind her. As she slowly slid toward the floor, but Dun jumped forward and grabbed her arm to hold her up. As he did, one of her high-heel shoes fell off and she pirouetted around in an arc and slammed into him. He slipped his other arm under her armpit to hold her steady and they ended up almost nose-to-nose.

She was not a pretty sight; her hair disheveled, her legs spread wide apart, one shoe missing and the other tilting her like a car jack. Seeing the look on her face, Dun wasn't sure whether to laugh or profusely apologize.

Fortunately for him, he chose the latter. Collecting himself, Dun steadied her while she worked her feet back into her shoe and straightened her skirt.

"I'm so sorry," he said, backing off and removing his hands. Brevity seemed the best course of action right now. "I'm not this klutzy most days. Today is obviously an exception. Just point me in the direction of the better men's belts and I'll get out of your hair."

She just stared at him as though she were trying to decide whether to scream, place her pointed shoe in his crotch, or just walk away. Again, fortunately for him, she chose the latter.

He turned and looked for the ballpark exit.

Dun could think of several other occasions where his masculine charms had completely abandoned him, but those were too painful to recall.

"Dun! Are you listening?" Knott poked him in the arm to snap him out of his reverie. "I said I have some questions for you."

Dun nodded. "Sure. Me too."

No, he wasn't the casehardened gumshoe. And he hoped he never got to that point. But he was determined to make it in this crazy profession called private investigation. He had to. He had nowhere else to go.

CHAPTER 7

"QUESTIONS? What do you mean, questions?" Knott's last comment to Dun was just sinking in as he snapped out of his reverie.

"Oh, just a couple. No big deal."

"'No big deal coming from the FBI makes me nervous."

"Relax. Just wondering what you know about the Witness Protection Program?"

"Ah...let's see. It's run by the US Marshals, I think. And if I remember right, you guys get involved somehow." Dun scratched the small scar on his chin.

"Pretty close. Not bad for a new PI. What else?"

Dun thought for a moment. "It's set up to protect folks who testify against criminals, big time stuff. They get a secret identity and are established in a new location."

"A-plus, my boy. Anything else?"

"What the hell is this? Twenty questions?"

"Naw. Just wondering if you could use a little business?"

"Are you kidding? Of course, I could use a little business. I'm just getting started. Is this personal or government business?"

"Neither." From habit, Knott looked around the restaurant before continuing. "Seems like we've got a little problem. Internally. One of our witnesses has had his cover blown, and the bad guys are lookin' to erase his shadow."

"I assume 'neither' means unofficial, like no pay. Screw up and the 'Secretary will disavow any knowledge of you'—that kind of thing."

"You catch on quick, Dun. You musta' grown some new brains since high school."

"Sounds like if I get involved with this, what few brains I have could get a new hole in 'em. One's enough."

"Not much of a chance there, but I won't kid you, there could be some danger. However, you'll get all the protection I can give. Plus, while I can't give you any fees for this, I can cover your expenses. Generously cover, if you know what I mean."

"What's your role in this?" Dun's mind was churning like a whirlpool, with warning flags and buzzers going off all over.

"To find out who the internal mole is and nail him...or her."

"Internal to what? FBI or Marshals?"

"Whatever. Not sure yet. But I need someone who's unknown to handle some details and digging around. Once we get wind of who it might be, we'll set a trap."

"This is for real, Knott? No bullshit."

"No bullshit, man. Real serious shit. Whoever is doing this could endanger more than just this guy's life. Could compromise the whole program."

Dun unconsciously scratched the little scar on his chin again, trying to decide if this was more than he wanted to take on. Talk about jumping from the frying pan into the fire. He could get his ass burned big time on this one. Maybe more than just his ass.

"Why me? I don't have a lot of experience with this kind of thing. I was just hoping to work on skip traces for a while, until I can get on my feet. Taking on something like this, with no fees, doesn't sound like a good investment in the future, as they say in the commercials."

"There is no one inside I can trust. It could be someone I work with, or even the local AIC—Agent In-Charge. I can't take a chance that whoever this is will learn about the investigation. Besides, while your experience sucks, from what I read in your file you seem to have good instincts. If you're still the Dun Wheeling I knew when we were best friends in high school, there's no one I can trust more."

"Wow. Thanks, Knott. I hope I can live up to that."

"You will...or die trying." Knott laughed, and then continued. "Just a little humor there, buddy."

"Yeah, very little. So, why can't you hire me as a PI consultant, or whatever you do in this kind of thing?"

"Well, as you well know, most FBI agents look down their noses at PI's. No offense, but we FBI think we are the greatest and the latest, and PI's are piss ants."

"Well, I hate to tell you this, but this PI is no way a FBI wannabee. You can put me on the FBI nogoddamnwayabes list."

Knott laughed. "Further, if I hire you as a consultant, the paperwork gets around, everyone will know something is up. Your life wouldn't be worth crap if the mole found out what you were up to. Better to keep it between us. As I said, I can cover your expenses, and no one knows either one of us is checking this out."

"Sorry, but I'm a little confused. Won't folks inside know you are working on this, whatever 'this' is?"

"Nope. I'm a special agent, independent of the local office, so I don't have to answer to anyone here. I work various assignments, some internal investigations, but mostly liaison with other agencies, like the CIA, DIA, and…ah…others."

"DIA?" Dun was scratching his chin again.

"Yeah, Defense Intelligence Agency."

"Oh, yeah, heard of them. What do they do?"

"You don't wanna' know."

"So, who do you report to?"

"You don't wanna' know—someone much higher than I'll ever reach."

"Gee, this sounds like a whole bunch of fun. And I suppose, when it's over—if I agree to do it—you'll have to kill me."

"No. But just before you die of natural causes, decades from now, I'll have to inject you with bubble bath."

"And that will…?"

"Make you fart your brains out and garble your words with bubbles so you can't tell any secrets." Knott's grin was contagious, and Dun couldn't help but laugh.

"OK. Let me chew on this overnight. I'll call you tomorrow. If I agree—and that's a big IF—what's my first step?"

"Wait for the guy who's been compromised to make a call to you."

"How will he know who to call, or my number?"

Knott's grin started to fade. "He'll have your cell phone number, or rather mine, but it will be routed to yours if I don't answer."

"Cell phone? I don't have a cell phone."

"You do now. Every good PI should have one." Knott reached into his pocket and retrieved a small cell phone, smaller than any Dun had ever seen. "This little baby is good all around the world, from anywhere. Has built-in security and encryption. No conversations can be tapped or traced. Just don't lose it."

Dun looked at the phone. It was hard to believe something that small could have all that. He tried to turn it on, but couldn't find a switch anywhere.

"Just hold it close to your mouth and say 'on.' It's already programmed for your voice commands. No one else can operate it. To see the phone number, say 'ID,' and to call me, say 'Knott.'"

"Jesus!"

"Sorry, but that word won't bring help." Knott openly laughed at his own joke.

Dun held the phone up close to his mouth and said "on." The unlighted screen instantly displayed the word 'ready.' When he said "ID," the cell phone number displayed for two seconds and then went back to the 'ready' mode.

"How'd you program this for my voice? You must have recorded our phone conversation, right?"

Knott's eyes squinched a little and a thin smile appeared, then his expression went blank. He stared at Dun, until Dun began to laugh.

They both laughed at the same time and said, "You don't wanna' know."

CHAPTER 8

THE tap of leather heels on the tile floor echoed down the long narrow hallway. The only illumination came from the red exit sign at the far end. The short, slight-built man was wearing a white medical coat with no markings or badge. The stethoscope swung effortlessly from his neck.

He stopped at one door, put a key in the lock, and quietly opened the door into a darkened room. Lying on a solitary bunk was a young woman, her blond hair the only discernible feature in the subdued light. She was motionless, almost lifeless, with only a white sheet and dark blanket covering her body.

The doctor paused, as if to reassure himself that she was still alive, and then closed and locked the door. He walked back the way he had come, and exited the hallway through double swinging doors. Turning left, he strode through two more hallways before coming to a dimly lighted area that served as a lounge area for several offices.

"She okay, Dr. Shavitz?"

"Yes. The shot will carry her through the night." Dr. Mark Shavitz was CEO and trauma specialist at the small private clinic in the Catskills that catered to wealthy clients. He had relocated from Florida only ten months ago, and already the clinic was doing quite well.

"I don't know about all this. What if something happens?"

"Nothing will happen. We've been through all this before." Mark walked over to the nurse and put his arms around her waist. "Everything will be fine, Bev. Don't worry."

"But, what if…"

"Shhhh. I told you, I've got it covered. She's a trauma patient being treated for severe shock and depression. We have to keep her partially sedated for awhile, and then we'll start her treatment." Mark roved his hands over her body and started nuzzling her neck.

"I know. Still....oh Mark, you drive me crazy." Bev pressed her body close to his and curled her arms up around his neck, drawing him closer still. Her lips reached up toward his and opened in invitation.

As Mark steered her toward the oversized plush couch placed along one wall, he began unbuttoning her white nurse's uniform. She offered no resistance as he gently laid her on the couch and continued with the buttons as he kissed her neck and now exposed shoulders.

Bev closed her eyes and smiled. "Mmmm, this is wonderful…"

"Let's see if I can really drive you crazy," Mark murmured, as he began ripping the remaining buttons off her uniform.

Bev opened her eyes. "Mark! What are you doing? I don't like that look in your eyes!"

CHAPTER 9

AT first, he thought he'd gone blind. Alex's eyes fluttered, then slowly opened. As he became more conscious, he realized it was as dark as the inside of a deep cave. Barely perceptible lighting came from an old oil lamp scarcely glowing from its perch on a rough pine-board table.

After several moments, his eyes adjusted and he could make out crude wooden furniture, a large animal rug spread across much of the floor, and a stuffed chair covered with a faded Army blanket to hide years of use.

Sitting in the chair was an old man who'd just stepped out of a vintage mountain-man movie. It was hard to tell where the hair on his head left off and his beard began. A well-used pipe was between his teeth, and his clothes looked as if they had been fashioned from animal hides. He was staring straight at him, not saying a word.

"Uhmm…where am I?"

"Just relax, sonny. You've got a nasty gash on yore head."

Alex reached up and gingerly fingered the layers of bandages on his head. Long strips of cloth crossed his forehead, wrapped so they covered most of the back of his head. Something underneath had been used as padding.

Suddenly, a wave of pulsating pain hit him, as if someone was hitting the back of his head with sharp bricks. Alex put his arm down and held his breath, hoping it might help. It didn't.

With the energy of a man forty years younger, the old woodsman stood up from the chair and without a sound walked over to the cabin window and looked out. On a table just below the window lay a hunting rifle and a long-bladed skinning knife.

"Guess those men lookin' for ya' finally gave up. 'Bout time. Sure as hell weren't no woodsmen." The man spat a wad of tobacco juice into an old rusty coffee can.

"What happened? How long have I been here?" Alex tried to sit up, but the pain in his head made him think better of it.

"Just stay quiet, sonny. No need ta worry. Yore safe here. You'll be back on yore feet real quick. Get some sleep and we'll talk in tha mornin'."

Alex drifted back into sleep. Dreams of men chasing him, bullets seeking their mark, and cold water surrounding his body kept him twitching for several hours.

* * *

The old man picked up his hunting rifle and slipped out the cabin door. Outside, the predawn light and heavy ground fog gave everything a haunted look. The man moved through the woods without making a sound, his eyes and ears taking in everything around him.

His log cabin was located about two miles from the stream where Alex had fallen, and was nestled into a thick patch of briars and pine trees. Anyone not familiar with its location could walk by at ten yards out and not see it. The white mortar between the logs had long darkened with age, and the roof was camouflaged with layer upon layer of pine needles. The chimney, seldom used, was a black pipe that exited the rear of the cabin and blended in with the old pines.

As he approached the stream, his pace slowed and his senses sharpened. The hunting rifle lay crooked in his arm, ready for use if need be, and the skinning knife was sheathed and stuck in a rawhide belt around his waist.

He crossed the stream, easily jumping across where Alex had fallen, and continued on toward the camp where Alex had been. Following the half-mile trail was as easy as trailing a bull elephant across damp sand on an open beach.

He circled around the camp in a wide oval, stopping often to sniff the air and listen for unnatural sounds. Nothing. Dead quiet, except for the scampering squirrels and the crows off in the distance. He opened the hunting camp door with the tip of his rifle and eased inside, keeping his body low.

The camp had been tossed like a garden salad. Everything was upside down, clothes and furniture strewn around as if a tornado had danced through the place. The old man crossed to the front of the camp and looked out the window toward the lake. There wasn't even a ripple on the water; the men had left long ago.

He pulled a worn pillowcase from under his jacket and gathered up the few clothes and articles Alex had left behind. Without a sound, he left the camp and melted into the woods.

CHAPTER 10

SIDNEY followed Gloria up the stairs to her apartment. Her tight dress rode up with every step. He couldn't take his eyes off her.

"Here we are. C'mon in and get comfy. I'll grab the beers."

Sidney looked around. It was obvious she'd just moved in. A small, two-room apartment that had hardly any furniture. The living room/kitchen combination held one couch, one end table, and a TV on a stand. In the corner were a small table and two kitchen chairs. All the stuff looked new, like it was rented. The bedroom didn't even have a door, and the small bed was by itself. No bed stand, no dresser, no mirror. *Wow. Thought my place was bare.*

He watched Gloria as she opened the small apartment-sized refrigerator and bent over to get the beers. He quickly looked away—he didn't want to make a fool of himself.

"Okay," she said, handing him a beer, "grab a seat anywhere on the floor." She turned on the TV and changed the channel. The big special was due to come on any minute.

"Thanks. Nice place."

"Not much, but it'll do until I can find a job and get something better." She sat on the couch and tucked her feet under her. Her dress rode halfway up her thighs and looked as if it would split any second.

Sidney sat on the floor, his back against the couch and his legs extended in front of him. He twisted off the cap from the beer bottle and took a long pull. "Man, that testes good."

"Oops, almost forgot the subs. Thanks for buying them." Gloria moved off the couch and grabbed the bag with the subs. Handing one to Sidney, she plopped back on the couch in the same position.

Sidney put the sub sandwich on the floor next to him, opened the wrapper, and took a mouthful of roast beef. The mayonnaise dribbled out of the side of the sandwich and started to run down his cheek. Gloria laughed, grabbed a napkin, knelt beside him on the floor, and wiped his mouth. Her leaning over him, wiping his mouth, and slightly rubbing against him started to get Sidney aroused. He was embarrassed to death, and his face started to glow red.

"Gee Sid, glad to see you like me. I was hoping you would. I like you a lot. Was attracted to you right off. Dunno, but something about you really stirs me up. Maybe it's the heat, maybe it's being lonely, not sure, but wow you sure do get my juices flowing." With that, she cradled his head to her breasts and moved closer.

Sidney tried to respond, but with a mouthful of roast beef and his head nestled between her breasts, he was effectively muffled. He tried to swallow and nearly choked. His arousal was expanding, in spite of his efforts to lower his blood pressure.

Gloria moved over on top of him, and settled down of his lap with a heavy sigh and a quiver that seemed to move her whole body. That only served to excite him more, and in spite of his embarrassment, instinct took over. He moved his hands to her waist and then up the sides of her body, his fingers trembled as he reached her breasts.

She arched her back, and at the same time reached down and slipped her tight dress up to her waist. Again, her body trembled as they slid prone on the floor and his hands started nervously roving over her body. She adjusted her position and slowly began unbuttoning her dress. It was then that he realized she wasn't wearing a bra or underpants.

As her ample breasts spilled out of her tight dress, Sidney lost it. God, he'd never been so embarrassed in his life. She must think he was some sort of little kid.

Gloria laughed, stood up, and pulled Sidney to his feet. Still laughing as she towed him toward the bedroom, she said, "Don't worry, Sid. I'm not going to let you off that easy. I'm sure there's more where that came from."

CHAPTER 11

THE man reached over and grabbed the phone before it could ring a second time. His speed was surprising, given the hairy, beefy arm that extended beyond his rolled up shirtsleeve.

"Yeah?" With his other hand, he picked up the Cuban cigar resting in the scarred, wooden ashtray, tapping the long ash into the receptacle before placing it in the corner of his mouth.

He listened for a moment, then shook his head. "No way," he said in a low growl. "How tha hell that happen?" The obvious displeasure of the message he was receiving flashed across his face like angry graffiti on a schoolyard wall.

Still listening, he sat up straight and smashed the cigar into the ashtray.

"What do ya' mean you *think* he drowned in a stream? You left, not finding tha body?"

After listening for a few more seconds, he interrupted the caller. "Bullshit! The two of you clowns couldn't catch that little prick? Forget tha excuses…forget tha contract…you bums get nothin'. If I were you, I'd be heading out of town, looking for a new line of work. You're through…through! When tha word gets 'round, you guys won't be able to get work sorting shitty diapers in a dumpster!"

The phone slammed into the cradle so hard it actually bounced.

* * *

Alex woke, feeling a little better. The headache was still there, though not as intense.

"How's the head, sonny?"

Alex turned to find the Maine woodsman sitting in the crude rocking chair, still staring at him.

"OK, I guess. It still aches."

"Thought it might. Don't have no aspirin, but here, chew on this."

Alex took what seemed to be the root or bulb of a plant, and looked at the man. The woodsman nodded his head, so Alex started chewing on the root. It was dried and actually tasteless, crunching in his mouth almost like a macadamia nut.

"Will this take the headache away?" Alex would have chewed on anything if he thought it would help.

"Maybe...Indians thought so. Never tried it, myself. Doesn't look too damn tasty to me." The old woodsman chuckled, and then got serious. "Okay, sonny. What's going on?"

Alex tried to sit up, but only managed to get his head higher on the pillow. He took another bite out of the root and then related to the old man what had happened in the woods. He remembered slipping on the mossy boulder and sliding back into the cold stream. After that, everything was black.

"I found ya' downstream a ways, caught up on some branches of a tree that had fallen 'cross the stream. Almost didn't see ya' in the dark. Ayah, damn lucky."

"Thanks. Guess you saved my life. If you hadn't come along, well...ah. Alex reached up and touched his head again. It felt like it was going to split open like a ripe watermelon. After a moment, he continued.

"How long've I been here?"

"Just one night. It's 'bout near the end of July. Relax, yore not going anywhere for a while."

Alex didn't respond. He was trying to put it all together. Finally, he found his voice again. "By the way, my name is Alex. Appreciate what you're doing for me."

"Glad to do it, Alex. Name's Hermy. That's not my real name, but one I picked up, guess from being a hermit here in the woods fa' so long. Real name don't matter."

"Thanks, Hermy. I'd be dead if it weren't for you."

The old man ignored that comment, but continued with his question. "Why they lookin' for you, sonny?"

Alex hesitated, Should he trust this man? He wasn't sure, but the man did save his life and treat his injuries. Alex decided only to disclose what he had to, for his protection as well as for the old man's safety.

"I'm sure they're hired assassins. I'm in the Witness Protection Program because I testified against some big-time crooks that were into drugs and money laundering. They swore to get even."

"How'd they find out where you was?"

"That's the question of the year. Not sure. They somehow discovered where I was living. I could tell they'd been there, so I grabbed a few clothes and left. Must've watched my place and followed me up here. Gotta' be an inside leak; someone doing it for the money."

"A-yuh. Money can sure screw you up. Almost did me. Don't think ya' ought to stay here very long; those outsiders may come back lookin' for ya'."

Before Alex could question that, Hermy got up from the chair and went over to the stove. He rustled around for a bowl and spoon, poured the contents from a steaming pan into the bowl, and brought it over to Alex. "Here you go, sonny. Home-made stew, just what tha doctor ordered."

"Another Indian recipe?"

"A-yuh. Only this one works."

* * *

After he calmed down, the man with the beefy arms picked up the phone and punched in a speed-dial number. Sweat was collecting on his bushy eyebrows, and he wiped the palm of his left hand on his pants.

The ringing stopped as someone on the other end picked up the phone.

"It's me. Just heard from tha guys. They botched it. Think tha guy drowned in a stream, but can't confirm it."

The explosion on the other end of the line was not unexpected, but still he fidgeted in his chair. They paid him to get the job done, and he hadn't. Simple as that. Now he had to make up for it.

"Look, we'll get 'im. I'll personally send some guys up there and find out what happened. I'll put another team onto checking all tha travel terminals. If he's still alive, we'll nail the bastard. If he's dead, we've got a happy customer and it's payday."

After another moment he said, "Yeah, I know the price of failure," and hung up the phone.

CHAPTER 12

DUN almost jumped out of his skin. The sound was like a huge hornet, ticked off that its nest had been disturbed.

He looked over at the antique table (yard sale) to the left of his desk and saw the cell phone vibrating like an old wind-up toy. Dun picked it up, briefly crinkled his eyebrows, and slowly smiled. "On," he barked, a few inches from the phone.

The phone display lit up and the word 'Ready' appeared. The phone was still vibrating. Not knowing what to do next, he tried "speak," "hello," and "talk," in that order. Nothing happened.'

He muttered "Jesus" in frustration. The light went off, but the word "hello?" repeated several times came out of the speaker. He held the phone to his ear and said, "Hello, who's this?"

"Mr. Wheeling?"

"Yes, this is Dun Wheeling."

"This is Alex calling."

"Alex?"

"I'm the man Knott spoke to you about."

"Oh. Sorry. Knott never gave me your name."

"I don't suppose he gave you the code word either?"

"Code word? Are you kidding?"

"No, I'm not. Knott said you would ask me for a codeword so you'd know I was the person he spoke to you about."

"That dumb…OK, I'll play the game. What's the code word?" Dun's irritation meter was inching up on the scale. Patience was not his strong suit.

"High School."

"Wow, you got it on the first try. Congratulations. Boy, that's secure. I feel so much better, knowing that you could make up any code word and I wouldn't have a clue whether it's valid. Real slick."

Dun had little patience for bureaucratic BS—or any BS for that matter. He couldn't stand spoiled brats, trophy wives, pampered husbands, or folks with egos bigger than their heads. His humor, normally dry and slightly sarcastic, could get downright nasty in the right situation.

"I'm sorry, Mr. Wheeling. But I'm in a tough situation here. I was nearly killed two days ago. If it hadn't been for an old Maine woodsman, this would be over."

"OK, Alex. Knott did fill me in on your problem. Where are you?'"

"Andrews."

"Andrews what?"

"Andrews Air Force Base"

"Boy, this gets more fun by the minute. How the hell did you get to Andrews Air Force Base?"

"It's a long story, better discussed in person. Can you pick me up?'"

"Sure, Alex. I can be there in twenty minutes or so. Where do I go, once inside the base, and how will I know it's you?"

"I'll be waiting at the main gate. You won't have to identify me; I'll know who you are."

"And how will you know that?"

"Knott described you."

Dun scratched his chin. "Oh, he did? What did he say?'"

"Well, actually he said look for a big goof in a racing-green Miata."

"When I get my hands on him!" Dun yelled "off" into the phone, slipped it into his pocket, and left his office. As he passed Lucy's desk, he said, "I'm off to Andrews."

"Andrew's what?"

"Andrews Air Force Base."

"Oh, picking up the President?" Lucy started to chuckle until she noticed the look on his face.

"Yeah, and his whole damn Cabinet. In my Miata."

* * *

As Dun pulled up to the main entrance of Andrews AFB, a man about his age stepped out of the guard shack, waved, and walked over toward Dun's car. Alex was a little shorter than Dun's six-two height, had a medium build, close-cropped dark hair with just a hint of white at the widow's peak, and features most women would consider handsome. A large white dressing covered the back of his head.

"Hi, Mr. Wheeling. I'm Alex," he said, as he approached the Miata. It was such a beautiful day that Dun had put the top down.

Dun rose out of the bucket seat as best he could, held onto the windshield frame for support, and shook Alex's hand. "Get in, Alex."

Alex opened the door of the Miata, and struggled a little getting in. Dun was relieved to see he had only a small duffle bag for luggage. Apparently, most everything he had with him was on his body.

"Sorry it's a little tight," Dun said, after Alex had settled in and put on his seat belt. "It takes a little getting used to, but it's worth it."

Alex just sat there, staring ahead, his hands spread on his legs as if he couldn't decide what to do next. His whole body was tense, and Dun knew it wasn't the car.

"Look, Alex. I appreciate the situation you're in. Must be tough. You don't know me from Adam, and probably not real sure of Agent Harrison. But we're going to get you out of this mess, and keep you safe while we do it." He tried to look convincing, but underneath he wasn't quite sure he could back up that promise.

Alex turned to look at him, a small smile creeping at the corners of his mouth. "Thanks, Mr. Wheeling. I guess that's all I can ask."

"You can ask for a hell of a lot more, and deserve a lot more, but looks like this is about the best you're going to get right now. Harrison is a good man. A bit of a jerk at times, but I'd trust him with my life. And, call me Dun—we're going to be together for a while."

"Knott said you two guys had been tight in high school. 'Like skin,' I think he said."

"Yeah, I'm from the forehead, and he's from the opposite side of the belly button."

Alex's smile broke into full bloom, and he chuckled. "Thanks, Dun. Guess I'm a little up-tight."

"You've got every reason to be. Now, let's get the hell out of here." He started the Miata and pulled back onto the main road.

On the way back to his office, conversation was brief because of the road noise and wind. Alex put his head back on the seat and closed his eyes, as if he were trying to let the wind carry away all his troubles. Dun glanced over at Alex from time to time, initially wondering if he was sleeping. But when he saw Alex's closed eyes twitching, he knew there was a lot going on in that mind. He also wondered about the bandage on the back of Alex's head.

He parked behind his office building, and they walked around to the front entrance. Lucy greeted him with a big wave, and then spoke to Alex. "Hi. I'm Lucy Cannon, Dun's assistant. I'm glad you're here, and safe."

"Hello, Lucy. Thanks." Alex shot a look at Dun but said nothing.

As they went into Dun's office, Lucy followed right behind them with a tray of Coke cans, two glasses with ice, two coffee mugs, and a thermos of coffee. "You boys might want something about now, especially after riding in that wind tunnel."

"Thank you, Lucy. But, actually, I enjoyed the ride. The fresh air felt great." Alex reached for one of the Cokes.

"Yeah, thanks Luce." Dun picked up the thermos of coffee.

Lucy left the office and quietly closed the door behind her.

Alex waited a second after she left, then turned toward Dun. "She knows about me?"

"Yep. Everything. I'd trust her with my life—even before Knott. They could pull out all her teeth and pubic hairs and she'd still spit at her tormentors. I couldn't do this without her."

"OK." The look on Alex's face didn't match his words.

"Look, Alex. She's part of the team. Only the three of us know about you, and that's the end of that chain. She's a wonderful woman, with a heart of gold…and the fortitude of a middle linebacker."

Alex's smile was back again. "I can't argue with that." He poured the Coke over the ice and sat back in his chair.

Dun pointed to the back of Alex's head. "What happened?"

Alex reached up and touched the bandage, which was a lot smaller than the one put on by Hermy in Maine. "Banged my head against a rock trying to escape in the dark woods. I probably had a concussion, but the old guy in Maine patched me up and tucked me away in his cabin. He saved my life. I owe him a lot. Just hope I can repay it someday." Alex paused for a moment, his eyes staring at nothing. "Anyway, the Air Force medic changed the dressing while they were giving me a meal in flight."

"Tell me what's going on, why you went to Maine, how you got to Andrews, and everything in-between."

Alex started with his drive to Maine, using the hunting camp of an old friend, his flight from the killers, and Hermy rescuing him. He briefly explained how he got the wound on the back of his head and how the old guy had nursed him back to health. "We had to walk about a mile to where he kept his pickup. It was camouflaged under a pile of branches and pine needles. Looked like it hadn't been used in years, but it started right up. He drove me to some small town, haven't a clue what its name is, so I could use a payphone to call Knott."

"Why call Knott? Don't you work with a Marshall?"

"Yeah, I do. But frankly, I'm not sure I can trust him. After I'd been compromised the first time, Knott had given me his special cell phone number in the event of an emergency. So I called him, and he gave me your name and number."

Dun listened in amazement, his mug of coffee not touched. "Then what happened?"

"Knott told me to send the old man back to his cabin, and for me to wait where I was. About ten minutes later, two guys in a Humvee picked me up, whisked me to some local military base, and put me on a plane to Andrews. Here I am."

"Why the military?"

"I guess those guys were military…not in uniform, so not sure. Knott figured the killers were staking out all the transportation terminals, so the safest way to get me here was by MATS."

"MATS?"

"Military Air Transport Service."

"Oh, yeah." Dun knew that Air Force term sounded familiar. "How'd he arrange all that so quickly?"

"I don't know. But I'm glad he's on my side."

"Yeah, me too." Dun was beginning to feel he was getting way out of his league.

CHAPTER 13

GLORIA stopped in front of the bed and slowly let her dress fall to the floor. Without looking back at Sidney, she pulled back the blanket and sheet and slipped onto the bed.

"C'mon, Sid. Don't keep a girl waiting," she said, pulling the sheet up to her neck as though modesty had just occurred to her. The silk sheet clung to her body like plastic wrap as she stretched full out in the bed.

Sidney was standing in front of the bed, watching her while trying to remove his shoes and socks with one hand, and unzipping his now soggy pants with the other. As his pants curled down around his knees, he lost his balance and toppled onto the bed. Undaunted, he somehow managed to lose his shoes and wiggle out of his pants.

"Oh, Sid, please hurry." Gloria was beginning to move in slow rhythm under the sheets while uttering low moans, each moan followed by a slight shudder that seemed to begin at her toes and move up her body toward her breasts. She arched her back as the shudder moved through them, and then with a soft sigh began the cycle again.

He couldn't wait any longer. All hope of removing his socks, underwear, and shirt was abandoned as he scrambled under the sheet and moved toward her. She arched her back again, turned to face him, and threw a warm silky leg across his waist.

That was all it took. He lost it again.

"Sid. Sid. What am I going to do with you?" Gloria said, wrapping her arms around him and snuggling close. "You naughty boy, wasting that life fluid when I need it so badly."

"Ah…sorry. Guess it's been a while…"

"Well, we'll have to work on that, won't we? Let's see if we can start that engine again, before that tank runs dry." Gloria laughed, and then slowly moved on top of him.

She was hot and sweaty all over. Her hands and body caressed Sidney in slow, gyrating motions and she smothered his lips with her ample breasts. His mind was ablaze with emotion and desire, but he couldn't will his body to respond.

That's it. It's all over. God, she'll think this was my first time. Yeah, it's been awhile…well maybe a long while, but this was ridiculous. I get a chance like this and blow it. Man, if I could only start over. C'mon body.

"Oh…you are such a man. My God, you must drive all the women crazy."

Gloria kept gyrating and murmuring. Sidney kept talking to his body, trying to make it obey his urgent commands. Finally, he felt a faint stirring. Not much, but it was a start.

"Sid, you are amazing. I do believe there's life in you yet." With that, she slid down his body and enveloped him like a warm, moist blanket.

Sid held on. It was the proudest moment of his life. When it was over, he felt like his whole body had been through liposuction. He couldn't move, nor could he erase the smile on his lips.

"Oh, that was so wonderful. I don't know how you did it, but I'm sure going to keep it a secret. If the other women find out about you, I won't stand a chance. No sir, this man-bull is all mine." Gloria slid off him onto her side, and then wrapped her arms and legs around him as if she were afraid he'd get away.

"Well. I do my best. Just been saving it up for the right woman." Sid stretched and then cradled his hands behind his head. The non-erasable smile was still there.

He couldn't believe his luck. Just yesterday, he was lonely and depressed. Nothing going in his life except his dumb job. No one appreciated his talents. Now, that all changed. He was back on top—sorta'.

They both catnapped for a while. Gloria finally stirred and murmured in his ear. "Oh, Sid. Am I ever glad I ran into you. This has been the best night in my whole life."

He untangled her arms and legs, and sat up against the headboard. Gloria moved right with him, wrapping her arms around his neck, and placing her mouth close to his ear.

"Gee, Sid. I don't even know you, and here I am in bed with you. But loving every minute of it."

"Yeah, that was great. Maybe we can do it again if it's not too late."

"It's never too late for that, my man-bull. Maybe tomorrow night we can try your place?"

"Yeah, sure. Anywhere is fine, as long as it's with you, Gloria."

"Mmmm, oh yes. If you're up to it. Don't want to wear you out."

"Don't worry. I can handle it. Long as I'm on time for work."

"Oh, no problem. You may not be able to stand up, but I'll get you there. Then I'll rest up all day waiting for you to return." Gloria giggled and snuggled closer. "I may have to delay looking for a job for a while. Need to save my strength for my man-bull."

He laughed. Wow, she really liked him. Neat. Nice to be appreciated for a change.

"Speaking of work, Sidney, just what do you do?"

"I work for the FBI." He tried to look nonplussed, but a slow smirk crossed his face.

"What! FBI! You're kidding?"

"Nope." Without another word, he reached over and picked up his pants. Retrieving his wallet from the rear pocket, he showed her his FBI identification badge.

Gloria's eyes grew as large as melons as she took his wallet and rubbed her thumb over the badge. She drew the badge to her lips and caressed it with her lips and tongue, and then placed it between her breasts.

"Come get your badge, my man-bull," she whispered, as she moved on top of him again.

CHAPTER 14

HE'D been sitting in the old wooden rocker for two hours, waiting for the twilight to fade and night to take over. Now it was completely dark outside and a low fog was settling in, not uncommon for this time of year.

On a table near the rear door of the cabin laid his hunting rifle, a Marlin 30-30 carbine. Its short barrel was ideal for hunting in the dense woods typical for this part of Maine. The stock, once a rich polished walnut, was now faded and scarred from use, but the metal still glistened as if it were new. On the top of the barrel was the mounting for a Tasco 3-9X variable scope that he'd taken off years ago. No need for a scope in these woods.

The knife was in a sheath to protect its honed edge, ready to be tucked into his belt on his right side when he left.

He slipped out the rear door, the rifle crooked in his left arm, and entered the woods. This was his favorite time to explore. Most of the woodland creatures, including the noisy squirrels, blue jays, and crows—that always shrieked alarms of his approach—had bedded down, except for the deer and rabbits he normally hunted. But tonight was different. He wasn't hunting. He was on a mission.

The old woodsman headed toward the fishing camp on the lake. It hadn't been used in years, until the recent visit by Alex. He didn't like leaving Alex alone near the phone booth after the call, but Alex insisted that everything would be all right. He hoped so.

Crossing the stream about a hundred yards from where Alex had fallen, he took a wide circular path toward the lake. The fog was thicker here, lying like cotton candy under the bushes and trees, and helped muffle his movements. Every so often, he would stop and listen for unfamiliar sounds. Nothing. Not a creature was stirring, not even a mouse—he smiled at the recollection of the old Christmas poem.

He'd lived in these woods for over twenty years, completely on his own, living off the land. At times he got lonely, but his family was gone—partly his fault—and he had adapted to the solitude. There were others, some as close as a few miles away, but he mostly kept to himself. Better that way, let the past stay there.

More cautious now, he edged along the shore of the lake toward the camp. Each moccasin-clad foot was slowly placed in front of him, not putting weight on it until he felt for a stick or a leaf beneath. It had rained off and on all day and the moon was still tucked behind the clouds. The water on the lake was like a mirror, not a ripple to betray its depth.

The old hermit expected that the outsiders who had tried to kill Alex would be back, looking for his body or evidence that he had escaped. But so far, there was no sign of their return.

He could see the camp now, encased by fog, looking as though it was floating in air above the ground. Stopping behind a row of thick pines running along the shoreline, he crouched and waited. His eyes and ears took in everything around him. After several minutes, he moved on.

Approaching the camp from the east, he used the brush and trees for cover. Every ten yards or so, he stopped and listened for any evidence of the outsiders. Nothing. Quiet as a cemetery at midnight.

He crossed under the front windows of the camp and stopped at the corner, listening and surveying for anything that might be out of place. The only sound was his heart beating. Moving along the far side where there were no windows, he paused at the back of the camp. He could see the outhouse and woodpile. The back door to the camp was closed.

Had he closed it when he'd been there earlier to collect Alex's clothes? He couldn't remember. He thought so, but he wasn't sure.

Staying in place for over ten minutes, hardly breathing, Hermy strained his vision and hearing to the limit. If only his heart would stop beating. He smiled at the thought, and crept toward the outhouse. He could now see that the back door of the camp was just slightly ajar. That's how he had left it, he remembered now.

So, the outsiders hadn't come back. Or if they had, they were long gone. He relaxed a little, but still on alert, crept to the back door. Again, he opened it with his rifle barrel and slipped inside. No one. Completely empty.

The view out the front windows revealed an empty lake, still smooth as a baby's bottom. Everything inside was as he had seen it the last time. He breathed easier and left the camp, this time swinging the door shut. No sense letting animals in there to mess it up even more.

As he left, he angled toward the outhouse to make sure its door was also closed and latched. Damn animals, they get into everything.

He opened the door to test the latch, and started to close it again when his body stiffened and froze in place. His heart leaped into his throat. And stopped.

A long powerful arm snaked out the door and grabbed him by the shirt, jerking him inward. The other arm held a jagged military knife, its surgical edge gleaming as it slashed across his throat, severing the jugular and windpipe.

Hermy slumped backward to the ground. He hands went to his throat in a futile attempt to stop the blood pouring from the gash that nearly went ear to ear. As he tried to breathe, a horrible gurgling sound erupted. He was chocking on his own blood! Nothing he could do would stop it!

The blood covered his hands, arms, and chest like a thick blanket. It was warm, almost comforting. Except it was the life ebbing out of his body. *Funny, I'm dying, all alone in the woods, and no one that cares will ever know.*

He looked up at his attacker, but the man was already moving away toward the woods. The fog was getting thicker now, moving over him like a wet mist from dry ice. He thinly smiled for the last time. Not a creature was stirring…

CHAPTER 15

DUN leaned back in his chair and stretched. "Maybe you ought to fill me in on how this all started. I know some of the story from Knott, but I'd like to hear it from you."

Alex rubbed his eyes, using both hands to rub from the center out and back again. "I don't know where to start. It's a long story…too long."

"Try me," Dun said, leaning over and putting his hand on Alex's shoulder. "I know this is tough, and I hate to say it, but you look like you've been through hell. But, before we can fix this, we have to know everything. So, go ahead, give it a whirl."

Alex paused for a moment, obviously thinking of where to begin. "Okay, this started a few years ago. In another state, across the country. I was an OD Consultant—OD stands for Organizational Development. Anyway, I had a contract with a fairly prominent company—I really can't say who or where—and I uncovered some…ah, funny stuff going on." He paused again, as though he didn't want to relive the nightmare again.

Dun sat there, listening. He had a notepad in front of him, but his hands and the pen rested on top of the pad.

"So, since this company had major government contracts, I went to the Feds. They investigated, prosecuted, and nailed the principal owners. Of course, I had to testify. That's where the trouble began—they threatened that they would do whatever it took, for as many years as it took, to get me." Alex turned and looked at Dun.

"They put me in the Witness Protection Program, moved me here, and gave me a new life. Not one that I liked very much, but a new one." Alex rubbed his eyes again, before he went on.

"While I was here I fell in love with a local girl. We kinda' bumped into each other at the library one day. We started seeing each other, dating a lot…you know…and I was getting my courage up to ask her to marry me…" Alex's eyes glistened, and he looked away from Dun.

"…just about that time, someone took a shot at me. I was sitting in my apartment watching TV. Came right through the window, missed me by barely an inch, and blew apart the back of the lounger I was sitting in."

"Man! You were lucky!

Alex turned back toward Dun. "Lucky? I wish that damn bullet had hit! I've been running ever since. My life has been shit ever since." He reached for his back pocket and pulled out a handkerchief. Dun waited while Alex wiped his eyes and blew his nose.

"My handler, as I called the US Marshal assigned to me, whisked me off to another location. I barely got a chance to say goodbye to her. I knew I'd never see her again."

"Couldn't she have gone with you?"

"Yes and no." Alex wiped his eyes, this time not turning away from Dun. "Yes, if we'd been married. No, because she wasn't ready to marry me. No, because I wouldn't put her life in danger."

"Man, that's tough. Sorry."

"They took me to a small town in Northern New Hampshire, near the Maine border."

"Okay, I guess that's why you headed for the camp in Maine…"

"Yes, it belonged to a friend of mine. Told me a ton of stories about him and his dad going up there for a couple of weeks every year. Knew by heart how to get there."

"I would have thought they'd taken you across the other side of the country, or maybe even mid-West. But, New Hampshire?"

"Yeah, they figured that my pursuers would figure just as you did, and concentrate their efforts out there."

"So, I assume that in spite of that they found you again. In New Hampshire."

"You got it. Dirty bastards. But this time I had a warning. Came home one night from work and could tell someone had been in my apartment. Things out of place just a little, that kinda' thing. Packed my stuff, right then and there, and hit the trail. Didn't call anyone. Didn't look back."

"Wow. All that for being a good citizen." Dun paused, unconsciously scratching the tiny scar on his chin. "Now, here you are back in Alexandria. Any chance you could look up that girl?"

Alex's eyes flashed, then quickly dimmed. "No, 'fraid not. She doesn't need my problems."

"Well, you never know."

"Yeah. Thanks, Dun. But I'd better leave well enough alone."

"What's her name?" Dun turned away and reached across the table for the coffee thermos.

"Sally Olivia. Sally Olivia Sawgrass."

Dun's neck sounded like the crack of a bullwhip as it snapped around.

CHAPTER 16

SIDNEY and Gloria were seeing each other almost every night, alternating between his apartment and hers. Their relationship consisted of sex, more sex, and spontaneous sex in between. Sidney was exhausted. Gloria, on the other hand, seemed to thrive on that special diet.

He was glad he had to work every day, and was even beginning to impress his boss with the overtime hours he volunteered for with enthusiasm. Weekends were a problem, however, but he was working on creative solutions for that issue. Maybe if she found a job she would have less energy.

Not that he wasn't enjoying it. He did. He loved the attention and the whole affair was a turbo boost to his ego. Shaving became a daily routine, he was paying more attention to his clothing and hairstyle, and he walked with his head held high. His coworkers snickered behind his back, for they were sure Sidney was in love.

And he was. He just hoped he could endure the physical strain.

One evening, after playing U-turn bingo under the sheets for a couple of hours, Gloria finally ran out of steam and was resting her head on his chest.

"Sid. Didn't you mention last week that you worked for the FBI?"

"Yep. Sure do."

"What do you do there? You never talk about it. Is it super secret, or something?"

"Naw. I'm redesigning their whole computer system. What they've got goes back to the Stone Age."

"Gee, that must be exciting. Sounds like a real important job."

"Oh, yeah. A lot of responsibility. But I'm making great progress. I'll get them up to speed real soon."

Gloria smiled and hugged him tighter. "Well, if anyone can do it, my man-bull can." She wiggled and rubbed against him, knowing just what to do to get his juices flowing.

"Well, in some ways it's kinda' a pain. I'm working with out-of-date equipment, but they're slowly replacing that based on my recommendations. I mean, we're talking millions of dollars here."

"What's the system do? Run the whole FBI?"

"Just about. Some of its routine, but other sections keep track of such things as their thousands of agents, open and closed cases, evidence inventory, people on the 'watch' list, and the WPP, for example."

"WPP? What's that? Women Prefer Penises?" She started to giggle, and Sidney joined in, relieved they were doing something other than having sex.

"Not quite. WPP is the Witness Protection Program. That's where they protect people who testify against gangsters, terrorists, and the like. It's highly classified, and only certain people have access to that section of the system."

"And, of course, the man running the whole show has access. Right, my man-bull?"

"Right. I have access to everything the FBI has on file. Even certain areas, where they feel I don't have the need to know, I can still get into with my eyes closed. No big deal."

"Sounds like a big deal to me. Mmmm, I didn't know I was sleeping with such an important person. Makes me kinda' warm and fuzzy all over."

Sidney jumped out of bed and headed for the bathroom. "Yeah, me too. But right now I have to see a man about a horse."

"Oh, Sid. You are so funny. Hurry back. Gloria has a little surprise she's been saving up for the right moment. And this is definitely the right moment, so don't keep me waiting too long."

Sidney groaned inwardly. He was torn between excitement and fear. He just hoped he could walk up the stairs at work tomorrow.

CHAPTER 17

KNOTT Harrison went into his office, closed the door behind him, locked it, and sat down behind his desk. He pulled a small cell phone from his pocket, held it close to his mouth, and spoke softly to place a call to Dun.

"Wheeling Investigations."

"Hi, Lucy. It's Knott. Dun back yet?"

"Knott who?"

"C'mon, Lucy. This is serious. I don't have much time."

"OK, sorry Knott. Hang on."

Knott waited only a second or two before Dun answered. "Hi. Got Alex here. He's been briefing me on his situation."

"Good. Did he get to the part about the Maine woodsman helping him?"

"Yeah. Must be an interesting old guy."

"You mean must *have* been…"

"What?"

"They found him just a few hours ago. Throat slashed. Bled to death. Now you know how serious this is."

* * *

Dun couldn't believe it. This was getting too complicated. He now knew for sure this was out of his league. Alex is supposedly in the Witness Protection Program, but has been compromised twice. A nice old guy who lives in the woods helps him out and gets his throat cut for it. Now Alex was in his office, and he has someone from the FBI on the phone.

"Look, Knott—"

"I'm sorry," Knott interrupted, "but I wanted to let you know. I've got a meeting in a half-hour with the U.S. Marshal who's assigned to Alex's case. I don't know whether he's part of the leak or what, but I intend to find out. Keep Alex there until I get back to you."

"OK, but it's getting late. Alex is exhausted and probably hungry by now. How 'bout I take him out to dinner and then drop him off wherever he's staying tonight?"

"Considering what's happened, I think you better take him through a drive-in window for chicken or something. Then take him back to your place until we can figure out where to put him. I haven't had time to work that out yet."

"Sure," Dun answered. "This is real exciting."

"Look, I'm sorry, Dun. This wasn't expected to happen like this. It'll just be for one night. Oh, before I forget, I wanted to fill you in on something about Alex."

"What's that?"

"Seems like he had a girlfriend while he was here, got real serious with her, and—"

"I know. He told me. This is getting better by the minute. Bye."

Dun's brain was almost exploding. There was more stuff going on in there than he could process. The guy sitting across the table from him has been shot at twice, in spite of the supposed protection program run by the U.S. Marshals. All for being a good citizen. And what if he contacts Sally Olivia again? She'd at least want to see him, and that alone might put her in direct danger. Damn, what a mess.

Someone, somewhere, is leaking information to people who have plenty of money and no scruples about killing. They've already done it, to the poor guy in Maine who was just trying to help a fellow human. And they're trying real hard to do it to Alex.

And, there's another side of this with Sally Olivia. Does Alex still have a thing for her? Or, is it over? And, what about her? Will her feelings toward Alex return if she sees him? He didn't think so, but he didn't want to test that theory.

Dun hadn't seen Sally Olivia since they had whisked her away from the hospital in Florida to a private hospital—only God knew where. She went through three kidnapping attempts fairly well, but had a total collapse after she learned her pompous brother had become part of the scheme to save himself from financial embarrassment.

Sally Olivia's estate lawyers wouldn't tell Dun where she was. They said the doctors insisted on no contact with anyone relating to recent events until they could get past the trauma. Dun had protected her, saved her life—twice—and now was helpless to do anything for her. Not knowing her whereabouts was driving him crazy. He didn't want to lose her now.

Dun looked at Alex. "Guess you're stuck with me for the night. What would you like for dinner? Chicken, hamburger, tacos—your choice."

"I'll settle for a bullet-proof vest."

CHAPTER 18

ANOTHER long session of playing roulette under the sheets left Sidney exhausted. He didn't know how much longer he could survive this marathon mating ritual. And yet, there was Gloria in the bathroom, singing in the shower like she was just warming up.

As he heard the shower turn off, he groaned and slipped the sheet over his head. He wanted to leave, but that was difficult since they were at his place.

Her voice rang out from the steamy bathroom. "Sid, I need to talk to you."

Sidney brightened and sat up. "Talk?"

"Yes, I have a big favor to ask."

"Sure, Gloria. Anything." Anything except more of this. Pretty soon he would need bandages and a splint to hold together.

Gloria opened the bathroom door, and through a cloud of steam stepped out wrapped only in a skimpy bath towel. She smiled as she sauntered past the end of the bed and slipped in between the sheets. As she did, the towel came loose and fell on the floor.

He groaned softly and pulled the sheet higher over his body. To his amazement, however, she didn't wrap herself around him but propped up a pillow and sat up. The sheet barely covered her breasts. He had to admit she looked pretty nice.

"Sid, you mentioned that you have access to the Witness Protection Program information. Right?"

"Well…yeah."

"A close friend of mine has been wronged by that program. She spoke about it last weekend when I called her."

"Wronged?"

"Oh yeah. Apparently, her brother-in-law was wrongly accused by someone who's in the program. That someone gave false testimony to cover his own ass, and her brother-in-law went to jail. He's still there."

"Wow. That's crazy. That doesn't seem right."

"It's not. It's unfair. And my friend's sister and her three kids are about to be kicked out of their home. The bank is calling in the loan and selling the house at auction. She'll be on the street…with three little kids." Her eyes started to water.

"Man, that sucks. Did anyone complain to the FBI?"

"Oh sure, it went through the courts and everything, but they believed this guy who's now in the program. He walked away free, and my friend's sister's family has to suffer because of it. My friend was crying so hard over the phone that I could hardly get the whole story."

"Justice sure wasn't served on that one, was it?"

"No. Sure wasn't." Gloria began to cry and turned away from Sidney.

Sidney sat up even higher in the bed. "Jesus. Wish I could do something about that."

Without turning back to him, she whispered, "I think you can."

"I can? How?"

"I'll get the name of that person in the program and you find where he's staying. My friend and her sister want to talk to him, find a way to convince him that his false testimony is ruining the lives of this family. Maybe appeal to him about the three little tikes involved, who will soon be on the street, homeless and hungry."

"Just talk to him?"

"Sure. They have to try. The FBI and the courts have been no help. The lawyers can't do anything. They can't even find out where this man is."

"Geeze, Gloria. That's tough. I could lose my job for that. Maybe worse."

Gloria turned toward Sidney, wiping her eyes. "Oh, Sid. Please. Not for me, but for this poor mother and her three little kids. They're suffering because of this guy. They can't even figure out why he's in the program at all. No one has threatened him to their knowledge, so why's he being protected?"

"Yeah, you're right. I'll see what I can do."

Gloria snuggled into his arms and rested her head on his shoulder. "Thanks, Sidney. I love you." She began to cry again.

CHAPTER 19

KNOTT hung up the phone. He felt sorry for Dun, being caught in the middle like this, but he didn't have much choice. There was no one in this section of the agency—no one—he dared trust right now. He didn't know about the Marshall he was about to meet. Maybe he's a good guy, not involved in all this, but he didn't know.

Sure, the US Marshals Service runs the Witness Protection Program, but they couldn't do it without the FBI. We get 'em to testify, they protect 'em. Unfortunately, the records of the program are in huge computer files available to many insiders—not impossible for those with the wrong intentions to get access.

Knott scanned the file on his desk again. The guy's been with the Marshals for fourteen years, no unusual plusses or minuses, except a couple of minor infractions a few years ago. He dug deeper into the file and found the Marshal had been reprimanded twice for losing contact with his witnesses. He knew this wasn't always the Marshals' fault; the witness could just up and take off in the middle of the night. In spite of this, however unfair, the Marshal was responsible for maintaining contact at all times.

Just then, there was a knock on his door. He got up and unlocked the door, then turned around and went back to his desk. "C'mon in."

The man who stepped through the door was about average height, maybe a little shorter, and looked like he had eaten beef and corn his whole life. The file indicated he was late 40's, but he looked younger. Close cropped thick hair that had long ago turned white, and the build of a bricklayer's helper. The man obviously took pride in keeping in shape, and it showed.

Knott held out his hand. "Knott Harrison."

"Cob Ferguson. Nice to meet you, Knott. Heard lots about you."

"Don't believe a word of it. Take a seat." Knott sized up the man before him. His clear blue eyes seemed to say "Hey, I'm a good guy. You can count on me." But Knott knew from experience that eyes, like words, can lie.

"Cob? Little unusual for a name. Nickname?"

"Yeah. Short for Jacob. That, and my folks owning cornfields, made it stick. Actually, I like it better than Jacob. Short and to the point."

"Like you?" Knott raised one eyebrow as he continued to study the man. His instincts were giving him good vibes, but it was too early to tell.

"Yes, like me. I don't have much patience for long-winded bureaucratic tap dancing." Cob sat ramrod straight in his chair, his eyes never wavered from Knott's.

"You'll fit in." Knott smiled.

"Likewise, I'm curious about your name. Run in the family?"

"Well, Cob, there are a hundred family stories about how that originated. One is just as wild as the rest. My favorite is my mother refused to believe she was pregnant again. I'm number five. She only wanted two. When the doctor told her the news, she yelled, "I am not!" and started crying. She did the same thing to my dad. I became the "not" baby, and somehow a 'k' and an extra 't' got thrown in.

"Bet you took a lot of jabbin' over that when you were younger."

"Yeah. But, I was bigger than most of the kids in my class."

"You're lucky. I wasn't." Cob's smile indicated that it hadn't been a big problem.

"I suspect you can take care of yourself."

"Early on," Cob said, "I couldn't fight my way out of a sausage casing. But my dad was a Golden Gloves champ, so he taught me a few things. I still wasn't much for fighting, but it did come in handy at times."

"Looks like you work out a lot. Do you use the gym in the building?" Knott was there two or three times a week, and had never seen Cob before.

"No, I work out at home. Didn't have much money earlier, for gyms and stuff, so I figured out ways to do it at home. My dad helped me a lot. Then, when I came to work here and saw the big, fully equipped gym, my eyes bugged out like a little kid. But I couldn't get used to all those contraptions and went back to my home routine. Works for me, and I only have to smell myself."

Knott shook his head and laughed. "Yeah, now that's a benefit. For sure."

Knott got up from his desk and walked over to the window. Not much of a view. An inner courtyard with a couple of Bradley pear trees, three park benches, and seven trash barrels. He'd counted them before.

"Cob. Before I begin, I need to clear the air. And part of that includes, right up front, that anything and everything between us stays there. I know I can trust me, but I'm not sure of you yet. You're in the same boat. But we have to start off trusting each other, and let time disclose whether that was a good decision. Agreed?"

"You have my word," Cob said, standing and walking over to him with his hand extended. "I've been slapped twice for stuff over which I had no control. I'll be damned if I go there again."

Knott took his hand. Cob's handshake was firm, but not what Knott expected. Usually, guys who work out as much as Cob obviously does went overboard with the handshake, as if it were some sort of damn macho statement or badge. His was firm, but non-threatening, no statement.

"I don't report to anyone here, so no one's looking over my shoulder. You, on the other hand, have a boss whose head is so far up his ass he's afraid to open his eyes."

Cob almost fell over with laughter. With tears in his eyes, he said, "A fair assessment."

"So, I'm having you moved to a special detail. Your boss will get the word today."

"Who will I report to? Not that I mind getting out from under my boss." Cob sat down again.

"We'll report to POTUS." Knott wasn't smiling. He was referring to the President of the United States.

"The President? Are you kidding?"

"No, I'm not. He's extremely concerned about the breach of security here. It not only jeopardizes the lives of the witnesses whom we have sworn to protect, it has serious national security implications that I can't get into. It goes far beyond the credibility of the whole program and the US Marshals Service—not to mention the FBI, of course."

Cob opened his mouth to say something, then stopped. He shook his head and said, "Holy ..."

"Actually, I'll report to the President's advisor on security matters. You'll report to me. However, to keep this absolutely quiet, on the surface you and I have nothing to do with each other. We are on separate special projects, highly confidential, and report to no one but the President's advisor. We'll have to work out why we're meeting now, so as not to arouse any suspicions, and why we might be meeting again at times."

Cob looked like he was in shock. Knott figured his mind was probably whirring like spaghetti in a blender without the top on. Finally, Cob straightened in his chair and said, "Sorry, this is totally unexpected. Don't get me wrong, I'm excited about the opportunity. Not 'opportunity' like getting ahead...you know. But the chance to nail the bastard, or bastards, that are doing this to Alex. He's a nice guy, and doesn't deserve this."

"Glad to hear you say that."

"Glad I can even talk, after that surprise," Cob said, walking back over to his chair. As he sat down, he looked directly at Knott and said, "I'm in." After a short pause, a tiny smile peeked through the seriousness, "You'll have to work hard to earn my trust, but I think you have a shot at it."

CHAPTER 20

DUN'S apartment was a little unusual. He kept telling himself that he would soon move into something a little more upscale, but this was only an excuse not to fix up the place.

The apartment was located in an old brick building of some historical significance. During Colonial times, it had been used as a warehouse for the shipping trade in the Port of Alexandria. Dun swore he could still smell whatever it was that had been stored there, his guess was cow shit that was later used in fertilizer.

Dun's quiet little corner of the world was located on the third floor, which had the advantage of lower rental fees. But with no elevator, it had the obvious disadvantage of trucking up three flights with everything he brought home.

The unusual part came from the interior walls also being brick. He could relate long stories about his attempts to hang mirrors and pictures on those walls. After several attempts and about $300 worth of tools and supplies at the local hardware, he finally succeeded. What he lacked in skill he made up for with perseverance.

The heavy metal casement windows were covered inside and out with metal grills, making it a challenge to open them. In utter frustration, Dun broke one pane in each window and covered it with screen in the summer and cardboard in the winter.

The almost antique bathtub had tiger-paw feet that splayed out at angles—he covered these with day-glo tennis balls to minimize foot injury—and the toilet for some reason was mounted on a nine inch wooden riser, like a statue sitting on a base barely large enough to hold it. That made life interesting at times, especially for guests that weren't as tall as he was.

Dun did like a challenge, and this place offered him more than enough to keep him interested.

He used his key to unlock the door, and with Alex trailing behind, walked into his apartment. "This isn't exactly the Ritz, Alex, but it's safe. A 50-caliber shell couldn't get through these walls."

"Yeah. Double brick walls. You don't see them everyday." Alex looked around in the large living room and noted how Dun had framed the windows with boards so he could mount curtain rods. "I'll bet hanging pictures and mirrors is a real challenge here."

"Don't ask." Dun started to laugh, but the memories were still painful. "Make yourself at home. Your bedroom's just to the left of the bathroom, down that hall. My bedroom's on the other side, so we'll have to share the bath."

Dun didn't bother explaining the nuances of the bathroom. He'd found from experience that it was more fun to let the guest try to figure it out. "The kitchen's right over here, and that room is my supposed study. I don't use either very much. I'll get the chicken set up and you can wash up if you want."

"Thanks. Real sorry to barge in on you, but I don't know what else to do. Hopefully, Knott can get me to a safe-house tomorrow."

"No problem, Alex. Nice to have some company for a change. C'mon out to the kitchen when you're ready."

While Dun was setting up paper plates for the take-out chicken, his mind was churning with the fact that he didn't want to be in the middle of this mess. Someone's trying to kill this guy, and now he's staying at my place. And he was once, or maybe still is, in love with Sally Olivia. Throw in the 'pro-bono' aspect of the case, and that made him a three-time loser.

Sure, Alex seemed like a nice guy, but Dun was now going from investigator to body guard. This was not the direction where he hoped to steer his new agency, or the type of work he wanted to pursue. And, while danger was a part of his business, he felt like he was driving around in his Miata with the top down and a huge sign that said, 'Shoot Me.'

On the other hand, it would give him a contact at the FBI. Knott seemed to be highly placed. That could come in handy. Maybe other contacts would come out of this.

Or just maybe I'll end up like the Maine woodsman.

Alex walked into the kitchen and interrupted his thinking. "Man, that toilet is a challenge. Bet there's a few funny stories there."

Dun looked up from his distributing chicken, coleslaw, and mashed potatoes chore. "Oh yeah. This whole place is a bucket of laughs."

"I'd love to have a place like this." Alex was staring off somewhere.

Dun stopped what he was doing and looked at Alex. *Damn, I'm always bitching about this place, and this guy comes along and puts it all in perspective.* "You will. Just hang in there." To change the subject, he added, "What would you like to drink? I've got water, maybe milk if it hasn't gone sour, and Coke. Sorry, no beer."

"Coke would be great, thanks."

Alex sat down and dived into his meal as if he hadn't eaten in a week. Must be the tension, Dun figured, as he sat down to join him. When they had both finished, Dun brought up the subject that was tearing through his mind.

"So…ah, you knew Sally Olivia?"

"Yes, I did. But she knew me under a different name. I take it from your reaction earlier, that you were involved with her also."

"Met her in Florida. Her pompous brother hired me—"

"Aaron Suttle Sawgrass?" Alex interrupted. "Pompous isn't the word."

Dun laughed for a second, then turned serious again. "Right. Well anyway, he hired me to find Sally Olivia. She had gone to Florida to get away from him and all his phony social friends. She ended up getting kidnapped and—"

"What! Kidnapped?" Alex's face screwed up like a pretzel.

Dun filled him in on how Sally Olivia had been kidnapped, his involvement in her rescue, and the subsequent two other kidnap attempts all orchestrated by a rogue local police detective. When he got to the part about her brother being involved in the ransom to avoid financial embarrassment, Alex looked like he was in total shock.

"How did Sally Olivia bear up under all this?"

"She didn't." Dun's face showed the agony he was feeling. "She collapsed when she heard about her brother. I was the unlucky guy elected to tell her." Dun turned away as moisture came to his eyes.

"Jesus. I'm sorry. Where is she now?"

"I don't know...don't know." Dun looked down at his hands. They were trembling as he placed them on his legs. "She was transferred from the hospital that the ambulance had taken her to...to some private clinic somewhere in another state. I can't find out. Her doctors and trust lawyers refuse to tell me, saying she needs complete rest and avoidance of anything having to do with her trauma."

* * *

Alex couldn't think of anything to say. Memories of his involvement with Sally Olivia flooded his brain, especially the last time he saw her. While he was telling her goodbye, U.S. Marshals were waiting outside, ready to whisk him away to a new location and a new identity. Alex had been in love with her, ready to pop the marriage question, but his secret identity had been compromised. The criminals he testified against had hired killers to find him and even the score.

He knew she wasn't in love with him, not to the degree for marriage, anyway. Would she ever get to that point? He'd had a lot of time to think on that, tucked away in his new location, unable to write or call her. He had to admit the answer was probably 'no'. Besides, it didn't matter. A moot question. He wouldn't put her life in danger, at least not until this whole thing was over. But it looked like that may never come.

He wondered about Dun's involvement with Sally Olivia. He sometimes called her Sally. Was their relationship more intimate than his had been? And here he is, helping me, and not knowing where she is.

This has to be tough for him—must be torn between helping me and finding Sally Olivia. And worried about old flames rekindling. *Can I trust him with this conflict going on? Will his feelings for Sally Olivia get in the way of protecting me?*

* * *

Dun looked at Alex. He seemed lost in thought. Was being back here, where their relationship had taken place, stirring up old memories? Sally Olivia had told Dun about him, but thought she had called him Bruce, or something. He wasn't sure.

Was it long enough ago for Alex to have put away his feelings for her? Dun was almost glad Sally Olivia wasn't around. Would Alex seeing her rekindle his feelings for her?

Dun's mind was like confetti in a gentle breeze; blowing everywhere, but going nowhere very fast. Did he really want to help this guy? Was he willing to find out what feelings Sally Olivia might still have for him? Dun wasn't sure. He thought he should talk with Knott about this, maybe bow out because of the conflict of interest.

Or was that just an excuse?

CHAPTER 21

"NO body found anywhere, boss. Looked all over. Nothin'." The voice on the phone coughed once, then went silent.

"'Looked all over? Nothin'!' That's it? That's all you got to tell me? You guys botched it the first time. I give you a second chance to clean up your mess. And all I get is 'nothin'! NOTHING!" The sheer intensity and volume of his voice was almost enough to make the phone line vibrate. His muscles in his beefy arms were knotting as he clenched his fists.

"Look. Calm down, boss. We did tha best we could. Nobody coulda' done better. We couldn't find him tha first time because some ol' guy who lived in the woods musta' helped. Probably picked him up that night and took 'em back to his cabin, about a couple a' miles away, hidden in the woods."

"Why didn't you find the cabin that night? You had those IR glasses, or whatever the hell you call 'em." The volume was lower, but not much.

"We almost missed it in tha daylight. That guy musta' been a camouflage expert or somethin'. No shit. You couldn't see tha place from ten feet away. Unreal."

"That means Alex, or whatever the hell his real name is, got away. Shit! He could be in Alaska by now." The man sat back in his chair, a long Cuban cigar crammed in a corner of his mouth, his hands starting to tremble just slightly.

He wondered whether Alex would go back to the Marshal assigned to his case, or avoid him like the plague, thinking maybe the Marshal had been bought.

"You guys scour every inch of that area?" the man continued.

"Yeah. Went over it twice, real close. Pulled the guy's cabin apart. Nothin'."

"'Nothin'.'" The attempt to mimic the caller's voice wasn't even close, but the message was clear. "What happened to him? He get away, too?"

"Nah. I took care of 'im, boss. He came snoopin' around the camp. I was waitin' for 'im." The caller's voice was stronger now, more confident.

"You killed him? You dumb shit! Did you think about askin' him some questions before you killed him?" The man's rolled up shirtsleeves were absorbing the sweat from his arms.

A quick pause. "Sure. Of course I thoughta' that. But it happened too fast, boss."

"Bullshit!" He ripped the cigar out of his mouth and squashed the end in the old ashtray. The man was lying—he killed anyone, anytime, any chance he got. Young, old—didn't matter. Killing was his sex.

Now it was too late. Alex was on the run again. Could be anywhere. And he'd failed again. He stood up and slammed the phone into its cradle. Failure was not acceptable in the group he worked for. Failure brought severe penalties. Extremely severe.

Funny. He now had something in common with Alex. He was also on the run.

CHAPTER 22

"HI Sid. It's Gloria." Her voice over the phone seemed a little strained.

"Ah...hi, Gloria. How you doin'?"

"Just wondering if you're coming over tonight? You missed last night and I was afraid something was wrong."

Sidney swallowed. Nothing was wrong, except he couldn't get the information he'd promised her. Somehow, someone had locked down the whole WPP section of the computer system. And, he couldn't get access, in spite of trying every trick he had learned in the past.

"Well, to be honest, I'm just home for a snack, then going back to the office. That information I promised you has been moved, and I'm trying to figure a way to get to it. Something must be going on. For some reason I'm now locked out. Worked on it last night, too."

"Oh, God, Sid. I promised that poor woman that my genius of a boyfriend could easily get the information for her. Told her I'd have it for her today."

"I'm sorry. Not sure what's happened. Frankly, I'm a little nervous poking around right now, everything seems to be locked up tight. I've got to be real careful I don't leave a trail when I finally do find the info."

"But, you can find it, right?"

"Oh sure. Just taking a little longer than I expected. It's still in the system somewhere. I just have to find the door to its location. No sweat."

"Gee, that's great, Sid. I knew you were brilliant. I really miss you, and I'm sorry you can't come over, but I understand."

"No problem, honey. I'll have it for you tomorrow night. Count on it."

"Oh, I will, Sid. And then we'll celebrate."

"Yeah…celebrate."

As Sidney hung up the phone, he realized he was sweating a little. He wasn't kidding when he told her he was a little nervous. They didn't lock down that area of the system just for maintenance. Something serious was going on. Which meant his job just got a whole lot tougher.

It was one thing to hack a corporate computer. Another to hack into a computer owned by the government, especially one run by the FBI and the US Marshals. If he got caught playing games on this job, his parents would be long gone in Heaven before he ever saw the sky again.

On one hand, Sid was glad to have an excuse not to visit Gloria. His testicles were turning into swollen prunes from all the sexual activity. He wasn't sure what the true definition of a nymphomaniac was, but he was beginning to get an idea.

Gloria seemed to have no end to achieving sexual satisfaction. Just when he dared to hope her sex engine was running down, she seemed to switch gear and rev up again. She was in four-limb drive all the time.

He felt like the stubby nub of a worn pencil with a frayed eraser. She was some kind of a pencil sharpener, all right, with a high-horsepower electric motor.

On the other hand, he had promised to get her the information. That poor woman and her kids didn't deserve what was happening to them. Sure, the WPP was a good program. It was needed to protect honest folks that provided testimony against criminals, the mob, and other scumbags that would snuff them out to avoid going to jail.

But this case was a mistrial of justice. The guy had used the program to protect his own ass. The good guy's in jail, and this jerk was laughing up his sleeve as the government waited on him every day. Not right.

Sid finished his glass of milk and left his apartment for the office. He hoped he could solve the problem tonight. In spite of all his complaints, he missed Gloria.

* * *

"Yeah, I know. He promised to have it today. What can I do? He worked last night and again tonight trying to get it."

Gloria listened to the voice on the other end of the phone. He wasn't happy, but that was tough. She was doing everything she could. Making love to that jerk was like being screwed by a soft rubber Q-tip.

"You think I like this? You sleep with that toad every night! He's about as exciting as squeezing farts out of dead pigeons. And he thinks he's some kind of a stud. Well, let me—"

Gloria switched ears when she was interrupted. Her right one was burning.

"You're damn right he better get that info fast. Damn fast. I've just about had it. One more day of this and I'll have to start using wheel bearing grease. Not sure—"

She held the phone away from her ear to keep from losing her eardrum.

"Yeah? Well screw you. If you don't like it, find yourself another actress." She slammed down the phone, and with the back of her hand swept it off the table. She didn't even bother to look to see if there was any damage to the phone as she walked to the kitchen for another beer.

* * *

"Working late again tonight, Sidney?" The guard watched as he signed in.

"Yeah, getting behind on this project. I want to get caught up so I can afford to take a couple days off. This heat and humidity is killing me. My apartment is hotter than a whorehouse in the Sahara."

The guard laid back his head and laughed. "Know what you mean. Makes you glad you're working inside in this kind of weather. Weatherman says there's no relief in sight."

"The only relief I'm gonna' get is getting out of this moldy city and going as far north as I can. Maybe Canada."

"Sounds like a plan, Sidney. Don't work too late."

"Thanks. See you later."

Sidney walked up the stairs to the second level. The computer section was in the mezzanine area of the building, a separate level all by itself for security.

He punched in the code on the keypad next to the entrance door, waited for the latch to click, and opened the door. He didn't have to look for the light switch, they were on all the time. So was the air conditioning. A lot of folks didn't like to come here as it was always so cold, but that suited Sidney just fine. He hated the heat and he liked being alone. Especially now, with this little project he promised to do for Gloria.

He could kick himself for agreeing to get the information for her. But it seemed the right thing to do, so he'd better get started.

He sat down at his terminal and started by listing the sourcecode for the main program, the one that provided a menu of options for the users. It was a mess. The program had been patched a million times over the years, by a million different database geeks and stupid consultants. But he was better. Not one of them could match his skills. It was just a matter of finding the code that blocked access to the WPP area.

God, there must be a zillion lines of the stuff, with routines, subroutines, and loops that could make anyone dizzy. Trying to trace each one was a nightmare.

Then he got an idea. He recompiled the program and went to the main menu again. As he selected the WPP option, he stopped the code, and ran a little application he had designed to debug situations like this. It was a masterpiece of programming that he was proud of, but never dared to share with anyone. He had created it when he was into hacking corporate machines, and just having it could cost him his job. That's why he kept it on a floppy disk in his backpack.

As the application ran, it displayed on the screen what it was doing. Sidney watched as it backtracked the code through the system. Suddenly, it stopped and three lines of fresh code were highlighted. It worked! He studied the code, made a couple of notes on a pad beside his keyboard, and exited the application.

Now he had the key to the door he was looking for. He was in, and the information he promised Gloria was only a few screens away.

CHAPTER 23

THE next day, Knott and Dun met for lunch again. This time the location was a small out-of-the-way restaurant several miles south of Alexandria where no one was likely to know either one of them.

Dun took a seat with his back facing the wall—an old habit. "What's up?"

"How's Alex doing?" Knott was already scanning the menu.

"OK, I guess. A little nervous, but I don't blame him."

"He should be safe there." Knott looked up from the menu. "No one knows about you or your involvement."

"Hopefully." Dun looked away, knowing if that weren't true his apartment could turn into a war zone.

"Yeah. I've got to get Alex out of your apartment, but the usual safe house isn't an option. I can't trust anyone involved with that location until we can find the mole in the program. I need another spot, very secure, very quiet. Sorry to put you in the middle, but I'm having trouble finding a place that no one in the FBI or the Marshals service knows about. Almost there, just one detail to nail down."

Dun nodded. "I can handle it for a couple of days. But for his sake, let's get him in a bank vault somewhere. Sooner or later they're going to figure out where he is."

"Easier said than done. I'm working on a place near Annapolis, but it'll take a little more time. Hang in there."

"Why Annapolis? Isn't that a little busy?"

"Yeah, but perfect. They'll be looking for some remote location, not somewhere in the middle of the tourist hangouts." The look on Knott's face told Dun he was pleased with his logic. Dun hoped he was right.

"OK." Dun looked out the window at nothing in particular.

"What's wrong, buddy? This getting to you?"

Dun looked up, a little surprised. "No, not that. I'm just worried about Sally Olivia. No word on where she is. I can't find her anywhere, and I'm getting nervous. My gut tells me something doesn't smell right."

"Why? Isn't she in some doctor's care?"

"Yeah, but no one will tell me where she's being treated. I'm sure if she were all right, she'd have been in touch with me by now. All I get is that she's in private treatment, not to be disturbed until they can pull her out of the initial shock. Then, maybe, if she agrees, I might be able to see her. But no promises."

"Man, that sucks. What's her doctor's name?"

"That's part of the problem, Knott. I don't know. And can't find out."

Knott's brow furrowed. "Do you know that name of the last doctor that treated her?"

"Yeah, the doctor at the emergency ward in Jacksonville."

"OK. Write down his name and the name of the hospital. Let me see what I can find out."

"Really? You might be able to help?" Before Knott could answer, Dun sat up in his seat, took out a pen and his PI notebook, and began writing. When he was finished, he tore out the page and handed it across the table to Knott.

Knott glanced at the information, folded it in half, and slipped it into his shirt pocket. "No promises, but I'll try."

"Thanks. That'll be great."

"Let's talk about some logistics. If we're going to continue working together, we've got to make some changes."

"Changes? Like what?"

"Like your car, for example."

Dun half-smiled. "My car? What's that got to do with anything?"

"It's too small, too light, too conspicuous, and dangerous."

"Dangerous? That car couldn't hurt anything."

"That's the problem, buddy. Anyone hits you in that, you and Alex will have to be scraped off the pavement like bugs on a windshield."

"Look, Knott. I don't have any money to go out and buy something bigger. I'm barely making the payments on the Miata now. What the hell do—"

"Relax, Dun. Relax. I want you to go out and lease the largest and most powerful SUV you can find. And, make it black with tinted windows."

"Sure. No problem. And while I'm at it, I'll get one with a power winch on the front so I can pull my ass out of the poor house."

"Good idea. See if you can have it by tomorrow."

Before Dun could respond, Knott pulled out an American Express card and slid it across the table to Dun. It looked like it had been used for several years, but it had Dun's name on it.

"Wha'?"

"Take it. Use it for any expenses you might have. Don't worry, the bill comes to me."

"You're shittin' me."

"Naw. I wouldn't do that—you're my favorite turd." The expression on Dun's face must have been priceless. Knott started laughing, but quickly shut it off after looking around the restaurant. "Listen, Dun. I'm serious. Get that SUV. You're gonna' need it. And use that card for any expenses on this case. As I said before, I can't put you on the payroll, but I sure as hell can cover all your expenses."

Dun didn't know what to say. He just stared at the card. Then he looked up at Knott with a twinkle in his eye. "How 'bout a trip to Bermuda?"

"Don't push it, buddy. Just get the damn SUV, and do it quick."

Dun picked up the card, pulled his wallet from his back pocket, and slipped the card into one of the credit card slots. As he started to return the wallet, Knott reached across the table and grabbed his arm.

"You can start by using it to pay for this lunch."

Dun looked up and nodded. His mind was already twisting and turning about how deep this was getting. How far could he go before he drowned?

CHAPTER 24

LUCY opened the door to Dun's office and stuck her head in. "Can I talk with you for a minute?"

"Sure, c'mon in." From the look on her face, Dun knew something was up. When she walked in and took a seat at the old worktable, he turned around in his chair and got comfortable. A 'minute' was going to be an understatement.

"Ah…I've got a friend whose daughter wants to get into the investigation field. She's out of college a few years and not real happy with her current job."

"What's she doing?"

"She's working for a non-profit in D.C. Some kind of convention coordinator, or something like that."

"Convention coordinator to investigator. That's a logical career move." Dun started to laugh, but thought better of it. "Well, Luce, if that's what she wants to try, tell her to go for it. Not sure I can give her any advice, except to contact some of the larger agencies in the area and see if they'll take her on. She'll probably have to start in a support role of some kind, but if she's serious, she can work her way up."

"She's done that. Got nowhere. She doesn't have good secretarial skills, and the local agencies don't think her degree in Equestrian Studies will help them much."

"Equestrian Studies?" Now Dun did laugh. "You're kidding?"

"Nope. Always loved horses. Thought someday she'd manage a horse ranch. But, somehow pushing a broom through hay and horse poop burst her bubble. She found that starting at the bottom in that field meant under the horses' tail."

"Nice view. But now that I think of it, seems like some of the folks we have to deal with can be a horses' ass."

"Yeah. Anyway, she's heard me talking about what we do and is asking me a ton of questions."

"Questions? Like what?"

"Like could she get a job here and learn the ropes about being a PI?"

"Sure, Luce. No problem. We'll just put her on the payroll, plus full benefits. Then, after a week or so, she can move up to Vice President of Investigations."

"Seriously, Dun. She really wants to do this."

"Well, I'm not serious. I can hardly cover your salary, much less take on another investigator. That, Mrs. Cannon, is a long way off. Tell her to come back in ten years or so and we'll see what's open."

"She's willing to do it as an intern."

"Intern...meaning no pay?"

"That's what she said. She'll work for nothing just to learn the ropes. She's living with her folks, who are quite well off, so money's not an issue."

"I'm sorry, Lucy. I'd like to help. But right now, I'm up to my own horse's tail in problems, with Knott and Alex, and this Sally Olivia thing. I won't have any time for her. I don't even know where I'm going, much less teaching someone else. And frankly, between you and me, I'm scared I'm over my head. This Alex situation is a lot more dangerous than I bargained for, and we don't need another party involved."

"Look. I'll bring her in, have her work with me for a few weeks on general stuff. I agree that she shouldn't be privy to the Alex case—that has to be kept confidential. Plus, I don't want her put in any danger either. Her mother would kill me."

"Well...

"Let's give it a try. If it doesn't work out, I'll convince her to move on. That'll keep you out of it. I'll handle it completely."

"OK, Luce. Your baby. Just keep her out of my way."

"Agreed. Thanks Dun. I think you'll like her. She's really nice, just floundering a little right now."

Oh boy, what did he have himself in for? When women say another woman is 'really nice,' that usually means an ugly duckling with the social graces of a eunuch. Dun groaned as the vision of a baby whale flashed through his mind.

CHAPTER 25

KNOTT was in his office when his phone rang. He reached across his desk and picked it up. "Knott Harrison."

"Yes you are," came the reply, followed by laughter. "Sorry, Knott, this is Cob. I couldn't resist. Always wanted to do that."

Knott chuckled. "Morning, Cob. How's it going?"

"Well, you tell me. I haven't heard a word since our first meeting. What's going on?"

"Been meaning to call you. Unfortunately, there's a lot going on. And, I've had to make a decision."

"Oh?"

"This is no reflection on you…or, maybe it is. I've decided to put you on hold for a while. There's been some heavy activity with our boy, so somewhere there's a major leak in the dam."

"What's that got to do with me? I thought you and I were going to work on this?"

"We are, Cob. But until I get this situation stabilized, I have to isolate all possibilities. And, frankly, you're one of them."

Knott could hear Cob suck in some air on the other end of the phone. "Damn, Knott. I thought—

"I know," he interrupted. "Look. I can't take any more chances on this. For your protection, and mine, I'm closing and locking any doors that can open. I don't want you being a suspect when and if something else goes wrong. If I'm the only one working this case, then no one can point a finger at you."

"Wait a damn minute! This is my case, remember? Fingers have already been pointed at me. Accusations made. I need a chance to clear my name, and I can't do that sitting in a dark closet."

"Calm down, Cob. This *was* your case, remember? You've were reassigned to special duty for the White House. No one, including me, thinks you're dirty on this. Your past record speaks for itself."

"That's bullshit, Knott. Word gets around. You know that as well as I do."

"Yeah, and the word is you got special recognition with this new assignment. Everyone knows you are no longer the handler on this case."

"So, what's the problem? Why am I on hold? And, who is officially handling Alex?"

"I can't tell you that, Cob. For your own protection. All records on this case have been sealed, by order of the White House. That means you no longer have access to this area of WPP—nor does anyone else."

"Damn, Knott. Isn't that a little overkill?"

"Not to the President, it isn't. He wants this case locked down and resolved ASAP. He's put the highest priority on it until we can find the leak and plug it. There's more than just this case at stake—the whole program is at risk, along with some other security issues I told you earlier I can't talk about."

"What the hell am I supposed to do in the meanwhile? Sit around with my fingers up my ass?"

"Of course not. You're too valuable for that. Hang tight for a while. Clean up some of your current projects and be ready to jump in when I give you the signal. I'll need you on this, Cob. I just have to isolate you right now, again for your own protection and mine. I'll get back to you as soon as I can."

"OK, Knott. Doesn't look like I have any choice. I don't like it, but I'll be ready when you call."

"Thanks. I appreciate your support." Knott hung up the phone. He didn't feel very good about putting Cob's loyalty in question, but he didn't have any choice.

* * *

Cob sat back in his chair and looked at the phone he had just placed on its cradle. This wasn't good for what he wanted to do, what he was expected to do.

His face glowed red and his fingers trembled a little as he picked up a pen and scribbled a few notes on a piece of paper, which he then folded and put in his pocket.

When he finished, he swiveled his chair toward the window and stared out for a few minutes. Finally, he made a decision.

He turned back toward his desk, picked up the phone, and placed a call.

CHAPTER 26

DUN took a cab to the local Lincoln dealer. From what he could gather from the SUVs he saw on the road and the classified section of the newspaper, the Lincoln Navigator seemed to be as big as any.

As he got out of the cab in front of the dealership, a salesman with a plastic smile and a hearty step came through the double front doors and gave Dun a big wave.

"Good afternoon, sir. May I help you?" The salesman had just been through a new course on customer service and he was eager to apply all the wisdom he learned.

"No thanks," answered Dun, ignoring the outstretched hand. "I'll just look around for awhile."

"That's fine, sir. My name is Brad. I'll be right inside if you need any help. And your name…?"

"Wolfgang Schmidt of the FTC, Brad. After I check things out, I'll come looking for you."

"Oh, ah…sure, Mr. Schmidt. Actually, I have to leave early today, but I'm sure someone else will be happy to answer any questions you may have."

"I doubt it, Brad. Most people aren't real happy to see me. But, maybe today will be different."

Without another word, Dun brushed by the salesman and started for the showroom. Brad ran ahead and held the door for him, and then scurried around the corner and out of sight.

Dun looked around and saw a Lincoln Navigator on display in the center of the showroom. It was huge. Compared to his Mazda Miata, it looked like a Bradley tank. The paint was jet black, the tires were jet black, and with the exception of the windshield and the driver and passenger windows, the remaining windows were jet black.

He opened the driver's door and climbed inside. The seats were black leather, the dash was black walnut—even the carpets were black. It was equipped with digital instruments that had soft-tan backgrounds and black numerals.

Well, Knott had said big and black. They didn't get much bigger or blacker than this. Dun had to admit that if this thing ever hit his Miata head on, there'd be nothing left but his stained underwear.

As he climbed out of the vehicle and closed the door, he bumped into something soft. Very soft. Turning around, he faced a gorgeous dark-haired young woman with outstanding attributes. Outstanding as in very top heavy. He wondered how she ever managed to tie her shoes, much less see them.

He blinked twice, and then offered his apologies. "I'm sorry, Miss. I didn't realize you were right behind me." Actually, she could have been ten feet away and he would have still bumped into her.

"Mr. Schmidt, my name is Paula Hardbridge, and I'd like to welcome you to our dealership. I'd be happy to answer any questions you may have."

Dun blushed. The first question that popped into his mind was one he couldn't ask. The second one, like asking what she was doing for lunch, probably wasn't a good idea either. Looks like they brought out the heavy artillery, the big guns. Doing his damnedest to focus on her face, he had to admit she sure beat the other salesman.

"Well, actually Paula, I have a confession to make. My name is not Schmidt."

"I didn't think so. Hate car salesmen?"

"Good guess."

"And dentists?"

"Right again. But I do love dental hygienists." That thought almost made him blush again.

"Well, I'm not a salesman."

"So I noticed."

"Actually, I'm the General Manager, and while I don't usually sell vehicles, I'll be glad to work with you if you give me your name."

Dun was surprised. His first impression was that her position at the dealership was 'prone,' but maybe that was an unfair stereotype. "Fair enough. I'm Dun Wheeling, and I'm here to lease a Navigator."

"OK, Mr. Wheeling—"

"Dun."

"OK, Dun. What features are you looking for."

"Big, powerful, and black."

"Wow, that's pretty specific," she said, laughing. She had a dazzling smile. "What else? All-wheel traction, CD, GPS, lighting package, V-8, remote entry, roof rack?"

"Yes, all that and a power winch."

"I'm sorry, Dun, but the dealership doesn't install power—"

"Just kidding, Paula. An inside joke."

"Maybe if you tell me what you intend to use it for, I can suggest some other features."

"Well, Paula, that's not quite so easy to explain."

"Why don't your try me?" The gleam in her eye was hard to miss.

Dun paused and decided to let that remark pass. He turned around and pointed to the Navigator behind him. "This one have all that?"

Paula walked over to the Navigator and leaned against the front fender. "Yes. There's a lot more under here than you'd ever believe."

"Really?"

"Oh, yes. Would you like to see?"

Dun looked at her. Paula's face was expressionless, but the sparkle in her eye told him she was an expert at double-entendre. Maybe with a figure like that she had to be—self-defense.

"That's okay, Paula. I'll take your word for it. Wrap it up."

"I have a special running right now, with unique incentives you wouldn't believe."

"Fine. As I said, I'll take your word for it."

"Well…okay, Mr. Wheeling, er, Dun. Let's go to my office and review the lease terms, and I'll have one of the men bring this one's twin around so you can test drive it."

"No need for a test drive, Paula." He pulled out his American Express card and handed it to her. "Just put it all on here, and I'll be off."

"But, Dun. Don't you want to negotiate my lease?"

He shook his head; the woman wouldn't give up. "Sure. Just give me your best deal. I trust you."

* * *

Paula was speechless. This was new to her. She was geared for battle, to dicker, negotiate, pull out all the stops, and definitely use her figure to befuddle and intimidate. And yet this guy was leaving it all up to her. "I trust you," he said. She felt like she'd been kicked in the stomach and the wind driven out in one rush.

Was this guy some hick? Or maybe he had more money that he knew what to do with? He didn't want to explain what he planned to use the car for—a drug dealer? Nah. Or…or, the FTC after all?

He didn't look like a government guy. He was actually quite nice looking. Tall, sandy hair, good build, beautiful eyes, and a quiet confidence. Something about the way he walked attracted her.

When she first approached him, she thought she had him. He couldn't take his eyes of her. Which was the reaction most men had when they first saw her. But then he turned off, refused to play in sexual banter. She was disappointed. She enjoyed messing with men's minds, winding them around her little finger, dropping little hints here and there, playing up to their little sexual fantasies. It always had worked before.

But this one, he was different. There was no ring on his finger. Maybe if I ask him out to lunch, while the paperwork is being prepared, I can grab his attention.

She took a deep breath, sucked in her stomach, and said, "Dun, I'll make sure you get our best deal. Take my word for it. However, it will take a few minutes for the paperwork to be prepared, so how about if I take you down the street and we grab some lunch?"

"Why, thank you Paula. That's very nice of you. However, I'm not at all hungry. I'll just sit over there and wait until the paperwork is ready."

"A cup of coffee?"

"Thanks, but no. If you don't mind."

"No…ah, not at all, Dun. I'll put a rush on it." Paula turned and walked toward her office, Dun's credit card extended out in front of her in one hand, the other scooping her hair behind her ear.

She stopped, turned, and watched as Dun walked over to the seating area by the front window and pulled out his cell phone. Holding it close to his mouth, he said something, but she couldn't make it out.

After several moments, she heard him say, "Knott, this is Dun. What's going on? Any info on Sally Olivia? Please call me back."

She turned again and headed toward her office. She shook her head as she walked; she was stumped. She didn't know why, but something told her to give this guy a very good deal.

CHAPTER 27

DUN pulled up in front of the safe house in Annapolis. Knott had given him directions, even drew a small map. Not that he really needed it, with the Global Positioning System mapping feature in the car, but he felt a little guilty telling him that.

Yep, just as Knott said, located right on the waterfront, smack in the middle of the restaurants and gift shops.

"Here we are, Alex." Dun turned off the SUV and looked across at his passenger.

Alex looked around in surprise. "Here? This is what you call a safe house?"

"Sure. The last place anyone would suspect. Right in the middle of tourists, merchants, and local residents. You'll be staying on the second floor, right over that little pizza shop there. C'mon, let's meet your resident agent."

Dun opened the door, stepped down, and went around the front of the SUV to the sidewalk. After Alex got out, Dun popped the rear lid and took out the little sports bag that contained all of Alex's possessions. He pointed at the pizza shop. "Right up that flight of stairs on the side of the building. After you."

Alex walked to the top of the stairs and waited on the landing while Dun used the key given to him to open the door. Stepping inside, he found a small kitchen that looked like it had been decorated in the fifties. As he turned around to say something to Alex, he felt something like a cold pipe jabbed into the back of his neck.

"Good afternoon, Dun. I'm Roy."

Dun stiffened, then turned and faced a .45 automatic held in the hand of one of the largest men he had ever seen.

Without moving, Dun said over his shoulder, "Alex, meet Roy. Knott says he's an ex-NFL lineman, and the only guy he knows that can put out a squirrel's eye at thirty yards with that Colt clunker."

"Fifty yards. Nice to meet you, Dun." Roy smiled and held out his hand. Dun hesitated, wondering if he'd ever get his hand back.

Roy stepped around Dun and offered his hand to Alex. "Hi Alex. Glad you're here."

Dun and Alex both gaped at the size of Roy. He was huge, especially up close.

"I know," Roy smiled, "we look a lot smaller on TV."

Dun laughed. "Sorry, Roy. I always thought I was pretty big until now. Nice to meet you also. Knott thinks quite highly of you, so that's good enough for me."

"He said you guys go back a ways, Dun. Sorry for the greeting, but you didn't fit the description he gave me."

"Oh, Jesus. What did he tell you?" Dun couldn't wait to hear this one.

"That you were bald, fat, and cross-eyed."

"That dirty sonofa—"

Roy's laugh sounded like a bear's roar, and cut off Dun's sentence. "Just kidding, Dun, he finally told me the truth. I've worked with him long enough not to believe anything he tells me—at first."

Dun smiled and relaxed a little. Knott hadn't changed a bit over the years. "That guy's going to get me killed one of these days."

"Naw, he said you were his favorite turd."

"You know, Roy, I'm going to have to think real hard of how I can get back at him. It may take awhile, but it'll happen."

"Let me know if you need any help. I owe him a few."

"I'll just bet you do," Dun said, turning toward Alex, who was standing there looking as if he had blundered into a psychiatric ward.

"Don't worry. You'll be safe with Roy here. Just do everything he says. And I mean everything. Knott or I will be back to check on you in a couple of days. If you need anything, Roy can arrange it. But Knott was serious when he said that neither of you are to leave this place. Understood?"

Before Alex could shake his head 'yes,' Dun turned, took a chance shaking hands with Roy again, and was out the door.

* * *

"Come on in and have a seat in the living room, Alex. We've got TV, cards, magazines, and checkers. What's your pleasure?"

Roy turned and walked into the living room in front of Alex. Without seeming to move, he quickly tucked away the pistol in his shoulder holster. He could retrieve it even faster. An earplug, with the cord running down the back of his neck and under his shirt collar, was now obvious.

* * *

Across the street, on the roof of a two-story building with a false-front that held a large 'General Store' sign, a man watched as Dun drove away. He put down his binoculars, wrote down the license plate number of the SUV, and spoke into a cell phone. "Our man has arrived."

After listening for a moment, he said, "I know what to do. I'll take care of it."

He closed the cover of his cell phone, reached down, and unzipped a long leather case shaped like a rifle.

CHAPTER 28

AS Dun drove away from the safe house, he checked his cell phone. He was hoping for a message from Knott. He held the cell phone close to his lips and said, "Knott." To his surprise, Knott answered almost immediately.

"Hi, Knott. Assume you got my message."

"Yes. Where are you?"

"Just leaving Annapolis. Our boy is safe in his new location, well guarded. You can relax for awhile."

"How's the SUV?"

"Leased a Lincoln Navigator."

"Outstanding choice.'"

"Yes. And an outstanding general manager."

"What?"

"Never mind, I'll tell you later. Any news on Sally Olivia?"

"As a matter of fact, there is. I'll meet you at your office in two hours and fill you in."

"Can't wait. Thanks Knott. Really appreciate this."

"No sweat, buddy. Glad I can help. See you shortly."

Dun wondered what news Knott had for him. He obviously didn't want to discuss it on the phone, even though the cell phones were supposed to be super secure. So, it must be bad news. Great, just what he needed.

He tried to force the subject out of his mind and pay more attention to his driving. The SUV was like a cruise ship compared to his Miata, and he wasn't yet comfortable with all the controls and gadgets. A guy could get killed fooling around with all that stuff.

The GPS display really intrigued him, but even with excellent vision he found trying to read the information while driving very difficult. The woman at the dealership—what was her name, he forgot already—said it could be hooked up to a laptop and it would provide voice directions for any trip he had planned. Unreal. He laughed, thinking about the laptop screaming, "Take the next right…no, right, you dumb idiot."

He liked the advantage of being high off the road. The visibility was much improved, and safer since he could see farther ahead. However, he could understand where someone could become a road bully with the size and power the vehicle offered. Knott was right, if he got hit by one of these things while driving the Miata he'd be flatter than a bumper sticker. Structural mismatch, he thought they called it.

As much as he tried to get off the subject, his mind kept coming back to Sally Olivia. Where the hell was she? Why hasn't she contacted him? His gut told him something was wrong. That she was in trouble somehow, and needed him. Well, he had Alex safely tucked away. Alex, Roy, and Knott would have to fend for themselves for a while. No reason he couldn't pursue this. He had to do something!

* * *

Without waiting for a response, Knott switched off his cell phone and tucked it into his pocket. The news he had for Dun wasn't particularly good. Sally Olivia had been transferred to a private clinic in upstate New York. Assuming she was still there, it was a long drive from where Dun was located.

However, that was the good news. The bad news was that the hospital administrator had a long history of suspicious behavior. Nothing the law could hold him accountable for, but enough that he had aroused the interest of several Federal agencies.

He was suspected of holding wealthy patients hostage, keeping them heavily sedated, and treating them with various medicines that ensured they stayed ill and required long and specialized treatment before they got well. No one had been able to prove it, but by the time the patient was released, the final bill approached the level of the national debt.

A few of the patients never made it. They somehow managed to OD on stolen medicines, or were accidentally killed after they escaped from the hospital and wandered away in a mental fog. It was no surprise to the Federal agencies that these particular patients were suspected of being unwilling to pay the expected final tab.

However, no conclusive evidence could be found to prove this theory. Drug tests on the deceased revealed no unusual substances, only medicines that would be used in accepted medical treatment for the stated illness were evident. And then, only in normally prescribed amounts.

He pitied the doctor and his facility if Dun found Sally Olivia was there and being held against her will. Knott officially couldn't do much until a legal case could be built, but he smiled as he thought of a line from one of his favorite movies: "Ve haf our vays."

CHAPTER 29

SALLY Olivia Sawgrass awoke with a start. The room was dark, except for a narrow crack of light under the door. She strained her ears, but the only sound she could hear was her own breathing through the double surgical mask tightly covering her face. A scream erupted from her mouth, only to be muffled like a bullet passing through a silencer.

As the fog in her brain began to clear, a rush of panic washed over her body. She couldn't move, sit up, or flee from wherever was. Her arms and legs were restrained with webbed straps secured to the sides of the hospital bed. The collars attached to her limbs were padded with thick foam to prevent bruising.

After several minutes of straining against the straps, she was exhausted, but the effort helped her fight off the drugs. She relaxed her body but struggled to clear her mind. The drugs were still pulsing through her veins, coaxing her back to a warm dreamless slumber. She almost gave in, but something made her fight it, subdue the temptation, and try to rise above the fog to figure out where she was, why she was here.

She felt like she was winning. Her mind was clearing, her senses returning. She remembered collapsing in Dun's arms after hearing the news about her brother, him taking her in an ambulance to the emergency ward at the hospital in Jacksonville, and the kind doctor giving her a shot to make her sleep. When she woke, Dun was there; holding her hand, reassuring her everything was going to be all right, that he would stay with her as long as she needed him.

When she awoke again. Dun was not there. Another doctor was talking to her, telling her something about severe trauma, and that she would be transferred to a private facility for treatment. That's all she could remember. Until now. How long had she been here? Wherever 'here' was. Days? A week?

She tested her restraints again, and could taste the heavy cloth of the mask over her mouth. Why? Had she been violent, trying to cause harm to herself? Did they need to restrain her for whatever treatment she was undergoing? Maybe she had suffered a concussion when she collapsed; they were keeping her perfectly still so she wouldn't injure herself.

Suddenly she realized she was naked, with only a sheet and thermal blanket covering her body. Again, a rush of panic invaded her senses, but it was no use. The restraints were unyielding.

Footsteps in the hall. Two people coming closer. One with a heavy step, each far apart, with what sounded like leather heels clicking on the hallway surface. The other, a softer, lighter tread, and steps spaced closer together.

They stopped at the door. The sound of a heavy key inserted into the lock and the bolt retracted. The door, as it creaked slowly open, creaked as if it were metal.

Sally Olivia closed her eyes and tried to regulate her breathing. Every fiber in her body wanted to revolt, tear of the restraints, and push her body through the doorway to freedom, but she willed herself to act as if she were in a deep sleep.

"She's still out, Doctor. I thought she would be. That was a heavy dose you gave her the last time." The woman, most likely a nurse, had a pleasant voice with a soft British accent

"I just want to make sure she doesn't come around before we're ready. Another day or so, and then we can slowly bring her back to reality and convince her of the treatment she'll need." The doctor's voice was smooth, but clipped. Sally Olivia detected a slight accent, but couldn't place it.

"I still don't like it."

"You want her coming out of this while she's still in restraints? C'mon, Bev, if that happens we'll have a serious problem on our hands. You remember what happened the last time."

"Yes, I do. Vividly. That doesn't mean I have to like it. The poor dear. How she ever got her hands on all those pills is beyond me."

"That won't happen again, I promise. We're here to provide outstanding and advanced treatments for trauma patients, and we have a right to expect proportionate compensation—not the pittance the insurance or government hacks dictate."

As Doctor Shavitz approached Sally Olivia, he reached inside his breast pocket and took out a hypodermic needle already prepared with the sedative. He pulled back the sheet and blanket covering her and paused.

"Um, Doctor," the nurse said, "you either put a gown on that poor woman or I'll be giving her the injections from now own. I don't like the way you're looking at her."

"Don't worry, Bev. Just checking her over to make sure she didn't have any bruises from the restraints."

"Yes, and I'm Florence Nightingale. Just give her the shot and let's go."

"Sure. We wouldn't want our lovely patient waking up and finding out what we're doing to her, would we? Could be rather embarrassing. We'll bring her out of this very slowly and she won't know the difference. She'll think we're wonderful, and maybe even want to make an important contribution to our clinic, not to mention the tidy sum we'll collect for our medical services when we're through. Her stupid estate lawyers will surely gasp when they see the final bill, but they won't have any choice but to pay it."

The doctor leaned over the bed and gave Sally Olivia the injection on the inside of her left arm. He slowly pulled the covers back over her and turned toward the nurse.

"OK, that will hold her for another day or so. But it won't hold me, so what say we go back to my place for a bottle of wine and some soft music? I've got one more examination I need to make today."

"Whatever you say. You're the doctor." Bev giggled as she left the room and the doctor locked the door behind him.

Sally Olivia's body convulsed with shudders. She could sense the doctor staring at her as he had folded back the sheet, and she felt violated. She tried to memorize every word the doctor and nurse had said, and vowed that if she ever got out of there they would pay dearly. Dearly...pay dearly...were the last words floating through her mind as the new sedative took effect.

CHAPTER 30

DUN returned to his office only to find another car parked in the small space behind the building. He had left his Miata at his apartment parking area, so he'd have room at the office for the leased SUV. Now, someone else was taking his space. A customer? No, there was room out front reserved for that. What the hell?

He walked around to the front of the building and opened the main door to his office area. "Luce, who the hell is taking my parking space? I had to park on the grass, which you know will really piss off the landlord. He specif—?"

"Dun," Lucy interrupted, "I'd like you to meet my niece, Samantha Shovert. She's the intern we discussed a few days ago." If the look Lucy gave him could kill, Dun would be embalmed by now.

"Oh…Sorry, didn't know we had a…er, new intern today." Dun turned to find that most of his vision of Lucy's "she's really nice" was true. Except for the baby whale part. Samantha wasn't quite an ugly duckling, but close. About five feet five, with shoulder-length dull brown hair done in the multi-corkscrew style that he hated. What might be a somewhat attractive face didn't have a chance behind the thick-rimmed black, boxy glasses that made her look like a Greek accountant. He guessed her age to be about mid to late 20s.

Her frame seemed to be slim, although it was hard to tell with the ankle-length flowered skirt shaped like a lampshade and a drab puffy linen jacket that seemed about five sizes too large. The image was capped with white socks stuffed into sandals that looked like they were designed as an accessory for the Humvee. She looked like a refuge from a yard sale at Ellis Island.

"Hi, Samantha. Nice to have you're here. Lucy has told me a lot about you." *Though, obviously not enough.*

"Hi, Mr. Wheeling. I'm really excited to be here. Thanks for taking me on. I won't get in the way, I promise." Her voice was smooth and pleasant. One check for her side.

"Call me Dun."

"OK, you're done." Samantha laughed, pleased with her own joke. Erase that checkmark. "Yeah, funny, Samantha. And, please, move your car around to the front. It's usually reserved for customers, but I need the space in back. Maybe folks will see it and think we've got business."

"Please call me Sam, Mr. Wheeling. Er, Dun. Sorry for the joke, guess I'm a little nervous."

"OK, Sam. No problem. Joking is a way of life around here, so you'll fit right in. Lucy can show you the ropes. Right now I'm up to my ears with a heavy case, so you'll have to excuse me." With that, Dun shot Lucy a thin smile and went into his office.

* * *

"Gee, Lucy. That didn't seem to go too well," Sam said, a slight blush showing on her cheeks.

"Don't take it personally. Dun is in the middle of a life-threatening case—don't ask, I can't discuss it with you for lots of reasons—so he's a little uptight right now. Dun's really a nice guy."

Sam ran her fingers through her hair and looked at Dun's closed door. "Wow, you said he was good looking, but you didn't prepare me for this."

"Yeah, he is. Don't ever tell him this, but he's the son I never had." Lucy paused and blinked her eyes.

Sam moved over beside Lucy and put her arm around her. "Gee, Aunt Luce, that's sweet. Don't worry, I won't mention a word, but it's nice you feel that way."

"You better not, if you know what's good for ya'." Lucy's threat came with a smile. "OK, let's get to work. But first, move your car around front."

Sam smiled, glanced again at Dun's door, and hummed to herself as she walked toward the front door twirling her car keys.

* * *

Dun sat down in his office chair and cupped his hands over his face. His mind was grinding like a food processor trying to mix concrete.

Dealing with Knott, the FBI, Alex in the Witness Protection Program with killers after him, one man already dead, and Sally Olivia somewhere unknown and possibly in trouble, was more than he had bargained for. And now he had Sam to trip over.

Earlier, being in serious debt with collection attorneys after him was nothing compared to this. Was he up for this? Could he handle it?

Dun wasn't a pessimist, but he knew his limitations. He didn't feel he had the experience to cope with all this. He felt like he was being thrust into a whirlpool, naked, with no weapons to fight the alligators churning around with him, snapping with their powerful jaws and whipping their armored tails at him.

Dun sat up straight in his chair. There was no choice now, he was already in too deep to back out. His dad had an expression, "When in doubt, move forward like you know what you're doing."

OK, no problem. I can move forward. I just have to find the right track.

CHAPTER 31

KNOTT arrived at Dun's office an hour late. "Sorry, but got hung up in some stuff at the office. Had an interesting meeting with the US Marshal that's been handling Alex's case. Unless my instincts are all screwed up, I think he's okay."

"That's good to hear. What's his name?"

"Cob Ferguson. Been around for a while. Good man. You'll meet him later."

"The only problem I have is that the ring of folks who know what's going on is growing wider," Dun said, tapping his pencil on his desk.

"Yeah, good point. I'll have to think on that. Cob is, and has been, part of the case. Hard to keep him out unless we can prove he's behind the leaks."

"Yeah. True. So, where do we go from here? Alex is nestled in the safe house. Met Roy the mountain. Glad he's on our side."

"They don't get any better, or bigger, than Roy. I'd bet my life on him."

"Hope you don't have to." Dun leaned back in his chair. "So, were you able to find out anything about Sally Olivia?" Dun's heart rate went up. He wasn't sure he wanted to hear the news.

"Yeah. Good and bad. The good is that I think I know where she is. The bad is I don't know if she's still there. Also, it's a long ways away from here."

"Long ways meaning what?"

"In the Catskills."

"Hell, that's not too far. I thought you were going to say Seattle or something. Even that's not too far if I can find her. C'mon, give me some details."

"OK. Some of my boys in Jacksonville spoke with the doctor at the emergency ward you mentioned. At first, he didn't want to cooperate, said it was confidential. They convinced him that the FBI was looking into interstate medical fraud, and he might be a material witness. That got his attention."

"Good. Go on."

"The doctor felt Sally Olivia needed specialized treatment, so he tried to contact a local specialist, only to learn this guy had moved to upper New York. He apparently had a top reputation in the area, so the doctor contacted Sally Olivia's estate lawyers and made arrangements to have her transferred to this clinic."

"So? I gave the doctor the contact for her estate lawyers. That sounds pretty normal."

"Yes, it does. So far. However, my boys checked out the specialist, only to find he'd left the area suddenly, like real quick. He's under investigation for over-treating wealthy trauma victims and running up bills that would choke a horse. There's also a question of why a couple of his patients died."

"What? How'd they die?" Dun's heart rate was really cooking now.

"One accidentally OD'd on meds, the other left the facility while heavily medicated and walked in front of a truck."

"God! I've got to get up there and get her out before—"

"Slow down, Dun. I've got some guys up there checking out the place. She'll be okay."

"Okay isn't good enough! Who is this guy, and what's the name of his clinic?"

"Dr. Mark Shavitz. Shavitz Trauma Clinic."

Dun was writing this down. "And where do I find him?"

"Look, Dun. No sense racing off without a plan. You can't go barging in with a club and drag her out. The local—" Knott stopped mid-sentence.

The skin on Dun's face was as tight as a kettledrum, and his neck muscles throbbed as the blood and adrenalin surged through his body. His words were barely above a whisper as Dun asked again, "Knott, I need that address. Don't worry, by the time I get there, I'll have a plan."

Without a word, Knott slid a piece of paper across the desk to Dun. "OK. Hope you know what you're doing. Be careful. On the back of that paper is the contact for one of my local boys in case you need it. Take the Lincoln; you may need the space and the power."

Dun looked at the address and nodded his thanks. "Guess I'd better buy a map. Never heard of this town."

"Think it's just above Glens Falls. Not sure. But with that GPS system you have in that tank of a SUV, it should be a piece of cake to find."

"Thanks, Knott. Appreciate this." As if he were in Knott's office, instead of his own, Dun got up and left. Knott just smiled and leaned back in his chair.

CHAPTER 32

"YOU hungry, Alex?" Roy was sitting on the couch, watching a golf match on TV.

"Not really. Guess I'm too nervous right now."

"No problem, I'm going to call downstairs and order a pizza. Sure you won't have some?"

"Thanks, but think I'll go into my room and lie down for awhile."

"OK, let me know if you change your mind."

Alex went into his bedroom and swung the door closed, stopping it just before it latched. He sprawled on the bed, cupped his hands behind his head, and let his mind wander.

He was beginning to think this would never end. Is this what the rest of his life was going to be? Running, hiding? Never having the chance for a normal life? It's one thing to say he could never marry, never have kids, always be alone without any real friends. It's another to realize his pursuers were never going to quit, would probably find him again, make him relocate one more time, and have to live with some gorilla guarding him. Sure, he liked Roy. Nice guy. But not his idea of a lasting intimate relationship.

There were times when he wished he'd never testified. Walked away from that company, not saying a word. They'd get caught sooner or later anyway. But he knew he couldn't do that and live with himself.

He almost laughed out loud. *Live with myself. That's what I'm doing, for Christ's sake! What a life!*

Alex's mind wandered several more minutes, until the noise of the doorbell caught his attention. He heard Roy answer the door, speak to the boy delivering the pizza, and return to the couch.

Roy called out, "Sure you won't change your mind? Looks pretty good."

"No thanks, Roy. I'm fine." The last thing his stomach needed right now was hot greasy pizza. Just the smell was starting to make his gut quiver.

He returned to his daydreaming, wondering what the future might hold, whether this nightmare would ever be over. Where did he go from here? Another safe house? Another apartment somewhere in the bowels of the country? A long lonely life without a partner, no kids, no normal job, no long-term friends? Nothing.

He must have dozed off. As he rubbed his eyes, he noticed there wasn't a sound in the apartment except for the soft drone of the TV. He called out to Roy, asking how the pizza was. No answer. Could he have fallen asleep? He doubted it.

Alex swung his legs off the bed and opened the door. He was wrong. Roy was asleep, with a piece of pizza still in his right hand. Funny, would a bodyguard fall asleep so easily, especially on a new assignment?

He walked into the living room and over to Roy. Putting his hand on Roy's shoulder, he gave him a shake. "Roy, you're missing the golf match."

Roy didn't budge. Alex shook his shoulder. No reaction. "Roy. Roy! Wake up!"

He shook Roy's shoulder again, then removed the half-eaten slice of pizza from his hand. He noted that the pizza box was nearly empty. Using both hands on Roy's shoulder, he shook him vigorously, but Roy only slouched over on his side.

Hands shaking, Alex searched for a pulse. There was one, but it was weak. He stood up and looked at the kitchen. He quickly crossed to the outside door and checked that it was locked. Then he returned and looked at the pizza. Roy must have been poisoned or drugged! Something in that pizza.

Not again! *Will they ever leave me alone?* Alex's heart was racing and his mind whirring like helicopter blades. They'll be coming. Just as soon as they figure whatever was in the pizza has taken hold. They probably think he's out also, so it would be simple to kill them both and not leave a trace. How the hell did they get the drugs into the pizza?

He realized he was starting to panic, and took deep breaths to calm himself. Then he remembered the cell phone Knott had provided through

Dun. His hands were shaking so much he had trouble unclipping it from his belt. Holding it up to his lips he whispered, "On" and then "Knott."

Within ten seconds, Knott answered. "Knott here."

"Knott. It's Alex. Something's wrong. Roy's been drugged, or worse."

"What? How the hell did that happen?"

"No time to explain. They'll be coming for us. Soon. Probably figure I've been affected too." Alex was having trouble keeping his voice steady.

"Alex, right now, go into the bathroom and lock the door! Someone will be there in five minutes."

"Hope that's not too late, Knott." Alex didn't even bother to turn off the phone as he turned and started toward the bathroom. He stopped, turned back toward the outside door, and listened.

No sound. But they'll be coming. Probably before Knott's men can get here. And he'll be a sitting duck in the bathroom. No way. He had to get out of here.

He quickly walked to the kitchen door, stopped, and listened again. No sound. He approached the outside door and peered through a corner of the curtain covering the small window in the door. No one outside. He could hear traffic in the street, and muted voices of folks walking by on the sidewalk below. If he could reach the street, he could blend into the crowd and disappear.

The door was locked and the bolt latched. He turned the lock button on the doorknob, unlatched the bolt, and slowly twisted the knob until the door came free of the jamb and started to swing inward. So far, so good.

Alex stepped outside and stood on the landing while he closed the door behind him. He let out a breath of air. All clear.

He never heard a sound as something red-hot smashed into the side of his head. His body slammed into the side of the building and slowly slid to the wood landing. A long trail of blood pointed to where his head rested on the deck.

CHAPTER 33

THE location was perfect for what he had to do.

Dun drove by the front of the clinic, driving as slow as he dared to avoid attracting attention. The clinic was situated about a hundred feet back from the road and nestled in a large stand of dense oak trees. The building, a one-story brick structure, was much deeper than it was wide, and looked recently built. A small sign, placed beside the stone walkway that led to the side entrance, was the only identification of the building's purpose. The nearest building on either side was a good one hundred yards away. Across the street was an empty lot. The dead branches, leaves, and debris were evidence that it had yet to be developed.

It was obvious that this area was being planned as a suburban office park, with each building on at least an acre of land. Driving to the end of the street, Dun passed by engineering companies, research firms, and a small manufacturing plant—all having one thing in common: no high volume of customer traffic.

Several hundred yards past the building, Dun made a U-turn, drove back to the clinic, and pulled into the driveway on the left side of the building. A small parking area was located on the side just opposite the entrance. The driveway continued around the back to an employee parking area, which, from its size, indicated a very small staff.

Perfect.

Dun parked and walked to the entrance. A sign to the right of the doorway indicated that Dr. Mark Shavitz, Trauma Specialist, was the only physician on staff. Under his listing were the names of two RNs. That would help; less people to get by.

Dun entered the building and walked up to the reception desk. Behind it was a full-figured nurse with an attractive smile and a perky demeanor.

"May I help you, sir?" she asked.

"Yes," Dun said. "My name is Ned Holmes and I'm here to visit one of your patients."

"Well, sir, we don't have visiting hours here. This is a restricted facility for patients with severe trauma symptoms."

Dun paused, thinking of where to go next. "Yes, I can understand that. My cousin, Sally Olivia Sawgrass, was admitted here. I've just come by to pay my respects. I live about sixty miles away and just happened to be in the area today."

"Just a minute sir, while I check the records." The nurse looked at her computer screen and punched in a few keystrokes. "I'm sorry, sir. I thought that name was familiar. She's no longer here. Been transferred to another facility for extended treatment."

"What? She just got here not long ago. Where's she gone?"

"I'm sorry, sir. I'm not at liberty to divulge that information. It's a part of her confidential medical records."

"That's crazy! I'm her closest living relative, and you can't even tell me where she's being—?"

"Just a minute, sir. I'll page Dr. Shavitz."

While the nurse picked up the phone, Dun looked around. Beyond the reception desk was a cross-hallway that connected the two other hallways that ran down each side of the building. Another nurse was walking by while Dun was talking, and Dun noticed the look of panic on her face. She hesitated for a moment, then picked up her pace and walked around the corner.

"Sir. Dr. Shavitz will be right with you. Just a moment, please."

"Thanks, nurse. I'll have a seat."

A few minutes later, Dr. Shavitz walked into the reception area. He was wearing the obligatory white coat and stethoscope. A slight man with dark wavy hair, the doctor smiled as though he was meeting a major benefactor of the clinic.

"Mr. Holmes?"

Dun smiled. Brilliant deduction. He was the only person in the reception area. "Yes. Dr. Shavitz?" He couldn't resist.

Dun stood up and they shook hands. The doctor's grip was like touching a wet eel in a kelp bed.

"I am so sorry about Miss Sawgrass. I understand you're a relative?"

"Yes, her only cousin. Both her parents are deceased, as are mine. I'm the only one she has, besides her estate lawyers, that is." Dun looked directly at the man with the broadest smile he could manage, while his instincts were telling him to punch out the man's lights, choke the shit out of him, grab Sally Olivia, and run.

"That poor woman. She's been through a nightmare, and I'm afraid will require serious and extensive treatment to get her back on her feet."

"Yes, I'm sure, after what she went through in Florida, and her brother being in jail and all."

"How did you find out she was originally here?"

"Well, through one of her lawyers. We had a discussion about her estate, should anything happen to her. He accidentally let it slip, so please don't mention it. I don't want the man to get into any trouble, he's only trying to do what's best for her."

"Absolutely not. I understand. However, I cannot disclose where Sally Olivia has been transferred. She requires special treatment, which, unfortunately, we cannot provide here. You can be assured she's in the best of hands, and I suspect in another month or two will be back on her pretty little feet and doing very well."

As Dun was fighting his instincts, he looked over the shoulder of the doctor and saw the nurse in the hallway again. She was peering around the corner, looking as if she was holding her heart in her mouth. Their eyes met, and the nurse quickly looked away and left.

"Well, we want nothing less than the best for her, doctor. I'm disappointed that I can't see her, but I understand. I was told that seeing anyone connected with her recent past could delay her recovery, so I don't want to interfere. Thanks for your time, and I'll keep in touch with her progress through her lawyers.

"That's wonderful, Mr. Holmes. I'm sure she would appreciate your concern. Now, if you'll excuse me, I have some minor surgery to perform on a patient that was just admitted last evening.

"Thanks, Doctor. I appreciate your time. Good day."

Dun turned and quickly left the building. He backed out the SUV, drove back to the street, and turned left. He hoped that no one in the building had noticed his out-of-state license plates.

He returned to the coffee shop where he'd had breakfast that morning and ordered a cup of coffee while he reviewed the events brewing in his mind. *Man, that doctor is a smooth crock of lying shit. Love to get my hands around his throat. And what's with that nurse? She obviously was panicked that I was there inquiring about Sally Olivia. She is still there. I know it.*

Dun then focused on how he would get into the building and find her. There had to be a way. After a few minutes, his face brightened and he asked the waitress if he could borrow the yellow pages.

CHAPTER 34

A dark four-door sedan pulled up in front of the pizza parlor. Two men, both dressed in jeans, short-sleeved shirts, and sneakers, casually crossed over the sidewalk and strode up the outside stairs.

Alex was lying partly leaning against the wall. His head was bleeding profusely, and the deck, long overdue for weatherproof sealing, was absorbing the dark red stains.

As one of the men attended to Alex, the other scanned the surrounding buildings, bushes, cars, and rooftops for the shooter, but there was no unusual movement anywhere. Whoever did this was long gone.

People were walking by on the sidewalk below, unaware that anything had happened. The silent assassin had made no noise whatsoever, and slipped away from his hiding place.

Both men grabbed Alex under the arms and dragged him into the kitchen, careful to close the door behind them. A quick look at the wound on Alex's head told them it wasn't life threatening, but would require a doctor's attention soon to stop the bleeding. The men propped his head on a chair cushion and applied compresses to the wound.

The first man whipped out his cell phone and dialed Knott.

"Knott here."

"Bravo team. One man shot. Need a doctor quick."

"Who and life expectancy?"

"OK on A, with quick attention. Not sure of R yet."

"Someone there in ten. I'll be right behind."

"Better make it five."

The man pocketed his cell phone and turned his attention to Roy, who was still unconscious on the couch. Roy's face was stark white, his pulse steady but weak. Depending on the substance used, they may have to fight for his life. It took both men to lift Roy off the couch and onto the floor. There was nothing more they could do for him but prop his head on a pillow found in the nearby bedroom.

Returning to Alex, they carefully cleansed the blood from his head and saw that the shot had creased the side of Alex's skull, just over his left ear. The angle of the wound indicated the shooter had to have been above Alex.

One of the men searched through the kitchen cupboards, retrieved a first-aid kit, and bandaged Alex's wound as best he could.

Alex was breathing shallowly, but steady. He'd be okay.

"From the angle of that wound, the shot must come from a rooftop, probably the store across the street with the false front." The other man nodded and placed another call, explained the situation, and asked for assistance.

The men checked the perimeter of the apartment and grabbed a blanket off the bed to cover Alex. Then they sat on the floor and waited.

In less than ten minutes, a doctor was at the apartment. No ambulance, no police cars, just a man in plain clothing parking on the street and climbing the outside stairs in seemingly no hurry.

* * *

A short time later, a figure across the street scanned the rooftop, looking for evidence or clues. A bullet casing, 7.62 caliber, was lying in a crack between the sloping roof and the false front. It must have rolled down after it was ejected. The shooter probably lost track of it in his haste to leave the area. The man, wearing latex gloves, put the casing into a plastic bag and left.

* * *

Knott looked over at Alex on the couch. He seemed to be resting comfortably. They were lucky on this one. The shooter was either new, nervous, or just a lousy shot.

The men gave Knott a full briefing of the situation as they had found it. Knott's cell phone buzzed and he got a report on the rifle shell casing found across the street. "I doubt that it'll do any good, but take it to the lab and see what they can find."

Knott thought for a moment. "We've got to make some arrangement to throw those guys off the track."

"You mean move him?" one of the men asked.

"No, something much better." Knott stood up, moved toward the window, and made a quiet call. When he was finished, he turned to the men. "An ambulance will be here in a few minutes. Two men will come up carrying a stretcher."

"An ambulance? That doesn't sound logical, boss. I'm sure there's a spotter out there, and they'll follow Alex to the hospital."

"That's what I'm counting on."

CHAPTER 35

THE next morning, after breakfast, Dun took a trip to a city about fifteen miles away. The store he was looking for was right on the main street. He parked the SUV and walked in.

"Help you, sir?"

"Yes, I called yesterday. Need to rent some supplies."

"Oh, yeah. Got some stuff put together for you. Right over here." The man walked toward the back of the store where he had some items piled on a table.

Dun checked over each item, marking off a list as he went.

"Big party?" the man asked.

"Kinda'. Family reunion."

"Sounds like fun."

"I doubt it," Dun said, concentrating on his list.

* * *

The nurse looked up, surprise evident on her face. "Is there a problem, sir?"

"No ma'am. I'm Lieutenant Mick Conner from the county Fire Marshal's office. Here to do a fire inspection."

"This is a brand new building, not even a year old. It must have been inspected after it was built."

The Lieutenant checked his clipboard. "Maybe so, but it says right here an inspection is due. No mistake about that."

"Just a moment, sir." The nurse picked up the phone and spoke quietly. After she hung up, she said, "Dr. Shavitz will be right here."

The lieutenant stood his ground. "Fine. But let's get moving. I've got two more to do today."

"Yes, sir. It'll be just a minute."

Dun was nervous in his Fire Marshall uniform and disguise. If he got caught playing this ruse he'd lose his PI license, everything he owned, and his freedom for longer than he'd cared to think about.

The pants and jacket fit perfectly. The shoes were a little tight, but manageable. The hat, with the distinctive badge on the crown, felt like it weighed fifty pounds.

His hair was a problem. No wig he could find even came close to fitting. Dusting his hair white was not his idea of fun, but it had to be done.

The steel-rimmed glasses with the thick lenses were already giving him a headache, and the white bushy mustache itched like hell. The cotton in his cheeks, to make his voice change, were sucking up all his saliva and giving him a sore throat. However, he had to admit, even he didn't recognize himself in the mirror when he'd finished.

The nurse's voice brought him out of his daydream. "Dr. Shavitz, Lieutenant Conner is from the country Fire Marshal's office. He's here to do an inspection."

Dr. Shavitz smiled and took Dun's hand. It was all he could do to keep from mashing the doctor's fingers and shoving his fist down his throat.

"Good afternoon, Lieutenant. I'm afraid an inspection at this time will be a problem for us."

"Oh? How so, doctor?"

"Well, you see, we have severe trauma cases here, and some of them are in a situation where they can't be disturbed."

Dun smiled at the doctor. *I'll bet, you smuck.* "Doctor, we do fire inspections at the hospitals, including the emergency wards and the surgical theaters, as well as at the county psychiatric ward. No problems there."

"Well, I'm sure. But they are different—"

"Look, doctor," Dun interrupted, "you can either cooperate or I shut this place down right now. Then I get the county judge, who's my fishing buddy, to issue a warrant and we tear this place apart. Your choice." Dun smiled even more. If this didn't work, he was going to push in the doctor's face, lock him and his two nurses in a room, and bust down every door until he found Sally Olivia.

The doctor never lost his smile. "Doesn't look like I have a choice, do I?" The doctor was still smiling. "I'd like to accompany you, if I may."

"Sure. No problem. Bring your keys. I want to see every room and corner in the place."

The doctor turned and put his hand out toward the nurse. She reached into a desk drawer, pulled out a large key ring, and handed it to him. She never lost her smile.

"Follow me, Lieutenant," the doctor muttered over his shoulder as he headed down the left hallway. Dun trailed right behind. In every room, Dun made notes on his clipboard, forcing himself to take his time and not look too anxious. All the rooms so far were either for storage, examination, X-ray, or in-patient surgery. All clean and very well organized. Even a novice could see there wasn't anything there that might cause a fire.

"What's that room over there?" Dun pointed to a steel door at the end of the hallway.

"Just the furnace room. Nothing else in there.'"

"Good. Open it up."

Dun held his breath as the doctor unlocked the door, but he wasn't lying. Inside was a shiny new furnace, quietly pumping air into the building. Dun took his time, checking all the valves and gages, and making notes on his clipboard. He paid particular attention to an outside air grille that provided fresh air for the furnace.

"Looks good, doctor. Nice system. OK, let's hit the other hallway."

"Those are the patient rooms. We'll have to be very quiet here, please." Now the good doctor had lost his smile and acted nervous.

"Sure. Let's see 'em." Dun was starting to enjoy this. If there hadn't been so much at stake, he'd run this quack through the wringer and leave him for the cleaning crew to mop up.

The doctor moved down the hall and unlocked the first door with his key. He opened it a crack and stepped aside. The doctor apparently assumed the lieutenant would peek inside, but Dun opened the door and checked every corner of the room and the ceiling sprinklers. Some poor patient, a man, lay on the bed as if he were in a coma.

"Is this guy okay?"

"Oh yes. He's been sedated and will be kept that way for a few days, until we can start intensive treatment. This allows his system to relax, so to speak, before we begin." The doctor looked at Dun as if he were a dumb Irish firefighter who wouldn't have a clue what the word 'trauma' meant.

"I didn't realize that heavy sedation was an approved treatment for trauma, doctor." *Let's see you work around this one, you dumbass quack.*

"Well, typically it hasn't been. But just recently, there has been some research suggesting that a trauma patient is best treated after stabilization with sedation. This allows the patient to physically recover from the traumatic experience before the psychological convalescence begins."

Dun just smiled. "Thanks for that technical explanation, doc. Lead on."

The doctor took Dun to several more rooms. Each one had a patient who appeared to be heavily sedated.

"Did all these folks come in at the same time? When the sedation wears off, you're going to have your hands full." Dun could hardly wait for that explanation.

"As a matter of fact, two of them did. A terrible automobile accident in the fog. The others are in various stages of treatment."

"Sure," Dun replied, reigning in his temptation to grill the doctor on the nearest barbeque pit.

The doctor turned and approached the next room. Only two more to go, Dun noted. As the doctor unlocked and opened the door, Dun could see a woman lying on the bed in the same state as the others. As he looked closer, her hair color and features made him involuntarily suck in his breath. It was Sally Olivia!

"Something wrong, Lieutenant?"

"Oh, no. I was just struck by her beauty. Real sad to see a lady with her looks in this condition."

"Yes, it is. Most unfortunate. Only one more patient room to go. Then just the office area. We're nearly done."

"Fine. Looks good so far, doctor."

"Glad to hear it, Lieutenant. We want to be good neighbors in the county."

Dun almost had to prick himself with his writing pen to keep up the deception while he checked out the doctor's office, lounge area, and nurse station. Finally, it was done.

"Well, doctor, got a fine place here. Just a few minor suggestions to offer, nothing serious. I'll type up my report in the next day or so and send a copy to you. If you have any questions after you get it, I'll be glad to answer them."

"Thank you, Lieutenant. I appreciate your handling of our special situation here, and your concern for our fire safety. I look forward to receiving your report."

"No problem, doctor. See you next year." He watched as the doctor crossed over to the nurse at the reception desk, handed her the keys, and then walked back toward his office. Dun tipped his hat to the nurse and left the building. He was relieved to see it had clouded up and was raining in torrents. That would make identifying his SUV difficult if anyone looked as he left.

Returning to his hotel room, he tore of his uniform and the false mustache, stripped to his skin, and jumped into the shower. The white dust in his hair he found difficult to remove; that might take a few washings. But meanwhile he could get rid of the makeup and the sweat. And plan his next step.

CHAPTER 36

PEOPLE turned and stepped aside as the ambulance shrieked down the street and screeched to a halt in front of the pizza parlor. Two men jumped out of the front cab, opened the rear doors of the van, and pulled out the gurney. Without any seeming effort, they carried the gurney up the steep outside stairs to the apartment above.

Knott met them at the door. "Inside, in the living room." He pointed the way.

The men positioned the metal stretcher in front of the couch and prepared to lift Alex onto it.

"No, not him. He stays here. Take this one." Knott motioned to one of the agents whose height and weight most closely matched that of Alex.

"Excuse me?" the ambulance driver blurted. "He looks pretty healthy to me."

Knott laughed. "Oh, he is. Very."

"I don't understand sir," the driver said, looking at his companion.

"Me neither," said the agent.

"I'll explain as we proceed. We need to hurry," Knott said. He turned toward the agent. "You're going to be Alex's replacement, since you are the unfortunate one to be the closest to Alex's height and weight. Okay, hop up on the stretcher."

The agent did as ordered, although his face showed he was befuddled.

"Okay," Knott continued, looking at the EMTs, "cover him completely with that heavy sheet and strap him in as though he were dead."

"What?"

Knott laughed again and then explained. "You guys will carry him out, put him in the ambulance like he's dead, and drive to the morgue. The spotter will think they've erased Alex and their job is over. Since he doesn't need hospital attention, we'll keep Alex right here until we can plan what to do next."

"What about Roy?" the other agent asked, looking down at Roy still flat on the floor.

"The doc says Roy will be all right. Whatever was in the pizza wasn't poison, as we initially thought, but some kind of heavy sedative. It'll wear off in a few hours and Roy will be up and around. With a huge headache."

The agent on the gurney raised his head and looked at his partner. "Boy, he sure doesn't look fine." The other man nodded.

"Yeah, it's heavy stuff they doped him with, but the doc gave him something to counteract it. For sure, I'll bet Roy won't be eating pizza for a long time." Knott laughed at his little joke, his way of relieving tension.

The EMTs covered the agent and strapped him in. Without another word, they carried the gurney back down the stairs and put it in the back of the ambulance.

* * *

Across the street, amongst the crowd of watchers, a man quietly spoke into his cell phone as the ambulance drove away. "They've brought him out, fully covered with a sheet. Looks like he's dead, but you better follow the ambulance just to be sure."

He listened for a moment and then replied. "Yeah, I'm leaving. No use hanging around here. Too many Feds."

* * *

"Okay, I've got him," the FBI agent said softly into his cell phone. "He's about 30 feet from me, giving a report. I could actually hear him on his cell phone, but I moved away so he wouldn't spot me. Advised his contact to follow the ambulance to make sure."

The agent was using the latest technology cell phone rather than a walkie-talkie with a microphone. The earplug and mike wires were a dead giveaway to anyone looking for it. However, half the world was using cell phones and no one would notice anything unusual. For all the people around him knew, he was just calling a friend or his wife and reporting the exciting scene before him.

The agent had been standing in the crowd, across the street from the pizza parlor, watching the EMTs load the gurney into the back of the ambulance. Actually, he was watching the people around him who were watching the scene.

"Okay, he's moving now. Six feet, Caucasian, 190 pounds, long dark wavy hair, about forty-five. Walking north, now crossing the street right in front of a tour bus. Still talking on his cell."

He followed the man, trying to keep his quarry in sight at all times, but having difficulty because of the traffic backup caused by the ambulance. Suddenly the ambulance lights went on and the siren pierced the air as the ambulance driver tried to clear a path through the crowd. People and cars scrambled on the narrow street to make a path for the vehicle they assumed was taking a life-or-death emergency to the hospital.

"I've lost him. Crowd and vehicles jostling to get out of the way of the ambulance. Following his last known track, which was north on east side of Main Ave. Other units converge."

The agent hustled across the street and moved as fast as he dared through the crowd. At the intersection of Main and Market, he paused and tried to pick up the trail again.

"Main and Market. Nothing. Going right on Market toward parking garage."

He half-ran toward the city parking garage, looking in all directions as he went. He was getting nervous. Losing his target now would not be good. He hoped the other team was following the ambulance, trying to pick up the other spotter's car. He assumed so, but gave a report just to be sure.

"Advise ambulance to take circuitous route to morgue. Might be easier to ID spotter car. Approaching parking garage, target still not in sight."

A late-model Buick was just paying the parking fee and waiting for the gate to lift as the agent arrived at the garage. He stopped and turned away, still talking on the cell phone as though it was a casual call. As the Buick left the garage and stopped to check traffic, the agent turned and started walking again. It was the quarry.

"OK, just leaving garage in late-model Buick, 4-door, solid blue, stainless rocker panel molding, American flag sticker on back window. Virginia plates, 57J-126. Let him get out of the area and then pick him up."

As he ended the call, he let out a long sigh of relief.

CHAPTER 37

DUN spent the day preparing for that night. While he was nervous about what he had to do, the urgency spurred him on. He had no choice. At 11 p.m., he left the hotel and drove back toward the clinic. About a half-mile from the driveway to the building, he shut off his lights and parked on the side of the road. He wanted to have ample time for his eyes to adjust to the dark. Fortunately, there were no city lights nearby; it was as dark as a frog's ass in a tar pit.

He almost laughed at the thought. He always had senseless observations when he was tense. But he had good reason to be tense. The consequences were serious if he were caught.

As he sat there, he went over his plans step by step and checked the tools he purchased in a hardware store a great distance from there to avoid possible identification. He made one more check of his Beretta handgun, and then tucked it into his belt at the small of his back. He was wearing black sneakers, black jeans, and a black long-sleeved shirt. He threw the black stocking cap he had purchased to match the outfit into the back seat, thinking that might be overkill. Pulling on his latex gloves, which only came in white, he looked like an unemployed French mime.

Dun made sure the car's dash lights were off before starting the SUV. He approached the driveway, going slow enough so he wouldn't have to use his brakes and show any lights. He turned in and drove past the building to the employee parking lot around the back. After reaching up and turning off the overhead light, he opened the door, collected his tools from the passenger seat, and left the SUV, leaving the door open. About ten feet from the SUV, he changed his mind, returned to the vehicle, and cautiously closed the door. If someone came by, he didn't want to raise any suspicions.

Dun's heart rate was starting to rise. This was his first B&E. He had sworn to uphold the law and here he was breaking it. While he didn't always buy that the end justified the means, in this case he was making a clear exception.

The back door to the building was dark, with the outside light turned off. Score one for him. He walked past the door to the corner of the building, paused to listen for any strange noises, and then moved around the corner until he was just below the outside grate to the furnace room.

As he looked up, the grate was about eight feet above the ground, with a solid brick wall surrounding it. Not a hand or toehold anywhere. Damn! He hadn't thought of that.

He concluded he ought to make a career out of this. He'd be great. He could break into five or more buildings each night and make a fortune. He got the urge to kick the wall, but thought better of it as he considered the structural difference between the brick wall and his sneakers.

He laid his tools on the ground and fingered the small scar on his chin. He looked around and could find nothing in the vicinity that he could use to stand on, but as he walked around to the back of the building, he spied a large dumpster in the back corner. Beside it was a wooden crate that must have been used to ship some medical equipment. The side label was printed with the words 'Fragile: X-Ray Equipment.'

With the crate on its side, he stood on top to test its strength. It seemed sturdy enough, and it gave him about three feet of height advantage. Great so far. He picked up the crate and struggled with it until he had it placed under the grill, and then laid his tools on the top of the crate and climbed up. He was pleased with himself.

Standing on top of the crate, which was a little unsteady because of the slope of the ground, Dun picked up his bolt cutters and started snipping away the grill from its frame. He figured right; the frame would be bolted to the wall and thus too difficult to remove with ordinary tools. Score another one. He smiled. Maybe he was good at this after all.

Working for about fifteen minutes, he removed the grate and stuck his head through the open frame. He could see inside the furnace room, although it was pitch dark and everything looked fuzzy and smudged.

Reaching down to the top of the crate, he felt around for his other tools that he would need inside. As he did, he heard a sharp crack, and felt the crate begin to crumble, folding over like a cardboard box with the end flaps unsecured.

Just before it collapsed, Dun leaped for the opening and got his head and shoulders through. His sneakers scrambled for traction on the brick wall, without much luck, as his arms frantically searched for something inside to grab on to. Finding a water pipe running down the interior wall, he latched onto it and pulled his body up and through the opening. As he did, the now sharp edges where the grate had been removed tore long rips in his shirt and pants. He almost cursed out loud as he could feel the cuts on the skin of his chest, stomach, back, arms and legs start to bleed. He figured he'd look like a damn pincushion, thanks to his careful planning.

Halfway through, he realized too late the grate was also eight feet above the inside floor. The concrete floor was unyielding as he hit it shoulder first. Rolling forward to break his fall, his feet got tangled in long cartons of fluorescent light tubes which sounded like target practice in a light bulb factory as they hit the floor.

Dun lay there, partially stunned, bleeding, and afraid to move. What else could he screw up? After a few moments, he heard footsteps in the hallway outside, and a key inserted in the lock. He quickly rose to his feet, pulled his Beretta, and stepped behind the door. His heart was racing like a bug trying to escape a flushing toilet.

A nurse's cap showed beyond the door as the furnace room light went on. The nurse stepped into the room and surveyed the damage all over the floor. As her eyes looked up at the open grate and her hand went to her mouth, Dun closed the door behind her. "Don't move, Miss."

The nurse whirled around and was about to scream when recognition crossed her face. "You! You're the cousin. And the Fire Marshal? Wha..."

"Guilty on both counts. Please don't panic. I won't hurt you. I'm here to take Sally Olivia Sawgrass out of here."

"You can't do that. She's a patient. That would be kid..."

"It might be saving her life, nurse. I know she's held here against her will, and that your wonderful Dr. Shavitz is up to his ass in fraud. I'm leaving here with her—with or without your help."

Dun paused, trying to size up the situation and figure what to do next. As he did, the nurse noticed his shredded clothes.

"You're bleeding all over! You look like a pincushion."

"Yeah, it's part of my new disguise."

The nurse started to say something, then hesitated.

"Look, I know what Dr. Shavitz is up to. So does the FBI. They've been watching him for some time, but don't have the proof they need for a conviction. But they will real soon, after I get Sally Olivia out of here and to a doctor."

The nurse's shoulders sagged and she looked as if she were going to cry. "I told Mark this wasn't going to work, that this wasn't right. But he insisted that all he was doing was giving specialized treatment to those that could afford it."

"But, you knew better." Dun lowered his Beretta and placed it behind his back.

"Yes, I guess I did. I believed him because I loved him. But after a while, I began to suspect that something was wrong, especially after a few patients were—"

"Killed? All accidents, of course."

The nurse choked up and couldn't answer. Dun took her by the shoulder and steered her into the hallway.

"Anyone else in the building?"

"No. I'm here until 2:00. My relief comes on then." She choked up again, with tears now staining her starched white uniform collar.

"OK, here's the drill. You help me get Sally Olivia out of here and I'll put in a good word for you with the FBI. Otherwise, I'll have to tie and gag you, and leave you for the FBI to collect. Your choice."

"Oh, I'll help. That poor girl. She shouldn't be here at all. And I saw the way Mark looked at her, and at the front receptionist. He doesn't love me; I know that. I thought he would over time, and maybe I could convince him to go legitimate, but I've been kidding myself. He's in this for the money and nothing else."

"I'm sorry you got involved. But Dr. Shavitz is going down. Tonight."

Dun thought the nurse was going to collapse on the floor, but he caught her in time and moved her over to a chair in the hallway. "Look, I haven't much time. You've got to pull yourself together and help me. Once I leave, I want you to call the FBI and tell them what's going on. OK?"

"Yes. I'll be fine. I'll get the keys to her room." The nurse strode off toward the front desk, while he went around the hallway the other way towards Sally Olivia's room. As he reached the door, he wondered if the nurse would cooperate or just take off. However, a moment later she rounded the corner with the keys.

She quickly unlocked the door, pushed it wide open, and turned on the lights. Dun rushed over to Sally Olivia's bed and checked her pulse. She was fine, but still under the influence of the drugs. He pulled the blanket and sheet from the mattress, wrapped Sally Olivia in them, and scooped her up in his arms. His eyes were wet as he turned toward the nurse.

"Please listen carefully and take mental notes. Inside my shirt pocket is a piece of paper. On the backside is a local number. Call that number and tell the person who answers who you are, that Dun Wheeling has Sally Olivia Sawgrass, and to bring a doctor to the Bergen Motel just south of town. Also tell them to get a warrant to inspect this place and that you will be here to cooperate. Got that?"

"Yes, I think so." She reached into Dun's shirt pocket and removed the card. "Call this number, Dun Wheeling has Sally Olivia something-or-other; bring a doctor to the Bergen Motel. I'm to stay here to let them in with the warrant."

"Good. If you do all that, I'll make sure you get special treatment from the FBI for your cooperation."

"Thanks. I think I'll need it. But you know, I'm already feeling better knowing this is almost over. Good luck, Dun. Please apologize to Sally Olivia for my stupidity."

"Geeze, I almost forgot. I don't have your name."

"Bev. Bev Stillman."

Dun smiled. "Thanks, Bev. I won't forget this."

Dun turned, Sally Olivia still in his arms, and half-ran toward the rear door.

CHAPTER 38

"GOOD morning, Aunt Luce."

"Hi Samantha. Be with you in a minute." Lucy didn't look up as Sam arrived at the office. She was busy doing some work she'd arranged on her own, and wanted to finish it before Dun returned from New York. He'd been gone a couple of days and she expected he'd be back in the next day or so. Crazy man, off running to rescue Sally Olivia again.

She was proud she had negotiated and signed this contract for Dun's new agency by herself. The first one. She hoped he'd be pleased, and she was working hard not to screw it up. While it was a fairly simple job of doing a skip trace—she had helped Dun with others a few times—she wanted to complete it and get the billing in process before he got back.

"OK, let me fill you in on what I'm—Sam! What happened to you? My God, you're beautiful!" Standing before her was her niece, though she would have hardly recognized her anywhere outside the office. The plain Jane had been transformed in to a stunning woman.

Sam was blushing, but her expression showed that she couldn't have been more excited with Lucy's reaction. "Well, I figured it was time to get rid of that old 'I am woman and don't need to be attractive to prove my worth' look. Like it?"

Lucy stood up and walked around Sam, not believing her eyes. The dull, frumpy baggy-clothes look was gone. Sam's hair had been completely restyled from the corkscrew frizzy look to a smart, swept-back fashion. Makeup was applied in all the right places, and she was wearing a sharp Coral-colored suit that accented her figure—an attractive figure Lucy didn't even know she had.

"Wow. You look like a Monarch butterfly that just came out of its cocoon. I can't believe it. And why the hell have you been hiding that figure all this time? You are one knockout, my dear. My, oh my, will the men ever be chasing you."

"Gee, thanks. But not sure I want all the men chasing me."

"Like your love life has been all that good?"

"Well, no…not really."

"Well, it will be now, honey. Turn around for me and let me look again."

Sam turned around slowly as Lucy checked her out. The skirt was a tad tight through the rear for Lucy's taste, but that was the 'show it all' look of today, she guessed. The hem was above the knee, displaying long silky legs that most women would kill for. Under the jacket, which was worn open, was a sea green knit top that also left little to the imagination. Lucy was stunned.

"You must have hired a fashion consultant for all this."

"Nope, did it all myself…with a little help from the cosmetics gal at the shopping center. You really like it?"

"Like it! I'll have to get a restraining order for all men within fifty miles."

Sam began to laugh. "I'm glad you approve. I was a little nervous that you'd think I'd gone too far."

"Oh, you had—before. Frankly, you looked like something the cat dragged in. This is sensational. Bet you've got someone new in your life."

"Well…not really, I guess.

"This wouldn't have anything to do with Dun, would it?"

"Dun? Of course not. Just decided it was time for a change."

Lucy just smiled. "Sure."

She was pleased that Sam had gone to all the trouble to look nice for Dun, but she was concerned that he might be too preoccupied with Sally Olivia to notice. Though he didn't talk about it much, it was obvious he had fallen hard for Sally Olivia after rescuing her in Florida. Since he'd been back, that woman had occupied most of his thinking, and Lucy knew he was worried sick wondering what had happened to her.

She hoped he didn't get burned from all this. Dun didn't deserve that.

Now there was another complication. Sam had come into the equation. Her niece. Who had set her sights on Dun. One of them was going to get hurt. Either way, she was in the middle.

CHAPTER 39

DUN carefully placed Sally Olivia in the rear bench seat of the Navigator and buckled her in around her legs, waist, and shoulders. After ensuring she was comfortable—even though she was still unconscious—he jumped into the driver's seat and roared out the driveway.

Turning left, he drove back toward the motel he'd been using. As soon as he felt under control, he took out his cell phone and put in a call to Knott.

Knott didn't answer, so he left a message. "Knott, I've got Sally Olivia. Had the help of a resident nurse named Bev Stillman. She promised to call the local contacts you gave me and have them meet me with a medic at the Bergan Motel where I'm staying. She also will let them into the clinic when they arrive with a warrant, and will testify about what's been going on there. I promised her she would receive leniency for her cooperation. Will call again once I meet your guys at the motel."

Dun glanced down at the dash and realized he was speeding. This was not a good time to get pulled over by the locals, so he forced himself to slow down. His heart was racing so hard he could almost hear it, and he had to wipe his hands on his sleeves to dry out his sweaty palms. Now that the initial action was over, he was feeling the aftershock of the adrenaline rush.

He looked over his shoulder at Sally Olivia. He though she had stirred a moment ago, but she was lying in the same position.

As he neared the motel, he looked for any vehicles that might belong to the FBI. Nothing. The parking lot looked normal. Dun began to panic. What if Bev hadn't called the FBI as she'd promised? What if she called the police and reported a break-in and kidnapping of one of the patients? He had given her the motel where he was staying. Those thoughts hadn't occurred to him until just now, and he cursed himself for being so dumb.

Well, so be it. At least Sally Olivia would be safe. Or, would she? He cursed himself again. Maybe he should take off and head south until Sally Olivia could regain consciousness? He was tempted to do just that, but then the thought that she might need medical attention overrode his fears. No, better to make sure she is okay and worry about the rest if and when it happened.

He pulled up in front of the door to his room, turned off the SUV, and looked around. No FBI. No police. No one. Quiet as a whore in church.

Dun sucked in a deep breath, exited the vehicle, and opened the door to his room. He had purposely left the lights off when he'd left earlier so he could carry Sally Olivia without anyone noticing. He turned back toward the SUV to get Sally Olivia when a hand clamped on his shoulder.

"Dun Wheeling?" The voice was low and gruff, and the hand that grabbed his shoulder was a warning not to run.

"Yeah," Dun said, trying to clear the lump in his throat.

"Agent Samuels of the FBI. Where's the patient?"

Dun felt his knees start to melt, but he caught himself. "Buckled in the back seat."

"We'll get her."

Dun turned just as the lights went on in his room. Inside were two other agents and a doctor standing by the bed ready to examine Sally Olivia. The agents brushed by Dun, opened the rear doors of the SUV, and carried Sally Olivia into the room.

"Hey, guys, she's naked under that sheet and blanket, so I'd appreciate it if you'd stand back a little." Dun didn't know where that had come from, but he was glad he'd said it.

"Sure," said Agent Samuels, "let's take a walk while the doc checks her over." The three FBI agents left the room and steered Dun toward one end of the parking lot.

"Man, am I glad you guys are here. I was beginning to wonder if the nurse had called."

"Oh, she called all right. She was still spilling her guts out over the phone when our men arrived with the search warrant. They've got the clinic secured, a medical team is on the way, and a warrant is out for Doctor Shavitz."

Dun sat down on a curb that bordered the lot and cupped his hands over his face. He didn't know whether to cry or shout with joy; his emotions were running around like mice in a forest fire. The agents must have sensed this, for they refrained from peppering him with questions.

Finally, Dun stood up and faced Agent Samuels. Before he could say anything, the agent said, "You know, your ass could be in a wringer if you didn't know Knott Harrison."

"Yeah, I know. But I would have done it anyway."

Agent Samuels smiled. "Well, if it makes you feel any better, we're glad you did. Of course, we'll have to handle the fact that you illegally broke into the clinic, but considering how long we've been trying to nail our little friend, Dr. Shavitz, I guess we can overlook that."

"I'm just glad he wasn't there. I would have strangled the bastard myself."

"That might have been harder to cover up," said the agent, still smiling. "Once the doc has finished with your girlfriend, I want him to take a look at you. You look like hell."

Dun looked down at his shredded and blood stained clothes and erupted with a nervous laugh. "Yeah, looks like I lost a fight with a vegamatic. Just scratches from climbing through a vent."

"Well, you get points for gumption, if nothing else."

Just then, the door to Dun's hotel room opened and the doctor approached the men. Dun held his breath.

"She'll be fine. Shavitz loaded her with drugs to keep her unconscious, but those should wear off by morning. She'll have a little hangover, but it won't take long for her to get back on her feet."

"Thanks, Doc.," was all Dun could say, as his shoulders sagged and the tension started to ease from his body.

"You'd better come into the room, Mr. Wheeling, so I can look at you in the light. Seems like you ran into Edward Scissorhands, or something."

Dun laughed. "Or something."

As he walked into the room, he couldn't believe he'd pulled this off. Not exactly without a hitch, but not bad. Now, he had one more thing to do, and that he didn't look forward to.

CHAPTER 40

AFTER the FBI and doctor left, Dun went over to the bed and checked Sally Olivia. She was breathing comfortably. He rearranged the sheet and blanket that covered her, turned out the lights, and then sat in the armchair next to the bed.

Wow! What a night. He couldn't believe it was over. It was like the distant memory of a dream. A good dream, as it turned out. Sally Olivia was safe, Shavitz was headed for serious jail time, and Dun didn't have his ass in a crack. Yet.

He realized how lucky he was. Lucky it turned out so well, lucky he didn't get picked up for breaking and entering, and lucky he had Knott on his side.

Before Agent Samuels left, he briefed Dun on what was expected. Allowing a few days for Sally Olivia to recover, she'd have to provide full, written testimony on her experience. He hoped that at some point she'd been conscious enough to realize what had been done to her. However, even without that, the agent felt that the nurse's testimony would be more than enough to convict Shavitz.

Dun was also expected to give Knott the full details of his involvement as soon as he got back to Alexandria. Dun promised, vowing that he would do anything to help put that bastard behind bars.

Now, sitting there in the dark, Dun wondered what would happen next. What would Sally Olivia's reaction be? Of course, she'd be grateful for her rescue, but then what? Would they return to their former relationship?

Sometime in the middle of the night, Dun realized he had fallen asleep in the chair. As he tried to clear the fog in his brain, he heard Sally Olivia stir. She was mumbling something, but he couldn't make it out. He stood up and went over to the bed. As he sat on the edge, he stroked her long honey-blonde hair with one hand.

"Sally Olivia, it's me. Dun. I'm here. You're with me now. You're safe."

Whether she heard him or not, he wasn't sure. But she seemed to smile before she rolled on her side and went back to sleep.

Dun sat back in the chair. Relieved that Sally Olivia appeared to be fine, he instantly went back to sleep.

The next morning, Dun woke and stretched. He looked at his watch and saw it was nearly 9:30. His back and neck were stiff from sleeping in the cramped chair, but the events of the past evening whirled through his brain and he smiled. As he looked toward the bed, thinking again how lucky he was, he noticed Sally Olivia's eyelids beginning to flutter.

Not wanting to disturb her, he remained in the chair. After a few minutes, Sally Olivia stretched one leg and rolled on her back. With her eyes still closed she said, "Dun, is that you?" Her voice was weak and barely audible.

Dun jumped up from the chair and sat on the side of the bed. "Yes, Sally Olivia, it's me. You're fine now. Nothing to worry about. You can go back to sleep for a while."

"I don't want to go back to sleep. I feel like I've been in bed for a century." With that, she opened her eyes and smiled at Dun.

His heart skipped a few beats and his throat caught as he tried to respond. All he could manage was a weak "Hi. Nice to have you back."

"Hi, Dun. Nice to see you again. Thought I never would."

Dun felt his eyes begin to water. "Sally Olivia, you should save your strength. Sleep for awhile."

"I feel like I've got a hangover," Sally Olivia said, pulling one arm from under the blanket and rubbing her forehead.

Dun stood up and went to the dresser. "The doctor left some pills just for this purpose; he'd said you'd probably have a hangover." He went into the bathroom, drew a glass of water, and returned to her bedside.

Putting one hand behind her head, he propped her up enough to take the pill and swallow a little water.

"Thanks, Dun. Seems like you're my savior in more ways than one."

Dun didn't know what to say, so he just smiled. Then, after a moment, he said, "Why don't you doze a little longer. I'll be right here, I promise."

In spite of her protests, she napped for another three hours. Dun's worries eased some when he saw her stirring again. After a few minutes, she opened her eyes and looked around. "Dun. Dun? Are you here?"

He stood up and walked over to the bed. "Right here. How you feeling?"

"Better. I think those pills helped, but I still feel like someone injected jelly into my brain."

"That'll pass. Here, let me help you sit up." He propped pillows behind her back and helped her change her position so she'd be more comfortable. As he did, she stiffened.

"God! I'm naked. How long have I been like this?" She pulled the sheet and blanket up to her neck.

"That's the way I found you in the clinic. Sorry, but I didn't want to leave you to go clothes shopping."

"Ah, that's okay…I guess. Who else saw me like this?"

"Just the doctor who examined you."

"Oh."

Dun smiled, but knew she must be totally confused. "As soon as you're feeling better, I'll run out and buy you a few things."

A look of alarm crossed her face. "Do you really have to leave?"

"Sally Olivia, it's all over. The FBI has Doctor Shavitz, the clinic has been shut down, and you're completely safe. I just need to pick up a few things and then we can leave."

After a short pause, Sally Olivia nodded. "OK, but hurry back please."

"You bet. I'll be back before you can say Rumplestiltskin three-hundred and twenty-eight times."

"I don't think I can say it once." Her eyes were already closing before she finished the sentence.

Dun sat on the bed for a few minutes to make sure she was sleeping peacefully, changed his shirt and pants that had been shredded breaking into the clinic, and then slipped out the door and unlocked the SUV.

He was in a dilemma. Sally Olivia needed some clothes, but he didn't have a clue what size she wore. He tried to think of items that wouldn't be size limiting, but decided he'd better rely on a salesperson for advice.

About a mile from the motel, he had noticed a small store that seemed to specialize in women's clothing. He figured that would be his best bet. As he entered the store, a young saleswoman approached him.

"May I help you sir?" She was about Sally Olivia's age, height, and weight. Great.

"Yes. Please. I need to buy some women's clothing, and you, coincidently, are about her size."

"What is it you need?"

"Ah...everything?"

"Everything?"

"Uhmm...yes, that's right. One complete outfit."

"Oh, I see. How complete is complete?"

"Well, you know, maybe a pair of slacks, a top, some shoes, and ah...underwear."

"Wow, sounds like this poor lady is naked." She laughed, but then caught herself. "Sorry, that was a stupid comment, don't know why I said it."

"Yeah, uh...actually she is."

"Really? That sounds interesting. She's not in your car, I hope." The woman laughed again, obviously thinking Dun was going along with her joke.

Dun tried to stifle a nervous laugh. "No, she's back at the motel."

"Oh. Motel... I see."

"It's not what you're thinking."

"Sir, it's not my place to think about those things."

For some strange reason, he felt the need to explain. "You see, she was in a local clinic. We left, uh...rather in a hurry, and I wrapped her up in a sheet and blanket and brought her back to the motel."

"Oh, that explains it." The saleswoman was looking around, probably hoping her supervisor would come to her rescue.

"Well, sorta. But not really." Dun had hit a brick wall, and he couldn't find the right words. Finally, he lowered his voice and said, "Look. This is FBI business. The young woman was being held at a local clinic against her will. I broke in and rescued her last night. The FBI has closed down the clinic and the doctor now has a warrant out for his arrest. You'll read all about it in tomorrow's papers."

"Sir, could you please excuse me for a moment?" The saleswoman did a perfect about face and headed for the back of the store. The look on her face told Dun she thought he was a nut case. He was sure she'd probably call the police.

As the woman reached the end of the display area and went through curtains to the back room, Dun gave up and left. He didn't seem to have much luck with saleswomen.

Next stop: Wal-Mart.

CHAPTER 41

ALEX woke with a start. As soon as he opened his eyes, he knew he was in trouble. The room was completely dark and his head felt like a watermelon dropped from the Eiffel Tower.

As he reached up to touch his head, Knott's voice pounded in his ears.

"Easy, Alex. You've got a new crease on the side of your head, and I imagine the mother of all headaches."

Knott's voice sounded like a 55-gallon drum full of bricks rolling down a rocky slope. Each word was a painful jolt that produced pain.

"Hmmmm. My head is killing me. Please whisper." The shades and heavy drapes were fully drawn; he could barely make out Knott's form in the darkened room.

Knott came over to the bed with a glass of water and painkillers. "Here, take these and go back to sleep while they start to work. You'll feel much better when you wake up."

"Okay, Knott. I'll do that."

Alex turned over and was snoring before Knott could put down the water glass.

Knott returned to the apartment living room and sat down. That was close. Another half-inch and Alex would really be at the morgue.

He was baffled. How did these guys figure out their every move? They must have known the safe house in Annapolis was going to be used and had a man planted on the rooftop across the street. His men were checking on the pizza parlor, but his guess was one employee called in sick and the replacement was a plant—now long gone from the scene.

Roy had finally come around, feeling a little stupid about what had happened, but after a short while they sent him home via the emergency exit so no one would see him leaving the apartment. The outside staircase was the only obvious way in and out of the apartment, but they had rigged up a steel-telescoping ladder from the rear bedroom window. The ladder could be deployed from the window, and dropped down the backside of the building through heavy trees and brush. The eight-foot stockade fence, just five feet behind the building, had a hinge-less gate, with a small section that could be easily taken away and replaced if you knew how.

Now it was just Knott and Alex left in the apartment. All Knott had to do was figure out how to get him out of there without being seen. He assumed the ploy of taking the 'body' to the morgue had worked, but Knott couldn't bet on that. Nothing had worked up to this point, so he had to assume they still knew Alex was alive and recovering in the apartment.

Getting Alex out and to another safe place was going to be easy compared to finding out where the leak in the system was. Somehow, someone was following their every move. But who?

Knott ran down the list of those that knew Alex would be in the Annapolis safe house.

Roy? He doubted it. Roy had been with the service for a long time, and he and Knott had been personal friends for many years. Knott had saved his life once, many years ago, in another country, so Roy would be the last name he'd put on the list of leak suspects.

Cob? Nope. Knott had purposely kept Cob out of these arrangements for that reason, to isolate him from any suspicion.

Dun? No way. His little buddy—he used to call him that just to piss him off—wasn't even in the picture when Alex's troubles began. Could they have followed Dun when he dropped off Alex? Maybe, but unlikely. Dun was an unknown in the equation, at least up to now.

Who else? There was no one. He and Roy had personally made the arrangements for the safe house. No one else alive even knew that location existed. So how?

Knott racked his brains trying to think of an answer, but he kept coming up with an empty piece of paper.

He looked at his watch and wondered how Dun was doing. He had received a report that the 'mission' had been successful, and he smiled thinking about the details he had received about Dun's break-in to the clinic. "That boy has a lot to learn," he muttered, as he took out his cell phone and placed a call.

"This is Dun." The voice sounded weary and frustrated.

"Hey, little buddy. Hear you just passed your first lesson on B&E. The doctor said you looked like a cat's favorite scratching post."

"Screw you."

Knott laughed. "What's going on right now?"

"I'm out looking for clothes for Sally Olivia. My first attempt almost got me thrown in jail, so I'm at Wal-Mart picking up a few things. As soon as she comes around fully, we'll head back."

"Seriously, Dun, nice job. You accomplished what we couldn't. I could get used to having you around."

"Yeah, well you could get used to having ticks up your ass, but don't count on it. I don't think I'm cut out for this rogue PI crap. I'm tired, cut up like I went through a paper shredder, and frustrated."

"But, you've got Sally Olivia."

"Yeah, I've got Sally Olivia. Thanks for your help, Knott. I owe you big time."

"Oh, don't worry. You'll get a chance to pay me back." Knott was still laughing as he said, "End," into his cell phone.

CHAPTER 42

WHEN Dun returned to the motel room, Sally Olivia was gone. His heart leaped into his throat until he saw the bathroom door closed and heard the shower running.

He threw the shopping bags onto the bed and knocked on the bathroom door.

"Dun? I hope that's you."

Dun opened the bathroom door a crack. "Yup, it's me. How you feeling?"

"Got any more of those hangover pills?"

"Sure, couple more. Plus I bought you some clothes."

"Great. Throw them in here and I'll try them on when I finish. Right now I'm staying in the shower until the hot water runs out or I drain the reservoir."

Dun laughed. He could imagine how she felt, being in that clinic with that slimy doctor. God knows what he had done to her.

He put the shopping bags just inside the bathroom door, reached in and got the last of the hangover pills, put them next to a glass of water on the sink, and then closed the door. As he sat in the chair, he reviewed the events of the previous evening. One thing for sure, he promised himself, he'd never enter a building through the fresh air grate again. Beyond that, he was secretly pleased with himself. He'd pulled it off, and Sally Olivia was safe again. Not quite back in his arms, but hopefully that would come. He decided to give her all the space she needed, realizing that her mind must be brim full of conflicting emotions.

His mind was so preoccupied that he didn't notice Sally Olivia had finished the shower, or that she had dressed and was standing in the room looking at him. As he looked up, Sally Olivia smiled and crossed over to him, almost tripping over her new shoes that were about three sizes too small.

Without a word, she threw her arms around him, buried her head in his shoulder, and softly cried. Dun didn't say a word. He held her close and let her cry. At one point, she picked her head up and started to say something, but buried her head again in his now wet shoulder.

Dun could have stayed there all day. The smell and closeness of her flooded his brain with memories of when they'd been in Florida. Dun knew he was hopelessly in love with her, and he thought she felt the same. At least she did before this all happened. If he ever saw that Shavitz character again he would probably rearrange his face and other body parts on the spot.

His mind floated back to Jacksonville, Florida. After her kidnapping and several attempts on her life, they became lovers. Dun had worried about whether she'd been suffering from the 'my hero' syndrome, but as time went on that became less of a concern. Sally Olivia had her head on straight, until she found out about her brother's involvement in the kidnapping scheme. Then it all fell apart, and she was rushed to the hospital. That was the last place he had seen her, and couldn't find out where she'd been taken until Knott uncovered the information.

Now she was back in his arms. She seemed to fit like she'd been molded for his body. Another rescue by Dun. Would she feel obligated to him? Did she still love him for just him, or would she doubt her own feelings?

Finally, Sally Olivia gave Dun a quick kiss on the cheek and stepped back. "Seems like you are all the time goin' 'round and saving me, sir," she said, mimicking an earlier statement she'd made in Florida.

"Sally Olivia, I —."

"Shhhh, let's not talk about it right now. We've got plenty of time for that. What do you think of my new clothes?" She took a few steps back, whirled, and almost lost her balance.

Dun thought she had never looked more beautiful, although he had to admit that the shoes seemed a little tight, and the slacks were a bit short.

"Guess I wasn't too good a picking sizes, huh?

"Nothing that can't be easily fixed. In case you're wondering, the underwear fits perfectly."

"Guess I got a feel for that, so to speak."

Sally Olivia blushed a little, kicked off her shoes, and gave Dun another hug. "Thank you. I feel so much better already. Couple more pills and I'll be dancing in the streets."

"Not in those shoes you won't."

"Right." She smiled and stepped back. "Okay, I need to do two things. Take those hangover pills, and get out of here as fast as we can."

"Yes, ma'am. Let's do it. And, we can stop by Wal-Mart on the way."

"No thanks. These will be fine until I can get back to my apartment. I just need to get as far away from here as possible."

Without even speaking, Dun handed Sally Olivia the hangover pills, scooped up the few clothes and shaving supplies he had brought with him, opened the motel door, and bowed as Sally Olivia walked out.

As he opened the door to the Navigator, Sally Olivia asked, "What happened to the Miata?"

"Still got it. This is leased for uh, a special job I'm doing."

"Oh, sounds interesting. You'll have to tell me all about it as we drive."

"Yeah, guess so." He closed her door and walked around to the driver's side, wondering if he really wanted to tell her about Alex.

CHAPTER 43

AS they were driving back toward Washington, D.C., Sally Olivia seemed lost in thought. Dun realized her mind must be in turmoil, with all that had happened.

She'd been through more than ten people would see in a lifetime. First, she was kidnapped, knowing that her abductors were planning to kill her. Followed by two more kidnap attempts by a man who had meant to kill them both. And finally, learning her brother had gone along with the final scheme to save financial embarrassment.

To make matters worse, just when she and Dun thought it was over, that smuck of a doctor comes along and decides he's going to squeeze her estate by trumping up phony trauma treatments in an exclusive clinic.

While his heart was aching for her, and he wanted to hold her and make it all go away, he knew he had to back off, give her some space and time to work it out. But it was killing him.

Her voice brought him out of his reflections.

"Dun, I don't know what to say. You keep rescuing me and I'm running out of ways to say 'thank you.'"

"No need. None of what's happened to you is your fault. You just hit a string of bad luck, but it's over. Done. Final. Just stay away from trauma doctors." Dun laughed, trying to make light of it, but he knew it didn't work.

"How did you find out where I was being held?"

"I've got a new contact in the FBI. An old high school buddy that I ran across recently. We hadn't seen each other in years. He found out, after I bugged him a little."

"And you risked your life, and your career, to rescue me again." Sally Olivia reached across the seat and placed her hand on his knee. There were tears in her eyes.

Dun took one hand off the steering wheel and covered hers. "I'll always be there for you, Sally Olivia. No matter what. You know that."

"Yes, I do. But it's not fair. How can I ever repay you for all you've done?"

"Just being near you is all the payment I need."

Sally Olivia removed her hand and used it to wipe her eyes. She turned toward the window and stared out again.

"Once, when I was starting to come out of the daze, I heard the doctor and some nurse talking about me. They were nervous that I would wake up before they were ready and cause some trouble. I remember every word they said, and as I was going under from another dose of whatever they had me on, I swore I would get even."

"Good. Remember every word, for after we get back you have to give a statement to the FBI. The more you remember, the longer that jerk doctor will spend in jail."

"Like my brother." The statement dropped like a bomb. He didn't know what to say.

After a few minutes, he looked at her. "Your brother was misguided and dumb for doing what he did. But I know under all that ego he loves you, and I'm sure being in jail is the least of his punishment."

"I know. Once I get through all this, guess I'll have to visit him."

"Well, that's something you can work out later. But, you know, I've decided he did one thing right."

Sally Olivia turned toward him. "What's that?"

"Called you Sally Olivia. It's a classy name, for a classy woman. And you're all of that, and then some, Sally Olivia."

"I noticed you calling me that. I thought we'd agreed that you'd just call me Sally."

"I did, but then as I thought of it, it didn't do you justice. You'll never be just a Sally."

"Dun, that's sweet, but sometime I have to learn how to take care of myself, and not rely on you to follow me around and keep me out of trouble."

"That's not how it happened, and you know it. None of it was your doing."

"You're right. It was my money's doing. If it weren't for me being rich, none of that would have happened."

"You forgot to mention beautiful. And educated. And wonderful. And caring. And probably a hundred other attributes. If you're looking for items to put on your 'pity me' list, I can give you a whole bunch."

"I'm sorry. That wasn't too smart of me. Guess my mind is going too many places at once."

"You don't need to apologize. You need to get back home and get on with your life, whatever you decide that is."

"Does that include you?"

"Only if you want it to. I think you know how I feel about you. But I also understand what you're going through, so I'm not going to crowd you. You've a lot to deal with right now, so as I said, I'll always be there for you. When, and if, you need me."

"I don't know how I ever got so lucky to run into you. But, I do need some time to sort everything out."

Dun's throat ran dry, but he needed to continue. "One other thing you should know about."

Sally Olivia turned and stared.

"An old flame of yours, Bruce, who now goes by the name of Alex, has surfaced." He would have rather cut out his tongue than bring up that subject, but she would find out anyway.

Her hand flew to her mouth, and he could barely hear her words. "Bruce! The Witness Protection Program? My God."

"Yeah, that Bruce. He had to change his name to Alex, but the bad guys found him again, and he's been having a few problems. I'm now involved in trying to protect him. Sorry, but I felt you need to know."

"Bruce? Alex? Is he OK? Has he been hurt?"

"He just narrowly escaped death in Maine. Now he's in the D.C. area. I'm working with the FBI to uncover who's after him."

"God, that's terrible. Can I see him? Talk to him?"

"I don't know. I'll see what I can do."

"Oh, please. I need to see him…thought about him often." Sally Olivia turned toward the window, lost in thought again.

Dun's heart dropped two notches. This wasn't going the way he'd hoped.

CHAPTER 44

DUN pulled up in front of Sally Olivia's condo in Alexandria, Virginia. "Here we are, safe and sound."

Sally Olivia sat up in her seat and looked around. "Yeah, I guess this is home. Been awhile."

"If you'd rather stay at my place, or check into a hotel, that's fine."

"Thanks, but I need to get back to my life, whatever that is. Besides, I'm feeling a thousand percent better now that those sedatives have worn off."

"Are you sure you want to be alone? What if you get sick? You've been through a hell of a lot, and I'm not comfortable leaving you alone. Maybe having someone around to talk to would be best for a day or so."

"No, being alone will be good for me, let me sort out a few things."

"Sure?"

"Yes, I am. No need to be concerned."

"Fine. You know where to find me. I'll check on you every so often, but I promise I won't pester you." Dun reached into his pocket, pulled out his wallet, and handed her a business card. "Office and home numbers on there. Don't hesitate to call."

"Dun, you are too much. You've rescued me from kidnappers, killers, my own brother, and now a doctor who has probably killed a few of his patients. We fall in love, but now I need to be alone. And all I can say is 'thank you.' This isn't fair to you. Maybe you should get back to your life and quit waiting for me to figure out where the hell I'm going with mine." Tears rushed to her eyes and she looked away.

"Look, Sally Olivia, you have nothing to apologize for. You've been to Hell and back, more than most people will ever see. None of it was anything you did—it just happened. I want to help in any way I can, but I understand you need some time to come to grips with it all and figure out where you go from here."

Sally Olivia turned toward him, tears streaming down her cheeks. "I have to be honest, with myself and you. Do I love you just for who you are, or is it because of what you've done for me? If it's the latter, will it last?"

"Sally Olivia, don't—"

"I've lost what little family I had, Dun. Sure, Aaron is still alive—in jail—but can I ever forgive him for what he did to me? I don't know…don't think so. I want to desperately hang onto you, have you make it all go away for me, but I know I have to do that myself. I leaned on Aaron, now on you. It's time I learned to lean on myself for a change."

"You're stronger than you give yourself credit for. You broke away from Aaron, in spite of social pressures. Don't sell yourself short, Sally Olivia."

"That sounds nice coming from you, but I have to reach that conclusion myself. Can you understand?"

Dun paused, looking away out the windshield. "Yes, I can. I've been there a few times."

"I've got to go. Thank you…thank you for all you've done for me. I won't forget it."

"This may sound silly, but thank you for what you've done for me. You've given me something I never had before, maybe never will again. I won't forget that, either."

"I'll call."

"Wait! How will you get in? Your key?"

"My neighbor, Mrs. Beach, has a spare. I'm sure she's home."

Sally Olivia leaned over and kissed him on the cheek. Tears still moist on her cheeks, she opened the door and stepped out. "Bye."

Dun watched her walk up the steps and ring the bell for Mrs. Beach's condo. He sat there as she entered the building and closed the door. She never looked back.

His mind seemed to go blank, as if his brain was all used up and had no energy to process anything. After five minutes, he started the SUV and drove away. As he drove, her words rang in his ears...*"Do I love you...because of what you've done for me?... will it last?... Maybe you should get back to your life and quit waiting for me..."* He had an awful premonition it was over.

CHAPTER 45

"GOOD morning, Dun. How'd it go?" Lucy was all smiles, hoping on hope that everything did go well.

While Dun felt like he'd been hit with a blivit—his dad defined that as ten pounds of shit in a one-pound bag—he decided it wasn't fair to take out his frustrations on Lucy. That was one sure way to lose a valued assistant. And, valued she was.

"Fine, Luce. I got Sally Olivia out of the clinic and she's home. It will take her some time to get over this one, especially with what she'd been through before."

"That poor woman. I hope I get to meet her some day."

"I hope so, too." Dun walked into his office and closed the door. He sat at his desk and closed his eyes. He'd hardly slept all night, thinking about Sally Olivia and what she'd said when he had dropped her off at her apartment.

Her words were ringing in his mind like a bad song that wouldn't go away. The look on her face, the way she left without turning around, and her final words. She was trying to tell him something, but she was too kind to just come out and do it.

When he added it all up, there was only one conclusion: it *was* over.

* * *

Lucy turned and looked at Sam, who had been sitting quietly in the corner observing the conversation. Dun hadn't even noticed her. Dun's last statement hung heavy on Lucy's mind. It didn't sound good. From the look on his face, she guessed the relationship was over.

"Give 'em a little time, Sam. I don't know the whole story yet, but I suspect he's been through a lot."

"Oh sure, no problem, Aunt Luce. I've got plenty to do."

"And, by the way, what's say we drop the Aunt bit and just go by first names. It'd be more professional in the office."

"Sure, I'll try. Might be tough to break the habit, though."

"Thanks." Lucy smiled and turned back to her desk. Poor Sam. Anxiously waiting to be noticed. Isn't that the way with men, when you want them to notice you, they act like dead fish. If you want them to go away, they're all over you like flies.

While Dun didn't talk about it much, she knew his heart was in Sally Olivia's court. She must be some kind of gal for him to fall that hard. And now Sam comes along and wants to throw her hat in the ring. Sure hope she doesn't get burned.

* * *

Sam turned back to her work. Her heart rate had soared when Dun had come into the office. He didn't even notice her! She'd spent a fortune to look this way and the guy just walks by. Unreal.

All her life she'd been looking for a guy just like him. Tall, muscular, intelligent, handsome. And he's in the middle of some other relationship. Just her luck. But... maybe she can change that.

Lucy told her that on his way back to Alexandria Dun had called the office and said he would be in the office the next afternoon sometime. He hadn't offered any details.

So, Sam had gone out, had her hair freshly done, got the nails painted— the whole bit. The outfit she was wearing really showed off her figure, maybe a little too much. She wasn't quite comfortable with the new style, but she had to admit it did make the guys take a second look. That was exciting. She wanted men to look, especially Dun.

All her life she had avoided men. She had almost gone out of her way to be unattractive. Then Dun came along and her blood pressure went off the Richter scale. For the first time, she wanted to be attractive, sexy, alluring. He was one hunk, and she wanted him. Any way she could get him. Long-term or not.

She looked up to see Lucy standing and preparing to leave for the day. "Gee, is it that time already, Aunt Lucy? I mean…Lucy. You go ahead; I'm just going to finish up before I leave."

"OK, Sam. Have a good night." Lucy waved and walked out the door.

Sam sat back and plotted her next move. Maybe this wasn't a good time. On the other hand, sounds like what he had going may be over. Maybe she could catch him on the rebound.

She was nervous, but determined to do something. Okay, maybe just talk to him, ask him a few questions, see if he notices, play it by ear. What questions? Let's see. What further education should she pursue if she wants to make this field a career? Good one. Better have another. Can she shadow him on a couple of cases, see what it's all about before she makes a decision? Another good one. That should do it.

She stood up, and smoothed the folds in her skirt. She smiled; she liked the feel of her curves under the tight skirt. Then she reached up and unbuttoned the top button on her blouse, so more of the tube top showed. She reached under the blouse and tugged on the front of the tube top to pull it down. Might as well put all her assets on the table.

Before she could chicken out, she walked over to Dun's office and knocked. After a short pause, she heard Dun say, "Come in."

Sam opened the door, stepped in, and closed it behind her. "Hi, Dun. Glad you're back. Got a minute? I'd like to ask you a few questions."

Dun looked up and stared. "Sam?"

* * *

Standing before him was a gorgeous creature that couldn't be Sam. Must be her sister; Sam never looked like that.

"Yes, it's me. I decided it was time to change my image and get more professional. Like the new look?"

"Well, hell yes, Sam. You look wonderful. I never would have imagined…" He was stuck for words. He didn't want to offend her by bringing up how dumpy she had looked, but man, she needed encouragement to continue with this one.

Sam sat in a chair opposite his desk, and slowly crossed her legs. The tight skirt rode high up on her thighs. As she continued, she leaned slightly toward him, exposing more of the tube top through the loosened blouse.

Dun's eyes were glued to her in disbelief. Talk about fairy tales. The ugly duckling has turned into a foxy swan.

"I can't get over how much you've changed…for the better. Much better. You don't look like the same person and…" Words failed him.

Sam leaned back in her chair and stretched. "Why, thank you, Dun. I'm glad you noticed. Sorry to bother you, but I do have a couple of questions I'd like answered."

"Well, I'll do my best." Bother him? Are you kidding? Dun's throat was as dry as five miles of dusty road. He could feel himself squirming slightly in the chair and his underarms were beginning to leak. He made a conscious effort to compose himself. This was ridiculous. But what the hell. His involvement with Sally Olivia was over. He knew it. Just from the way she had acted. Doesn't take a genius to figure that one out.

Was their affair in Florida just part of the hero worship reaction he'd been afraid of? Guess so. Then he goes and rescues her again. That probably didn't help, but he'd do it again, even knowing he would lose her because of it.

All she said was "Bye." Didn't even look back, or wave. Maybe she was right. Maybe he should get on with his life and let her sort things out. Maybe Alex coming back on the scene jolted her back to reality and she still has feelings for him. Well, screw it. He would get on with his life and leave her to her own. This was no time to get serious over some woman anyway. He had a business to establish. Might even get time to have some fun for a change.

Dun came back to the present as Sam shifted her chair closer and began. "I'd like to know what moves I should make if I decide to get involved in Private Investigation. I don't want to make a commitment, but I'm thinking involvement would be nice. Don't you agree?"

"Uhhh. Yes, involvement would be nice. It helps to get involved with whatever you're doing." *Boy, that was profound. Better engage your brain before you open your mouth again.*

"I like to throw myself into things. Not with wild abandonment, though sometimes that's fun, but with a slow, steady purpose so I can enjoy what

I'm doing to the fullest. Like, for example, working with you. I'd like to get to know you better, develop a solid relationship under you, work on coming together, and have some fun doing it."

Dun realized that Sam had leaned forward again and placed her hand on his knee. She was awfully close, and whatever perfume she was wearing was creeping into his brain and destroying all resolve. "Oh, I agree. Foreplay before work…I mean, all work without uh play is counterproductive."

"Are you hot?"

"Excuse me?"

"You just seem a little uncomfortable. It's a little stuffy in here, don't you think." Sam got up and walked over to the window. He followed her every movement. She unlocked the latch and tried to raise the window, but it seemed stuck.

"Here let me help you." Dun got up and went over to her. She didn't move, so he stood behind her and helped her lift. As he did, she arched her back and strained to pull up the bottom sash. His nose was almost in her hair, and it smelled wonderful. He also noticed that she had nestled gently into his crotch, and he could feel himself responding.

Once the window was up a few inches, she started to turn around but he beat her to it and quickly went back to his chair.

Sam turned around. "Phew. It was getting hot in here." With that, she unbuttoned her blouse and pulled it off, leaving only the tube top remaining. "There, that's much better, don't you think?"

Dun's jaw almost dropped into his lap. This couldn't be the same Sam. She'd either had a breast implant, or she'd done a great job of hiding them under her frumpy clothes. Her breasts were straining against the elastic top, and the top was working hard to contain them. Dun didn't know which would win, but he wanted to stay around and find out.

Clearing his throat, Dun managed to squeak out a "much better."

As Sam came back to her chair, Dun could feel his eyes shift from top to bottom and side to side as he followed her approach.

She raised her arms over her head and waved them back and forth. "Oh, yes. Much, much better. I feel I can breathe." He didn't know whether his eyes or her breasts would pop out first. Reaching her chair, she stayed standing and put both hands on the back of the chair and leaned forward.

She took a deep breath, pushed out her chest, and said, "That really helps."

"Helps me." Dun could have smacked himself. What the hell was he doing? Just yesterday he was pining over Sally Olivia, but now he was mesmerized by this awakened sleeping beauty. He averted his eyes and looked toward his desk. "Let's see, where were we? Oh, yeah, your plan of action."

"Yes, my plan of action, and also what I might do to get some practical experience. Some on-the-job training could really bring me up to speed a lot quicker. I'm all in favor of learning on the job. Makes the work more intimate, more intense, more fulfilling, so to speak."

Dun turned to look at her again and realized she was even closer now, sitting again, though he hadn't heard her shift her chair. He looked toward the window to see if it were still open. He was starting to sweat again.

"Yes," was all he could say.

"Doing it on the job brings a certain authenticity to the work. Textbooks are fine, but there's nothing like doing it for real." Her hand was on his knee again, but he made no move to discourage it. His brain was mush. Her perfume was doing a number on him.

"I think I'm going to like investigative work, Dun, especially being under you. We can explore exciting new areas, reach new highs, and achieve mutual satisfaction."

At that point, Dun didn't know what he wanted. "Well, on-the-job is fine, Sam, but there is a certain amount of study required before one can get beneath the skin…uh, so to speak."

"Oh, I agree. I'm all for study. Take your hair, for example—just as an analogy. Before I would run my hands through it, I'd want to look at it from all sides, study the way it curls in the back just a little, note its thickness." As she talked, she stood up and stepped closer to him. She put her hands on his shoulders and leaned over to view the back of his head. His eyes were about three inches from her chest and he thought the elastic top would lose the battle right then.

As she studied the sides and back of his hair, she reached up and began to weave her fingers through it while she continued talking.

"Now I can feel the texture of your hair." She pushed her legs between his to get closer. "It's warm and silky feeling, but strong like you." Her breasts were now rubbing on his forehead as she moved around and worked her hands. He feared which would explode first, his brain or the tube top, but didn't much care.

"Mmmmm, very nice, so far," she murmured, moving closer.

As she leaned even further to view the nape of his neck, her shoes slipped backward and she fell into him. Her arms went around the chair for balance, and her breasts slowly slid down his face to his mouth. As he opened his mouth in surprise, one breast worked its way in. He tried to back his head away, but the chair suddenly swiveled backward. The full weight of her body on top of him kept the breast in position, and he could feel it straining even more to release itself from its elastic prison.

He heard her moan softly. She shifted a little to the side and his mouth was relieved of the burden, but now the other breast was working its way into his mouth. This time it was without the tube top. Nature had won out over synthetics. It was wonderful.

She was almost lying totally on top of him now. He had the feeling she wasn't trying too hard to get up. Neither was he.

He felt her body quiver, and then she was moving down again, until her lips were on his and her tongue was working between his lips. Her lips were on fire, but moist, as they covered his mouth like a velvet blanket. He felt himself responding, in more ways than one, as his hands pushed her tube top down to her waist and slowly explored her now unrestrained breasts. They were more than ample, firm, and erect, and moved in rhythm with his hands.

Again, her body quivered as she pressed closer between his legs and began a slow dance with her hips. His loins, already aching, joined the rhythm. He tried to reach down to pull up her skirt, but he couldn't reach the hem. Sam slowly moved up until her breasts were at his mouth level again. He began using his tongue to search for her nipples while he slid her skirt up to her waist. Her wetness told him she wasn't wearing underpants and was ready. She moaned while electric shudders seemed to envelope her body.

She reached down, undid his pants, and slipped her hand over him. Now he was also unrestrained, and he felt like he would explode as she slowly slid down until she had completely enveloped him. Like her lips, she was on fire and moist. And all velvet.

What the hell am I doing? I must be nuts. Sally Olivia drops out of my life and I turn around and become the office stud? Conflicting thoughts were raging through Dun's mind. His body was sending frantic signals for more, more. His mind was telling him otherwise.

Dun tried to untangle himself. He knew if he went through with this his guilt would drive him crazy. Why couldn't he be like most guys and just say the hell with it? But he couldn't. All he could think of was Sally Olivia.

He turned his hips sideways, but Sam held on like the suction cups on an octopus. She writhed her body in excitement and he soon found himself hanging on for fear the chair would break. "Whoa, Sam! This is no good."

Just as Dun protested, the chair lurched farther backwards and sideways in one quick motion. Like lovers in a canoe, they capsized, with Dun hitting the floor first, followed closely behind by Sam. They rolled once, and Dun was now on top. Both were caught in a tangle of arms, legs, and tight clothing that restricted their ability to free themselves. Neither could move their legs. He finally pushed himself up with his arms, reached down and zipped up his slacks, and rolled off.

Sam, suddenly embarrassed, quickly pulled up her tube top, and then slid her skirt down over her waist.

"Oh my God, what have we done?"

"Saved just before the final bell," Dun said, straightening his slacks and standing up. Reaching down, he took her outstretched arm and pulled her to her feet.

She didn't look at him as she stumbled over to the chair and flopped down. Her clothes and hair looked like she'd been in a touch football match. Dun didn't look much better, as he tucked in his shirt and smoothed out his hair. They both looked like the 'after' photos in a domestic violence case.

She looked around for her new shoes and saw them squashed beneath the chair. One shoe had the heel snapped off. She began to cry.

"I'm sorry, Sam. Guess we got a little carried away." He reached down and freed her shoes from under the chair, examining them closely so he wouldn't have to look at her. "Looks like these can be repaired, no problem," he said, standing there not knowing what else to do.

Sam was crying harder now, hunched over, her shoulders shaking with uncontrollable sobs. Finally, she caught her breath and looked up at Dun. "Oh, I'm so sorry. This was all my fault."

"Don't go blaming yourself. I was a partner in this too."

"Yes, but I started it. I came in here determined to make something happen. I knew you were down about whatever happened between you and Sally Olivia, and took advantage of it."

"Now, look, Sam—"

"No, it's true. I planned the whole thing. I dreamed about this happening, and before I knew it, it was. I don't know what got into me; I've never done something like this before. Jesus, dress me up and I act like a tramp."

"Well, I have to admit I was caught off guard and a little uncomfortable at first. I guess being seduced by a beautiful woman did me in."

"Beautiful?"

"Man oh man, are you ever. When I first saw you, you had your beauty pretty well disguised. I didn't have a clue that under those frumpy clothes and frizzy hair there was a beautiful and sexy woman hiding. And now...wow."

"Really?"

"Really. You're quite stunning. If I wasn't already emotionally all wrapped up, I'd be chasing you like a rabid dog."

"And you are...uh, tied up?"

"Yes, guess I am. I don't feel real good about what I just did, but it happened. A ravenous creature with a body that won't quit came in and hit all my hot buttons. And I responded."

"Oh, yes, did you ever." Sam smiled, but couldn't quite look at Dun.

After an embarrassing minute of silence, Sam continued. "Dun, I have to admit that this PI business isn't for me. I don't know why, but I can't get excited about it. The only reason I hung around was to make a pass at you."

"Yeah, quite a pass. Sure helps the ego."

"And even though I didn't score a touchdown, you've done something very important for me. Something I'll be always grateful for."

"And that is...?"

"Wakening me to my real femininity. Before, I almost wanted to hide it. Wanted to be just one of the guys, compete on a non-gender basis. Now, I realize how exciting it can be to be female. I don't know what I'm going to do with my life, but whatever it is I hope they're ready for the new me."

"Well, I sure wasn't ready. You bowled me over." Dun started laughing at the image of them tumbling to the floor in a tangled heap.

"And neither was I, Dun. Neither was I." In a quick motion, she crossed over to him, stood on her tiptoes, and kissed him on the cheek. "Thanks for being so understanding. I'll gather up my things and leave quietly."

"What will you tell Lucy?"

"I'll call her tonight, tell her that you and I had a long talk, and I decided to pursue some other career path. She doesn't need to know about the rest."

Dun smiled, but was relieved to hear her answer. He doubted that Lucy would understand what just happened between him and her niece.

"OK, but if you ever need help, in any way, you know how to reach me. And once you get settled, please call and let me know what you're doing."

"Thanks, Dun. Sally Olivia is one lucky gal." Sam turned and left the office.

Dun righted his desk chair, pushed it over to his desk, and gingerly sat down. His groin still ached and he didn't need the damn chair tipping over again. While he knew the aborted ending was for the best, his mind was having trouble convincing his body. That was the true definition of frustration. And guilt. Seems like guilt is nature's way of reminding you that you've screwed up.

In spite of his guilt, he couldn't get Sam off his mind.

CHAPTER 46

JUST before Dun left for the evening, his cell phone buzzed. "Dun," he answered without enthusiasm.

"We've got a problem."

"You've got a problem. I've got a problem. What's new?" He wasn't sure he could handle any more from Knott. He wanted to go home and veg out for about two weeks.

"Settle down, Dun. This is serious." Dun could tell from the sound of Knott's voice that he was shaken somewhat.

"What? What happened?"

"They got to our boy again. He's all right, but he's got a new crease on the side of his head." Knott went on to recap the events at the safe house in Annapolis, including the ambulance ruse and the spotter on the street.

"How the hell did that happen?" Dun couldn't believe it. That place was supposed to be secure; no one knew it existed.

"I don't know. Somehow, they tracked us here. Only a few people knew of this location, and even fewer knew Alex was here."

"What happened when you apprehended the spotter?"

Knott let out a slow breath. "Nothing. Somehow he got rid of the cell phone he was using—must have suspected we were on to him and threw it out the window. We couldn't hold him."

Dun shook his head. "Damn. No leads there. And the car following the ambulance?"

"Never did. The spotter must have warned them off."

"Where are you now?"

"Still at the safe house with Alex. I've got to move him, but I don't have anywhere to take him."

"Oh, no. Not my place again."

"No other choice."

"Come on, Knott. He's about as safe here as a virgin in a biker's bar. Besides, I don't have any way of protecting him if he is discovered."

"You at the office?"

"Yeah."

"Meet me at your place in an hour. I'll bring Alex, and the protection." The line went blank. Dun threw the cell phone across the room.

* * *

Dun was sitting in his living room when he heard the door latch unbolt. He jumped up, went to the side of the doorframe in the front hall, and pulled his Beretta.

As the door swung slowly open, he heard Knott's voice. "Dun?"

The breath he was holding escaped from his lungs and his body relaxed. "Nobody home," he replied.

Knott stuck his head beyond the edge of the door. "Okay to come in?"

"Might as well, you've got a key. How'd that happen?"

"You don't wanna know." Knott stepped into the hallway and motioned for Alex to follow. Neither of them was smiling.

As he slipped the Beretta into its holster behind his back, Dun went into the living room and sat down. This was all he needed right now.

Knott walked into the living room and sat on the couch. Alex sat beside him, his hand unconsciously going to the bandage on the side of his head.

Dun heard a noise behind him and whirled around. Standing in the hall were four men who were dressed casually, with the exception that each had a handgun in a shoulder holster and was carrying a shotgun.

"What the—?"

"Meet the protection, Dun. On the left is Gary. Next to him is Carlos. Third from the left is Vinny. And the guy on the right is the ringleader, Harv. He'll be your contact."

The men nodded at Dun but stayed in place.

"Jesus, I'm running a hotel here." Dun wanted to stand up and shout "Out!" but knew he couldn't. He looked at Alex, who was still sitting in the same position, his eyes cast downward.

"Sorry, Alex. Nothing to do with you. It's been a frustrating day." Dun stood up and looked at Knott. "Can I talk with you in private?"

"Sure, buddy. Kitchen?"

Dun nodded, walked to the kitchen, and stood aside as Knott entered and sat down. He closed the door.

"Look, Dun, I'm sorry—"

"No, you look, Knott. You waltz into my life, turn it upside down, and now expect me to run a hotel for you. Yeah, I owe you for helping me with Sally Olivia, but this is too much. I'm trying to start my own PI agency, and here I am working for you for expenses. Well, guess what? Expenses don't pay my bills, Lucy's salary, my rent, and put food on the table."

"But, look at the valuable experience you're getting."

"Oh, wonderful. As a baby sitter and bodyguard. Bodyguard for a man who's got the whole damn world after him, wearing a bull's-eye on a cord around his neck, and killers with an inside track in your organization. That's just great."

"But—"

"Let me finish, dammit! I don't need that kind of experience. All I wanted was to start my own PI agency, do some skip traces, background investigations, surveillance of cheating spouses, and tracking runaways. The most dangerous work I looked forward to was nailing peeping Toms."

"Dun, if you'll let me—"

"Forget it. I've got to look out for myself. And Lucy…and Sally Olivia if she'll have me." Dun sat down and looked away.

Knott kept silent for a moment. "You're right. I have been unfair, expected too much, too fast. Seems like I've been doing this stuff all my life. I forget what it was like when I first started…didn't have any experience, no money. You're leagues ahead of where I was, Dun."

Dun looked up. "Great. That's supposed to make me feel better?"

"No, I guess not." Knott paused again, and then asked, "What happened with Sally Olivia?"

"I dropped her off at her place."

"And…?"

Dun looked away. "And, nothing. She said she needed time to think things through, that I should get on with my life without her. She didn't even look back when she left the car."

"Damn. After all you went through."

"I'd do it all over again if I thought she needed me."

"Give her time, Dun. She'll come around, you'll see."

"Well, if she does, I'd like to be around. Watching over Alex doesn't improve those chances, does it?"

"No, it doesn't." Knott stood up. "We'll take Alex somewhere else for tonight. I just thought of a place that might work." He turned and started to leave.

"Wait a minute, Knott. I don't want Alex in any more danger. He's had enough. He can stay here. No other practical choice."

"You sure?"

"Yeah, I'm sure. What the hell, with those four goons guarding him, he'll be as safe as a—"

"Yeah, I know…a virgin in a biker's bar."

Dun laughed. "Sorry, guess I got feeling a little sorry for myself."

"No problem. Understood. And, don't forget when all this is over to send me a bill for your hours on this assignment."

"What?"

"Oh, didn't I mention that before?"

CHAPTER 47

"HI, Mrs. Beach. How are you?"

"My land, if it isn't Sally Olivia. I'm doing fine. But frankly, my dear, you look a little haggard, like you've been crying. Been gone for awhile, haven't you?"

"Yes, I have. Too long. Can I get my spare key? I've lost mine somewhere."

"Sure, sure. Come on in while I find it."

Sally Olivia was lucky to have Mrs. Homer Beach as a neighbor, just down the hall on the opposite side of the building. While she was quite elderly, she was still sharp as a tack and quite capable. Mrs. Beach had always liked her, and watched over her like Sally Olivia was her own daughter—except she and her former husband had never had children.

"The last time I saw any activity in your place, that nice young man—what's his name?—was poking around, looking for you. Your brother—how is that silly ass of a brother of yours?—had hired him to find you after you had taken off again. Did he ever find you? He was one nice looking man. If I was just a little younger, I'd have thrown a rope around him and dragged…" Mrs. Beach's voice trailed off as she rummaged around in an antique desk looking for the spare key.

"Yes, he did find me. Thank God. It's a long, long, story. I don't have the energy right now, but after I get settled in, you'll have to come over for tea and I'll give you all the details. Right now, I need a long bath and some time alone."

"Sure, honey. It's plain you've been through a lot. Here's the key, right where I left it. Except I couldn't remember where I'd left it for a moment." She giggled as she handed Sally Olivia the key.

"Thanks. You're a dear. I'll call you in a few days and we'll get together." Sally Olivia gave her a kiss on the cheek, walked down the hallway, and opened the door to her condo. Stepping inside, she turned and bolted the door and put on the security chain.

It was just as she had left it. A little dusty perhaps, but the same. She tried to think how long it'd been since she'd been gone, but decided to work that out after a long, hot bath. Her skin seemed to have the 'creepies,' and itched all over. The thought of being in that clinic with that awful doctor made her shudder.

She went to the bathroom and began to draw the water for her bath. She turned the knob all the way to the left so that nothing but hot water escaped the faucet. Reaching over the tub to the marble shelf on the wall, she selected the strongest bubble bath she had and poured in the whole bottle. Steam and bubbles mixed in an aromatic mist that soon enveloped the bathroom and spilled out into her bedroom.

After a few minutes, she checked the water temperature, added some cold water, and shut off the flow. She quickly undressed, throwing her clothes on the floor to be dumped in the trash later. Without hesitation, she stepped into the tub, slipped down until the water covered her up to her neck, and laid her head back. As she closed her eyes, visions of the clinic flooded her memory, but the magic of the heated water and the scented bubbles seemed to cleanse her skin and soothe her nerves.

When the water began to turn cool, she stepped out of the tub, opened the drain, and watched her 'creepies' quickly swirl away. Once the tub was completely empty, she switched the water control over to the shower and stepped back into the tub. Running the water as hot as she could stand it, she lathered her body all over using a sponge and hand crème soap. Finally, she washed her hair, stepped out of the tub, and rubbed her skin vigorously with a Turkish towel.

Now her body felt back to normal. The soap and bubble bath left a clean scent on her skin, and it tingled in a pleasant way.

All that was left was to get her mind back to normal. That might not be so easy, she realized, as she walked into her bedroom to get fresh clothes.

As she dressed, her mind was flooded with images and voices. How vulnerable she had been, tied to that hospital bed, and that doctor hovering over her naked body like a vulture waiting to pounce on its next victim. Her body shivered and her stomach churned with revulsion just thinking about it. She knew people like that existed, but it was hard to believe that just a few hours before this had happened to her.

Only partially dressed, she lay down on her bed and tried to drive this madness from her brain. She knew she had to. Had to get on with her life, put this experience behind her and move on. But could she? Could she ever forget the horror, how easily she had been placed in that position and taken advantage of, and how lucky she had been not to become one of the unfortunate fatalities?

Her mind went to what might have happened to her had Dun not become involved. His persistence and bravery had saved her again. She loved him for that. But was that all it was? Gratitude? Obligation? Debt?

Someone once said the truth shall set you free. Would it? She was afraid of the answer.

* * *

Knott left Dun's apartment, and Dun sat on the couch looking at Alex. He felt bad about the way he had acted, but decided he had too much going on to beat himself up over that.

The four men left to guard Alex came into the room and sat down. The leader, Harv, looked at Dun. "Mr. Wheeling, you know this place better than we do. What do you suggest?"

"First of all, it's Dun. Second, I suggest you look around and see what you think. Then we can get our heads together and work out a plan."

"Sounds good to me. We'll do that."

As the men scouted the apartment, he turned back to Alex. "I'm sorry for what you've been through. I know it's tough, but I also know I can't put myself in your place. Your mind must be whirring like a tornado, and I'm sure you're wondering just who you can trust at this point."

Alex looked around at the FBI agents checking out the apartment, then turned his gaze toward Dun. "You're right. I don't know who I can trust. I think you and Knott are square, but then I wonder how these guys keep finding me. The first time they shot at me they missed by an inch. Up in Maine they got a little closer. This last time they got a piece of me. The trend isn't good." Alex reached up and touched the bandage on the side of his head.

"You've been lucky, Alex. Usually they only need one chance."

"Yeah, right. Lucky me. I'm so lucky I'm about ready to walk out on the street and get it over with. I've had it with playing hide and seek. My life is shit. Pure shit. And here I sit with you and four bodyguards and, frankly, I don't have a lot of confidence you guys can protect me."

Dun could feel his blood pressure rising. "Well, there's the door. If you feel like walking down the center of the street, I won't stop you. We all have our problems, and one of mine is watching out for you, which I didn't ask for either. So, go for it."

Alex looked like he was about to say something, but stopped.

"By the way, in case you're interested, Sally Olivia is back…at her condo."

Alex came out of his slouch and stared at Dun. "You found her?"

"Yeah. I assumed Knott filled you in."

"No, he didn't say a word."

"She fine. A little frazzled, but okay. I told her about you and she wants to talk to you. I suggest you give her a day before you do—she's been through a lot."

"God. I don't know what to say to her. She really asked for me?"

"Yup. Said she'd thought about you a lot." Dun turned his head away, pretending to see what the FBI agents were doing.

When he turned back, Alex seemed to be in a world of his own. He was staring across the room, his eyes unfocused. Finally, Alex came out of his reverie.

"I'll do that. Sometime the next day or so."

Dun stood up and approached agent Harv. "How you making out?"

"This place is like an old fort. Only two ways in and out, and both those mean coming up a narrow set of stairs. The walls are double bricked, and the windows covered with iron grills. This shouldn't be too hard to defend if we have to."

"Let's hope we don't have to. You guys are the experts, so set it up anyway you think best. Make yourself at home; anything in the kitchen is yours. Bathroom is over there, and sleep wherever you like."

"Thanks, we'll be fine."

"Just don't order any pizza delivered." Dun tried to smile, but he had difficulty.

Harv laughed. "Don't worry; we've got the food covered."

"Fine. I'm going to bed."

Dun turned, and walked to his bedroom. He turned on the light, closed the door behind him, turned off the light, and sprawled on his bed.

Lying on his back, with his hands cradling the back of his head, Dun tried to sort out all the thoughts running through his mind. He finally gave up and closed his eyes.

CHAPTER 48

DUN was awakened by his cell phone. He looked over at the clock on his nightstand. 6:30 a.m. What the hell?

"Yeah?" he answered, trying to shake off the cobwebs in his mind.

"Dun! You all right?" Knott's voice sounded like he was trying to climb through the phone.

"Ah...yeah. I guess so. Christ, why you calling so early?"

"Something's happened. I can't reach Harv."

"Harv? He's right in the next room."

"Dun, I've called him four times. No answer."

"OK. Hang on. I'll get him."

"Dun! Wait!" Dun was about to put down the cell phone, but placed it next to his ear again. "Take your gun!"

"You crazy? No one could get in here."

"Humor me. Take your gun."

Dun put down the phone, reached over to his nightstand, unholstered his Berretta, and slowly stood up. He crossed over to the closed bedroom door and listened. There wasn't a sound coming from the next room, not that he expected any this time of the morning. Knott was getting paranoid; Harv probably turned off his phone or it was out of order.

He slowly opened the door a crack and peered through. Nothing. Opening the door a little farther, he raised the Berretta in front of him and slipped through the doorway, keeping low just in case. Nothing. He couldn't see the guards anywhere. No Alex. Nothing.

Moving like a cat, he eased across the room and checked the spare bedroom, where he assumed Alex had slept last night. It was empty. So were the kitchen and the den. He checked the back door—locked and bolted. As he neared the front door, he heard a car leaving the parking lot, going much faster than it should have been.

He swore to himself and ran to the window in time to catch a glance of a white van exiting the lot and burning rubber as it sped up the street. It was out of sight behind buildings and trees in seconds; no sense chasing it.

He raced to the front door. It was closed but unlocked. No sign of forced entry. Turning, he ran back to his bedroom, careened off the doorframe going through it, and grabbed the cell phone.

"Knott! They're gone!"

"What!"

"Gone! The place is empty."

"Empty? That can't be."

Dun sat down on the bed. "Yeah, I know."

"How'd they get in?"

"That, I don't know."

* * *

Alex sat in the bench seat of the van behind the driver, his arms, legs, and mouth bound with duct tape. Behind him, on the floor, lay Harv and two of his men, also bound and gagged.

The other guard, watching him closely and pointing a nasty-looking silenced pistol in his direction, sat in the passenger seat—he couldn't remember his name. The guard was talking to the driver, whom Alex had never seen before.

"Okay, slow down. We're good. Take the next right, and then follow that road for several miles. When you come to its end, take another right and I'll tell you from there."

The guard turned to Alex. "Well, Alex. Hope you're comfy. We've got a long way to go before we sleep, so to speak. You might want to put that seat belt on, just to be safe." The guard laughed at Alex's inability to move.

For some reason, Alex didn't feel nervous. It was like watching a movie; all this really wasn't happening to him. In some ways, he felt relieved. It was over. No more running. Hiding. Never being able to use his real name. Always looking over his shoulder. Over.

The guard reached under his seat and picked up a cell phone. Punching in a speed-dial number, he held it to his ear.

When someone answered, he said, "We're out. Got the four boxed up and ready for shipment. ETA about one hour." The guard hit the End button, placed the phone in his shirt pocket, and turned toward the driver. "OK, coming up. Turn right, go about two miles and get on the Beltway toward Springfield."

Alex leaned back and closed his eyes. Over.

* * *

Knott arrived at Dun's apartment in less than fifteen minutes. Dun was slouched on the couch, his Berretta in his lap, staring at the television screen he hadn't turned on.

He reached over, gently took Dun's pistol, and set it on the floor. "What happened?"

Dun looked at him in surprise. "How'd you get in?"

"The door was open."

"Yeah, I know." Dun sat up and rubbed his eyes, as if he were trying to chase away a nightmare.

Knott waited a minute, then continued. "What happened, Dun?"

"Jesus, I don't know. You called. I was out like a light. I got up, checked out the apartment, and everyone was gone. Gone." Dun rubbed his eyes again.

"How the hell could that happen?" Knott's voice was starting to rise. "I had four guards that could defend the goddamn Washington Monument from a foreign invasion. This place is built like a brick shithouse. And they're gone? You slept through the whole thing?"

Dun jumped up from the couch. "No. Actually, they're all hiding under the kitchen sink." He turned toward the kitchen and yelled, "C'mon out boys. Surprise. Uncle Knott is here." He started to walk away, but turned toward Knott again. "Yeah, they're gone. And yeah, I slept through the whole thing. Next time, find yourself a bodyguard that doesn't need any sleep." He walked to the kitchen and began to clean the coffee pot.

Knott walked into the kitchen and sat down. "Sorry. I know it's not your doing, but I can't—"

"Oh, yes. It is my doing. I was here. And, I'm still here."

"Maybe whoever broke in didn't realize you were in the other room sleeping."

"Impossible."

Knott looked up at Dun. "Why?"

"No one broke in."

"What?" Knott stood up and walked over to the sink where Dun was filling the coffee maker.

"No signs of forced entry. The back door is locked and bolted. The front door is unlocked and unbolted. No signs of entry from the outside."

"That means—"

"Yeah. Either your men took Alex and left, or they opened the door for someone they knew and got surprised." Dun put coffee grounds in the hopper and turned on the coffee pot.

"As I was checking the front door, I heard a car racing out of the parking lot. I looked out the window and just got a glimpse of a white van."

"Yeah, you told me on the phone."

"Right. I did."

"We put out an APB, but nothing so far."

"Coffee?"

Knott looked over at the pot. "Sure, when it's finished."

CHAPTER 49

OVER coffee, Dun and Knott explored what might have happened. Dun started.

"I doubt it was someone surprising them from the outside. The front and back stairs were the only way in here, and those guys were guarding them like it was Fort Knox."

"I agree. They would have heard someone coming. I'm sure they placed listening devices in the hallways." The look on Knott's face showed he didn't like the conclusion he was coming to.

Dun paused for a minute, and then said the obvious. "Must have been one or more of your men, Knott. No other answer."

"I would have bet my retirement on those guys. I personally picked each one. I still can't believe this."

"Either way, Knott, you're in trouble."

"Yeah, I know. They were my picks and—"

"I didn't mean that."

"Huh? Don't follow you."

"Either way you're going to look suspicious. You've got a key to the place, or you could have arrived and they would have opened the door for you." Dun didn't like saying this, and certainly didn't believe it, but Knott had to know.

"Jesus. I didn't think of that."

"I hope nobody else does either. For your sake."

"Christ, me too. That's all I need…" Knott's eyes went unfocused for a moment, then he got his act together.

Dun shook his head, and then continued. "What I can't believe is why they left me behind? Wouldn't they have been afraid that I might wake up and spoil the plans?"

Knott ran his hand through his hair. "My guess is that they took shifts. Two on, two sleeping. One of them surprised the other. He would have had to knock the other agent out, so he couldn't warn the others. Then this bastard knocked out the other two while they were sleeping so he could tie them up. From there, it was easy to get Alex."

"He must have had help getting them out and down the stairs to the van, if that's what they used."

"Yeah, I'm sure of that. I've got a team coming over to sweep this place. If there's anything, they'll find it."

"Well, they'll find me. I'm still here."

"Look, they didn't want you. You would have complicated their plans. The only reason the guard or guards that weren't in on it were taken is so we wouldn't know who's involved. It'll take longer to track them down, not knowing who or how many of my men were part of the scheme."

"Doesn't look too good for them—those not involved, I mean."

"Or for Alex either."

Just as Dun was about to answer, his kitchen phone rang. He crossed over to the wall phone and picked it up. "Hello?"

"Hi Dun. It's Sally. Hope I didn't catch you too early."

He almost dropped the phone. He looked at Knott and rubbed his forehead. "Oh, hi Sally Olivia. Ah…how's it going?"

"Are you all right?"

"Oh, just great. What's up?" As much as he wanted to talk to her, he didn't have the heart to tell her about what just happened to Alex.

"First, I want to thank you for what you did for me. You were wonderful. If it hadn't been for you I'd still be at the clinic…and God knows what might have happened."

"No problem, Sally Olivia. Just Mr. Hero rushing in where angels fear to tread." As soon as he said that, he regretted it.

"You don't sound like yourself. Are you sure everything is OK?"

"Yeah, just a little sleepy."

"Oh, did I wake you?"

"No." Dun still felt like he was stuck in some horrid dream.

"Well…okay. You mentioned that I might be able to talk to Alex."

"Yeah. I did."

"Is…is that still possible?"

"Not real soon."

"Not real soon? What's that mean?"

"Ah, just not a good time. I'm tied up with some other stuff. That's all."

"But, Dun, I need to speak to him. You said I could."

"I know. Just take my word for it; it's not possible just now."

"Please, Dun. I need some closure on this. I'm trying to put all that's happened behind me. This is one loose end I need to wrap up."

Dun could feel his irritation meter starting to rise. He wasn't mad at Sally Olivia, just at the timing. Of all the luck. Problems were piling up. Plus, he was mad at himself over the Sam incident. Maybe more guilty than mad. Whatever.

"I'm sorry, Sally Olivia. I'm right in the middle of a situation here. I can't discuss it just now. I'll have to call you later."

Dun heard a soft click as Sally Olivia hung up.

* * *

Sally Olivia walked away from the phone and sat down in the chair facing the picture window. The view was of the Potomac River waterfront, and normally she loved sitting there, watching the river activity and folks strolling along the river walk. Today she didn't even notice, she was lost in thought.

Dun sounded different. Not himself. Something must be wrong. She hoped he wasn't in any trouble over what he did for her. She remembered him mentioning he was involved in some work for the FBI. Maybe that's why he couldn't talk.

But, as she sat there, another thought entered her mind. Maybe he wasn't alone. He said she hadn't wakened him, but he was a little sleepy. Had he been up all night?

And, if so, with whom?

CHAPTER 50

THE white van exited the Capitol Beltway that encircled Washington, D.C. and turned south on Interstate 95. The agent in the passenger seat seemed more relaxed and put his gun away, but he continued checking his side mirror and looking out the back window.

Alex laid his head on the back of the bench seat and closed his eyes again. They hadn't blindfolded him, so it didn't matter what direction they were taking or what the destination was. He had seen his abductors.

So this is how it would end. Somewhere in the woods, at the end of a long twisting path, or maybe even in the van once they were away from populated areas. A quick bullet to the head, a door opens, and he's rolled out into the brush.

Over. So be it. He amazed himself as to how calm he was and ready to accept his fate. He was sick of running, hiding, being shot at, moving to new places, changing his name, never able to make friends, never trusting anyone.

Even Dun. They had taken him out of Dun's apartment, and he never came out of the bedroom. Stayed in there until they were gone, he bet, and then called Knott or someone and screamed about him and the agents having disappeared. He had thought Dun was on his side, one of the good guys, trying to protect him. Well, shit, that was a joke.

The three other guards had obviously been knocked out and bound. He was dead asleep when the agent in the front seat and the driver stuck a pistol between his eyes and slapped duct tape over his mouth. Sure, everything was quick and done quietly, but Dun couldn't have slept through all that.

For all he knew, Knott was in on it too. Maybe the both of them worked this out, probably collected more money than they'd make in 15 years of working.

He was sick of thinking about it. Didn't matter. His only regret was that he never got the chance to talk with Sally Olivia. He had thought a lot about what he'd say to her. Maybe if they'd more time together it might have turned out differently. But, maybe he was just kidding himself.

She needed to get on with her life, and guessed she already had. Besides, she didn't deserve any more complications after what she'd been through; asking her to live the life of a fugitive's partner was ludicrous.

Alex could feel the van slowing and turning off the highway. As he opened his eyes he was surprised they'd reached their destination so quickly. He was even more surprised when he saw the wording on the exit sign.

* * *

"What the hell do we do now?" Dun didn't even look at Knott as he asked the question. He was staring into his coffee cup, stirring the luke-warm liquid with his finger.

"Well, I've got the whole agency looking for that white van. They won't get far." Knott stood up, took Dun's coffee cup, and walked toward the sink. As he poured the coffee into the sink and refilled Dun's cup, he continued talking over his shoulder. "Don't blame yourself. Those guys were pros. They didn't make enough noise to wake a watchdog."

"Yeah, sure. I was probably snoring so loud they didn't need to be quiet. They could have emptied all the furniture out and I wouldn't have heard anything."

"I didn't know you snored." Knott put the hot cup of coffee in front of Dun.

"I don't."

Knott almost laughed, but caught himself. "Look, nobody would have heard those guys. I mean it. They could steal the ring off the Pope's finger and he wouldn't realize it 'till morning."

"Yeah, but he's old. And he's not supposed to be protecting Alex."

"And neither were you, Dun. Those other agents are the ones that screwed up. They were protecting Alex, not you. You were just providing a place for them to work."

"Right. Some place. No one could get in, but they sure as hell got out."

The look on Knott's face showed he was frustrated. "None of us ever considered the possibility of them getting out. That was my job, and I screwed that up. So, don't go beating yourself up."

"Still, I feel responsible."

Knott put his hand on Dun's shoulder. "And I wouldn't respect you if you didn't. Now, let's move forward and try to figure this one out."

Dun picked up his coffee and took a sip. "What's there to figure? Our boy has been kidnapped, right from under my nose, and they've slipped away in a van. Alex probably won't see the sun set, and unfortunately neither will those agents that aren't involved. It's over. The bad guys won."

"Not necessarily." Knott had a wry grin on his face. "It's not over until the fat lady sings, and she's not even scheduled to perform until later."

CHAPTER 51

"HI Cob. It's Knott."

"Good morning, Knott. How's it going?"

"Actually, not too well. We lost our boy last night."

"What?" Cob had been standing at the side of his desk. With this news, he crossed behind his desk and sat down. "What happened?"

"Looks like an inside job. One or more of the agents turned sour on us. They were guarding Alex in a local apartment, and by morning they had all disappeared. Apparently got away in a white van."

"Jesus, Knott. That's terrible. I thought Alex was still in a safe house somewhere outside this area—you never told me where."

"Yeah, I know. As I said before, I had to isolate you and anyone else involved. Alex was moved temporarily to a new place right in Alexandria when the other location was compromised."

"Is Alex okay?"

"Well, he was, before last night." Knott scratched his head before continuing. "Someone took a pot shot at him outside the safe house, but he survived it with just a slight head wound. That's why we moved him to Alexandria. Now he's gone, and I don't have a clue where."

"Are we looking for the van?"

"Oh, yeah. Big time. But nothing so far."

"What about the agents that were guarding him?" Cob was writing notes as he spoke.

"Obviously, we know the names of the four agents guarding him. What we don't know is how many of them were involved in this scheme. I hope only one, but can't be sure. We're trying to track them, but these guys were all pros and skilled in avoiding detection. Doesn't look good."

"I agree. While I find it hard to believe that any or all of your agents would cross over like this, I actually hope they were all involved. Otherwise, the poor ones that weren't are history. Either way, doesn't look too hopeful for Alex." Cob wanted to say something about the FBI couldn't protect their ass with an iron griddle, but thought better of it.

Knott paused before responding. "Yeah, good point. However, any way you cut it, my ass is grass and the White House will be the lawnmower."

"What can I do?"

"Well, now that you mention it, it's why I called. I do need you back in on this. I have a plan in mind."

* * *

After Cob hung up the phone, he rubbed the back of his neck while reviewing his notes. This was unbelievable. How the hell could this have happened? It wasn't possible.

He reached for the phone on his desk and placed a call.

"Hi. Cob here. Is there something going on I don't know about? Otherwise, we've got a problem."

* * *

After Knott left his apartment, Dun sat over another cup of coffee and wondered where this was all going. If the kidnappers did kill Alex, Knott had inferred that his involvement in the case was over and he should submit a bill for his time and expenses.

He knew he couldn't do that. He couldn't bill Knott or anyone for screwing up on this case and allowing Alex to be put in harm's way.

Sure, Knott had tried to convince him that this wasn't his fault. He wasn't in charge of protecting Alex; that was Knott's job. But, any way you slice it, someone took Alex from his apartment and Alex could be dead right now. He'd be damned if he was going to submit a bill for that.

His mind shifted to Sally Olivia. He hadn't handled that too well. He imagined she was pretty upset about his response to her questions, maybe thinking that he didn't want her to speak to Alex for fear the two would get together again.

He decided to at least correct that error. He picked up the phone and called her.

"Hello?"

"Hi, Sally Olivia. It's Dun."

After a short pause, she responded. "Oh, hi Dun. Was just thinking about you, in fact."

"Yeah, I can imagine. Look, I wanted to apologize for my earlier conversation this morning. I couldn't talk right then, I was in the middle of something—."

"What's her name?"

"What…?"

"The woman that was there with you?"

Dun almost laughed. "Sally Olivia, there is no other woman in my life but you. The person here was Knott Harrison, from the FBI. We had…uh, a little problem this morning."

"A little problem?"

"Yeah, concerning Alex."

"Alex…oh, you mean Bruce?"

"You wanted to talk to him."

"I still do."

"Well…that may not be possible." His tongue felt like it was coated in lead.

Sally Olivia paused. "Why not? What's going on?"

"Maybe I should come over so we can talk."

"Can't you tell me over the phone?"

"I'd rather not." He didn't know why he said that, maybe his subconscious desire to see her, even if he was the bearer of bad news.

"Well, okay. I need to talk with you also."

"Be there in ten." Dun hung up. What did she want to talk to him about? He wasn't sure he wanted to hear it. Jesus, his whole life was falling apart. All he wanted to do was start a small private investigation agency, and look where he was. No customers and up to his nose in a gigantic barrel of shit. With waves. Huge waves.

CHAPTER 52

AS Sally Olivia opened the door, Dun stood there holding a key.

"Hi, Dun. What's the key for?"

"It's yours. Forgot I had it. Aaron gave it to me when I first started looking for you."

She held out her hand and took the key. Dun's heart skidded on the floor, knowing that he was right in expecting the worst.

"Come on in. Grab a seat in the living room. I've got some fresh coffee brewing."

"Thanks. That will be great." As he walked into her condo, he wondered just what the hell was so great about it. He was here to tell her the bad news about Alex, and she was about to tell him she'd decided not to continue with the relationship. Real great. He started to think what else could happen in his life, but he shut off that thought. No sense pushing his luck. If you could call that luck.

He chose a seat that faced the window; he might need a distraction.

"Here we go. Haven't done this in a while, so hope it's okay."

He reached over and took a mug of steaming coffee off the tray. She had remembered he liked coffee in a mug, not a cup and saucer. Never could balance those damn things. "Thanks, looks good."

She took a seat opposite him, and sat with her coffee mug in her lap, with both hands around it like she needed the warmth for comfort. "Okay, tell me why I can't talk with Alex, as you promised."

He stared at her. She was so beautiful. God, how he ached for her. He couldn't find the words to start.

"Dun, are you all right?"

He blinked. Where should he begin? Actually, guess it didn't matter. This will really cook his goose. He cleared his throat. Better to just do it. "We don't know where he is."

"What? He left, went off somewhere?"

"Ah, no. He was kidnapped. Early this morning."

"Someone took him?"

"Yes," was all he could manage to croak. His voice sounded strange.

"Where was he?" Sally Olivia was sitting on the edge of her chair, the coffee mug tipped at an angle, almost spilling its contents.

"My apartment." Dun turned and looked out the window. This wasn't going so well. He cleared his throat again.

"Dun! Your apartment? He's supposed to be in the Witness Protection Program, not staying at your apartment. Are you crazy?"

"Guess I am, Sally Olivia." He was torn between getting up and walking out, or just giving her the whole story. He concluded he might as well get it over with.

He turned to face her again. He noticed that she had spilled some coffee in her lap, and was using a napkin to daub the spots.

"He was there because the FBI couldn't find a safe house for him. The last one he'd been in had been compromised, and someone took a shot at him. He's got a nasty crease on this side of his head, but he's okay. Knott brought him over last night, with four agents to guard him. When I woke up this morning, they all had disappeared."

"The FBI couldn't protect him, so they put him in your apartment?"

"With four guards."

"And this morning they were gone?"

"Yep, I slept right through it." Dun turned his head away and stared out the window. He could see two small sailboats on the Potomac River, but they didn't seem to be moving. Neither was he.

"Oh, Dun. I'm so sorry." To his surprise, Sally Olivia got up, put her coffee down, and came over to his chair. She sat on the floor and rested her head in his lap. "That must have been terrible for you. No wonder you didn't want to talk on the phone."

He put his hand on her back. "Yeah, I really screwed up."

"You couldn't have done anything about it. I'm glad you slept. If you had heard them you might have walked out and been killed." She sat up, crawled in his lap, and put her arms around his neck. "I couldn't have dealt with that."

"Me neither." He choked out a short laugh, then put his arms around her shoulders and gently held her as if she might break. No way in hell was he ever going to let go now. Not ever.

She picked up her head and looked at him. She was crying, and just looking at her made his eyes start to mist.

"I thought you were stalling me, afraid that I might still have some feelings for him."

"Well, I have to admit that thought crossed my mind. But I had to tell you about him. You had a right to know."

Sally Olivia was now kissing him, on his neck, his cheek, and finally his mouth. His heart stopped for a brief instant. If he had to die, this was the time to go. He returned her kisses, and pulled her closer. Her tears mixed with his. Too late to die, he was already in Heaven.

Finally, Sally Olivia pulled away. She wiped away his tears, and hers. But she didn't move, she stayed right there, as if she was also afraid to let go.

"You can't blame yourself for what happened. It wasn't your job to guard Alex."

"It happened right in my place. Right under my nose. I can't forgive myself for that. In spite of being jealous, Alex is a nice guy."

"Yes, he is. And I wanted to talk to him about you and me. How I had found the man I love, and want to be with forever."

"You do? Even after what I did?"

Sally Olivia smiled. "Sure, you were probably snoring and couldn't hear a thing."

As Dun started to respond, laughter came out instead of words. She joined in, and they both laughed, and cried, sitting there, holding each other. The world was back in focus for both of them.

CHAPTER 53

SIDNEY picked up the phone and placed a call. He hoped no one would answer.

"Hello?"

"Hi, Gloria." His luck had run out.

"Sidney! I've missed you. Thought maybe you'd forgotten about me."

"No way. Been working on that project we talked about."

"And?"

"Got some information for you. Hope it helps."

"Gee, that's wonderful, Sid. Want me to come over?"

Sidney wasn't comfortable with that option. "No, that's okay. I'll be at your place in a few minutes."

"Mmmmm. And have I got something special for you, my little man-bull."

Sidney groaned as he hung up the phone.

He was still recovering from the last sex triathlon with her. She seemed insatiable, but then maybe she couldn't get enough of him. That must be it. At least, if he went to her place, he could find an excuse and leave at a reasonable time. Otherwise, it would be another all-nighter keystone cops under the sheets. He wasn't up for that. Literally.

* * *

"Sidney! Come in, come in. Oh, have I ever missed you. Little Gloria has been sad and lonely, deprived of her man-bull." She was all bubbly and smiles, wearing a shrink-wrapped, loose-weave knit dress over her bare body that left absolutely nothing to the imagination. She wrapped herself around him before he could even get through the door.

Sidney swallowed and handed her an envelope. "This is what I have." As he started to open it, she took it from his hand and threw it on the floor.

"That can wait, Sid. I need something else right now. I'll give you three guesses, and the last two don't count." With a smile as wide as a refrigerator door, she dragged him into the bedroom and threw him on the bed.

"But, Gloria," he protested, "don't you want to see what I brought?"

"Oh yes, I sure do." She unlatched his pants and unzipped his fly. "Oh, what a nice surprise! Just for me?"

She straddled his loins, lifted her knit dress up to her waist, and mounted him.

This is what it must feel like to be raped, he thought. However, as she worked her magic he found himself becoming less of a victim. Oh well, you can't rape the willing.

Afterward, he was exhausted, and Gloria wrapped herself around him like a starved octopus. Nervously, he brought up the subject again. "Got what you wanted. As I said, there's no door this wizard can't unlock. I admit it took me a little longer than I thought, but I got through. And, no one will ever know I was there." His grin was almost as big as his ego at that point.

"Oh, Sidney, I'm so grateful. Now, we—I mean, this woman—can find this guy and try to reason with him."

"Sure. What I found is a list of all the safe-houses within a radius of 150 miles."

"Gee, that's great. Which one is he in?"

"That I don't know, unfortunately."

"What? You don't know? He could be in any one of them?" She sat up in the bed, with her legs tucked under her. The angry scowl on her face gave him a hint she was extremely pissed.

"There is no record of where he is in the computer. They must be moving him around, and not updating the computer records so no one can track him. I don't know."

"I thought you said the computer records were locked, so no one could access them?"

"They are. Except for *moi*, of course."

"So, how could anyone access them?"

"They can't." Sidney was getting nervous. Gloria was definitely agitated.

"So, why wouldn't the person with access update the records, if no one else could see them?"

Sidney felt like he was a kid again, with his mother challenging him about some dumb thing he had done. "Gloria, I don't know. All I know is that any information about where he is currently is not in the computer. I checked several times."

"You dummy! I can't believe that! It's got to be in there somewhere. What the hell do you expect us to do, check out every damn safe house within 150 miles? Are you crazy?"

Sidney was speechless. Wow, this was a side of Gloria he hadn't seen before.

"But—"

"But, your ass. You'd better get your butt back there and look again. Otherwise, ol' Gloria here goes on strike. And, then what would man-bull do without Gloria to satisfy his needs? Eh?"

He wasn't sure that was such bad news. Without another word, however, he hitched up his pants and left.

* * *

"Jesus, I can't believe it. He screwed up again." Gloria was talking on the phone, her face flushed and sweaty. "I thought I'd be rid of him by now. But no, that little weenie only delivered half the goods."

As she listened, her face flushed even more, the red creeping down her neck and across her breastbone.

"Fine, I'll give him another shot. But if he doesn't deliver, I'm gone. Do you hear me? Gone." Her voice was rising in pitch and volume. She paced around the room, only limited by the length of the phone cord.

"Yeah, easy for you to say. You don't have to play with a puppy-dog that has a short tail. Every time I pat him on his head I'm afraid he'll wet all over my shoes."

She listened for several minutes. "OK. Yes, I'm calming down." Her face color slowly returned to normal. She stopped pacing and sat on the bed.

"Really? Oh, yes. I'd like that. That would be worth waiting for—I can handle that. Mmmmm, I can definitely handle that."

As she placed the phone back on its cradle, her body shivered with excitement.

* * *

Sidney was in a pickle. He didn't want to go back and break into the WPP section of the computer again. Every time he did the danger of detection increased. However, after Gloria's reaction, he didn't have much choice.

Well, actually he did. He was about to give up on Gloria. She couldn't talk to him that way. Besides, enough was enough. The thought of midnight romps, night after night after night, made him ache all over. He could see himself withering up and dying at thirty-five, with "He wasn't up to it" carved on his gravestone. And her standing by the gravesite, a sly smile on her face as she scanned the small crowd for her next victim.

He shivered just thinking about it. But then, he did promise to help. And it was a challenge to his title as the world's greatest computer programmer, even if that title was self-imposed.

Something hovering in the back of his mind bothered him. Her using the "we" and "us" words. He thought she was going to give the information to that woman, the mother of those little kids. Guess she was referring to her and the mother. Whatever, he had a challenge ahead of him, so better get to it.

After about thirty minutes of getting nowhere, he sat back in his chair and scanned the menu displayed on his screen. He could get in easily enough, but there didn't seem to be any information other than what he had already passed onto Gloria. However, there was one section he might try.

"Morning, Sidney."

Sidney almost jumped out of this chair. "Oh, hi Tony. Didn't hear you coming up behind me."

Tony was Sidney's supervisor, and was never in this early. Just his luck.

"You looked pretty absorbed. What are you up to?"

"Oh, just looking around, trying to get a handle on this great behemoth."
Tony leaned closer to the computer screen. Sidney held his breath.
"I thought the WPP section was locked out?"

Sidney exhaled. "It is. I'm just looking at the menu, trying to figure
how this whole mishmash of information should tie together. Once this
section is back online, I'll have to integrate it with everything."

"Yeah, that should be fun. Well, let me know if you need any help."

"Thanks, Tony." As he watched his supervisor walk away, he wondered
who Tony was trying to kid. He was about as useless as a tampon on an
elephant.

Sidney checked around before proceeding. Coast clear. His fingers
flew over the keyboard for several minutes, and then retrieved from his
backpack the floppy disk that held his special program. He watched it
work flawlessly, backtracking the code just as before. When it finished
and identified the new code, he thought he remembered only three lines of
code highlighted before. Now there were four. He had destroyed his earlier
notes, and he couldn't remember. He must be mistaken, probably because
he was so nervous.

Glancing over his shoulder every minute or so, Sidney worked at a
feverish pace. If he were caught, the moon would be over-populated
before he got out of Leavenworth.

Finally, he was in. And there was new information in the section he
hadn't tried before. Just what he was looking for. He smacked his hand
on the console, and in a whisper, celebrated, "Yes! I did it! The best!"

CHAPTER 54

DUN had to drag himself out of Sally Olivia's condo. He could have stayed there forever. All his fears of Sally Olivia rejecting him had disappeared. If there was a Heaven on Earth, he'd been there. But it sure was Hell leaving.

Knott had called, indicating that something critical had come up regarding Alex. He knew where Alex was located, and had found the leak internally. He wanted to meet Dun in his office in one hour.

Everything that surrounded Knott was critical. It was one crisis after another. He supposed that was part of the work Knott was doing for the FBI, but still, Dun felt like his life was out of control. He regretted ever getting involved.

He was grateful for the information and support Knott had provided in helping him get Sally Olivia back into his life. He owed him that. And, maybe this chapter was finally coming to a close and things would quiet down. But, somehow, he doubted it. Knott thrived on action and excitement. That was more than Dun had bargained for, and more than he wanted right now.

Sally Olivia was back. He wanted nothing to interrupt that. They had been talking about a long vacation together just when Knott called. Damn, that man had a way of interrupting everything.

Promising Sally Olivia he would get back to her as soon as possible, he had left her and driven back to his office.

As he entered, Lucy greeted him with a big smile. "Hi Dun. Nice to see you once in a while."

"Hi. Knott's coming over in about fifteen minutes. There are some new developments in the Alex case he wants to discuss." He briefed her on Alex's kidnapping and Knott finding the leak in the WPP program.

"Gee, that sounds like maybe this thing is going to wrap up. Wouldn't that be nice? You haven't been yourself since you took on this case. By the way, how's Sally Olivia?"

"Just wonderful, Luce. Wonderful." The joy in his heart was transmitted all over his face.

"I'm glad for you, Dun. I know this has been a tough time for you and her both. I do hope I'm finally going to get the chance to meet her soon. She sounds so nice."

"Luce, when all this is over, the three of us are going out on the town and celebrate. That's a promise."

"You're on. Sounds great." Lucy hesitated, but then continued. "I was sorry to see Sam leave. She's a nice girl. From the way she changed while she was here, I could tell she had a crush on you, big time. I hope you didn't say anything to encourage her to leave."

Dun had a brief flash of guilt thinking about Sam. "No, I didn't. You're right, she is a nice girl, and sure blossomed into a beauty. But she admitted that PI work wasn't for her; she couldn't get into it for some reason. I hope she finds something she's really interested in."

"She had. You. That was the only reason she stayed. I tried to tell her your heart was elsewhere, but I guess she had to take a shot at it."

"We had a nice long talk that night after you left. We parted as friends, and I asked her to keep in touch and let me know how she makes out." Dun well knew how she made out, but he couldn't mention that to Lucy. He was glad that was over, and it didn't go any farther. However, if he hadn't been committed to Sally Olivia…

"Thanks for that. I'm sure she'll be fine. She just has to find herself."

"I think she already has. Don't worry about her; I have a feeling she's ready to take on the world."

Lucy smiled. "I hope so."

Dun walked into his office and checked his messages. There were none, and he hadn't expected any. This thing with Knott had taken all his time. And it wasn't over yet. At least he would be able to bill the FBI once it was. And he hoped that happened very soon, for he was about to run out of money.

After several years of avoiding the collection attorneys, he was about to head back into debt. He wasn't going to let that happen, even if he had to close his agency and let Lucy go. But, he'd figure out something.

* * *

Sidney printed out the new information he'd found in the computer. It was only two pages, but the printer seemed to take forever. He kept glancing over his shoulder, expecting his boss or someone else to bounce in any minute and say, "Whatcha' doin'?"

He took the sheets of paper, folded them twice, and tucked them into an inside zippered pocket of his knapsack, the same pocket where he kept his special floppy disk. Then he returned to his console and exited the program. Done. If it hadn't been so cold in there, he would have been sweating.

The rest of the day seemed to drag more than normal. He kept glancing at the wall clock, almost wishing the clock hands to speed up in their slow recording of the passing time. Once he was out of the office, he would give the information to Gloria and that was the end of it. No more.

No more sex. No more sneaking around in the WPP section of the computer. And no more picking up girls in a bar. He'd had enough sex to last him for several years, and the way he felt it would take that amount of time to recover.

Finally, five o'clock. He waited another ten minutes, just to make it look good. Then he picked up his knapsack and casually headed for the exit.

"Good night, Tom. Have a good evening." The same guard was there every night. Must be the most boring job ever.

Tom waved as Sidney passed through the gate. Just as he had cleared it, the guard looked up. "Oh, Sidney. Mr. Wilson would like to speak to you before you leave."

"Mr. Wilson? I don't know him."

"Well he knows you. Said you should go to his office on the fourth floor before you leave. On the right as you get off the elevator. He just called a few minutes ago and said he had something important to share with you."

"Oh. Okay, I'll go right up." Sidney passed back through the gate and walked to the elevators. Wilson. Wilson. Nope, that name wasn't familiar. Oh, wait a minute, he's the guy in Personnel. Well, maybe they've recognized his genius. Wouldn't surprise him if they put him in charge of the whole damn department. His boss was an idiot, been there for a ton of years. Maybe the old fart was finally going to retire. And, guess who was next in line? He stood a little straighter and ran his hand over his hair.

The elevator doors opened at the fourth floor. Sidney turned right and walked down a hallway that seemed to go on forever. About halfway, he came to a small suite of offices labeled 'Personnel." The door on the right had Wilson's name on it.

He took the knapsack off his shoulders and knocked.

The door opened immediately. The guy standing there with a big smile looked like he might be Mr. Wilson, if his memory served him right.

"Sidney. Come in and have a seat."

"Thanks, Mr. Wilson." As he entered the office, he noticed two other men standing behind the seat he was supposed to use.

"Sidney. Meet agents Scalara and Quade. They have a few questions they'd like to ask you.

* * *

A knock at the door interrupted Dun's thoughts. Standing in the doorway was Knott. He had mixed emotions about seeing him, but he was anxious to find out what had developed with Alex.

"Hi. Come on in and grab a seat. Something to drink?"

Before Knott could answer, Lucy came in with a tray of refreshments.

"Lucy, I don't expect you to wait on us like this." Dun felt guilty about Lucy acting as a personal secretary.

"Don't get too used to it. But, I know you guys are heavily involved right now. Besides, it gives me something to do." Lucy exhibited a weak smile, put the tray on the table and left the office, closing the door behind her.

"Okay, Knott. What's so damn important that you dragged me here?"

"Gee, I thought this was your office?"

"It is, dammit. But Sally Olivia and I were just getting back together when you interrupted."

"This is a hell of a lot more serious than your sex life, buddy."

"Sex life? Yes. My life with Sally Olivia? No way."

Knott smiled. "I'm really happy for you, buddy. Glad it's all working out.'"

Dun shifted in his chair. "You can't imagine how happy I am right now."

"You're right. I can't imagine it. Maybe if I had played out my life differently, I could have. But, I didn't, and I'm sorry for that. However, life goes on."

He remembered what Knott had told him about his marriage not working out. He vowed he would never let that happen to him. Never. He looked at Knott, who was staring off at nothing.

Knott refocused and continued. "There's a lot going on right now. Some of it you're not going to like, and I'm sure you're going to have a few questions. Just let me lay it out before you react."

"Sure. You've got the floor."

"First, I lied to you."

Dun wasn't surprised to hear that. He suspected that some of that had been going on, or at least Knott had withheld some information from him. He figured it was Knott's way of working him into the case and judging his reactions.

Knott looked at Dun for a minute, then continued. "Alex wasn't abducted, as I told you. I planned that to get him away from your place. Just in case they had tracked him there. I didn't think anyone had, but I wasn't sure."

"What? You're kidding?"

"No, I'm not. We made it look real. Again, just in case."

"Why? That doesn't make sense."

"I didn't want anything else going wrong, and I wanted to make sure Alex was totally protected. I was close to finding out where the leak was, and I didn't want whoever is doing this to make another attempt before I was ready."

"Jesus. That's a little dramatic, isn't it? Where you'd take him?"

"To Quantico. I doubt that anyone will attempt to get to him in the middle of a Marine base."

Dun laughed. "No one with any brains, that's for sure. But, what if there had been a spotter. Wouldn't they wonder who else was involved in trying to get to Alex?"

"Sure. But we had the area totally secured in a half-mile perimeter. No one was watching your place. But, as I said, just to be sure, we made it look real. We had to take a chance, if for no other reason than to put Alex somewhere they couldn't get to him."

"Okay, I can buy that. But why the pretense with me? Am I suspect too?"

"I had to make sure you weren't. Nothing personal, but I had to isolate everyone I could before I could set up the next stage."

"And, what is the next stage?"

"We've discovered the source of the leak, and were using him to set up a trap."

Dun sat up in his chair. "Who is it?"

"A computer programmer newly hired to revamp the whole FBI system, including the WPP program. We locked out the WPP section, but then found evidence that someone had been tampering with it. With the insertion of a little unobtrusive tracking device, the next time he came in we had him."

"A computer programmer is after Alex?"

"No. His new girlfriend befuddled him with sex and blew up his ego so he would get information on Alex for her. Gave him a cock and bull story that he believed. Once we nailed him, he opened up completely. We put a tap on his girlfriend's phone, then sent him over to her place with false information on where Alex is located."

"And…?"

"She led us to Cob Ferguson."

Dun opened his eyes in shock. "The US Marshal assigned to him?"

"Yeah. He's the one. I would have sworn he was clean. Now I have to bring him in. We're going to set up a trap for him, just to make sure." Knott had a look of despair on his face. One of the guys sworn to protect Alex was dirty.

"Damn. I'm sorry for that, Knott. I know how that must hurt. But, at least you've finally uncovered the source. So, when's the trap set to be sprung?"

"The information we purposely leaked said Alex would be at a new location tomorrow night. Of course, he won't be, but I'm going to need your help then."

Dun looked across at the calendar on his desk. Tomorrow was July 31, the last of July, the night before August.

That last phrase surprised and bothered him. Why would he think of that? The night before August? Where did that come from? Dun didn't put a lot of faith in premonitions, but this one turned his skin cold.

CHAPTER 55

AFTER the meeting, Dun returned to Sally Olivia's condo. He told her everything that had happened with the Alex situation.

"You mean, Alex hasn't really been kidnapped, as Knott told you?"

Dun grimaced. "That's what he said. This guy is full of surprises."

"Then maybe I'll get to talk to him after all. I'd still like to close out that part of my life."

"Yes, I can understand that. Especially now that I'm not jealous anymore."

Sally smiled and gave him a hug. "If anyone should be jealous, it's me."

Dun tensed a little. "Oh? Why's that?"

"Knott's taking up all your time. Now that I've found you—and myself—I want you here all the time."

"Don't worry. This will all be over soon. Then I'm all yours. Try to keep me away."

"I'm nervous about this, Dun. This could be dangerous."

"I don't think so. We'll arrest whoever arrives at the location. That should take care of it."

"Then why doesn't Knott send in a dozen agents to do this? Why just you and him?"

He looked away. "I asked Knott the same question. He wants to take Cob by himself and try to keep it as quiet as possible. There will be enough embarrassment to both agencies, he feels, without spreading it all over town."

"Oh, Dun. Please, walk away from this. You've done your part. Let Knott take it from here."

"I'd love to, but I've made a commitment. I signed on for this project, and I'll see it through. When it's over, we can take vacation we talked about…if the FBI pays my bill, that is."

"Don't worry about that. There's plenty of money available for a vacation."

"This isn't the time to talk about that, but I won't hear of using any money from your trust to take a vacation. If I can't afford it, we'll camp out at my place for a week."

Sally smiled. "I'll camp out anywhere with you, and I won't bring up my trust funds again. I promise. I know a place where we can go for free."

* * *

The next morning, Dun and Knott met in Dun's office.

Dun placed a pad of paper in front of him on the table. "Okay, what's the plan?"

Knott smiled. "You sure you want to go through with this?"

"Sure. I need the billing.'"

"Tell you what. You prepare a bill and bring it with you tonight. I'll make sure it gets paid in a couple of days. Figure out all your hours, add in a few for tonight, and apply a healthy hourly rate. You can send in a supplemental bill for any extra hours and incidental expenses later. At least you'll have some money coming in."

"Great. That will help. I'm just about at the bottom of the barrel."

"No problem, buddy. Just have it ready and the money will be in your hands in a day or so. I promise."

"Terrific. I can pay Lucy and the rent, and Sally Olivia and I can take off for a week or so."

"You deserve it. Okay, let's get down to the specifics about tonight. The information Sidney delivered—he's the programmer, remember?—showed that Alex will be at a new location by late afternoon, when actually he'll still be at Quantico. This is an empty two-family unit in a not-so-nice part of town off South Capitol Street. It's not one of our normal safe houses, but it's been checked over by my guys. Just after dark, we'll slip into position and wait."

"Sounds good. How many men do you think will come for him?"

"Just one."

"Just one? You mean Cob?"

"Yeah. Sidney told Gloria that only one man would be guarding Alex. Cob is the one being paid to do this and he won't want any more mistakes. He'll come himself."

Dun relaxed a little. "I hope you're right. That will make it easy."

"Don't underestimate Cob, whatever you do. He's highly professional and can kill you with his little finger."

"OK." Dun didn't know what else to say. He was trying to stay calm, but it wasn't working. He poured himself another cup of coffee and then motioned toward Knott, who shook his head 'no thanks.'

"So," Dun continued, "we wait for him to show and arrest him. Is that the plan?"

"Basically. Except, you'll cover the rear entrance and I'll be in the front. Given the layout of the place, I think he'll come in that way. The rear doesn't have easy access, unless he wants to climb up onto a high porch using a ladder. There will be no ladder available, so he'll have to come in the front way. But you'll be the backup, in place in the event he tries to escape through the rear."

"What about if he tries to do another sniper routine?"

"He can't. All the windows are heavily draped, with no lights showing near them. And, since there will be no one in the apartment, we don't have to worry about shadows crossing the windows."

"Sounds easy enough."

"I hope so. But anything can go wrong."

CHAPTER 56

THEY met again at a little restaurant just west of Alexandria on Duke Street for dinner before the 'show' started. He handed Knott his bill for PI services. Knott smiled, glanced at it, and put it in his coat pocket. "Looks fine. I'll take care of it."

After they ordered, Knott turned to him. "We'll take your SUV and park a few blocks from the apartment. You can follow me from here so I can drop my car off. Assuming everything goes well, I'll call my agents to come and pick us up—Cob and me—and you can take your SUV back to your place."

"Okay. That's fine." He wasn't so sure everything was fine. He'd never been in a situation like this before and was nervous. As Knott had said, anything could go wrong, and it usually does. But, the plan was simple and that helped. What little experience he'd had in this type of thing told him that simple was better.

"Bring your piece?"

Dun snapped out of his thoughts. "What?"

"Did you bring your Beretta?"

Dun self-consciously reached around to his back and double-checked that he had his 9mm Beretta with him. "Yeah, all set."

"Why don't you get something with a little more stopping power? That pea shooter wouldn't stop a piss ant on the way to the men's room."

Dun laughed. It was good to break the tension. And tension he was feeling. His shoulder muscles were tight, and he found himself unconsciously stretching his neck from side to side to loosen them. Maybe all this was getting to him. It was going too fast, and he felt like he was being dragged headfirst behind a tractor through a field of geese shit with his mouth open.

As he looked out the window at the growing darkness, he muttered, "Oh, shit."

"What?" Knott turned around and looked at the window.

"It's raining like a cow pissing on a flat rock. That'll really help."

"*Au contraire*, my little PI buddy. That *will* help. It will be easier for us to stay hidden."

"Sure. With the rain dripping off my nose, along with fits of sneezing. Piece of cake."

"You'll be fine."

"What about you?"

Knott laughed. "Oh, guess I didn't tell you. I'll be inside, out of the rain in the lower hallway, waiting for our friend to show up."

"Seems like there is always something you don't tell me."

"Welcome to my world."

* * *

They drove up and parked on the side street. Knott pointed through the windshield. "The apartment is up one block, around the corner on the left. Second house. It's an old two-family with a detached building in the back. Only one like it on the street. You can't miss it; look for the high porch."

"If this damn rain doesn't let up, I'll miss having an umbrella."

"Trust me, you don't want an umbrella. It's warm out, so you won't get chilled."

"Yeah, just soaked." Dun's nerves were starting to jitter. He hoped everything would go smoothly and it was over soon. The thought of standing in the rain, protecting an empty apartment, and waiting for a killer to show wasn't his idea of fun. He was beginning to regret that he hadn't taken Accounting or something in school. One thing for sure, when this was over, he was done working with the FBI. Being a PI was dangerous enough; working with Knott was downright suicide.

"Ready?" Knott had his hand on the door handle.

"Sure. Let's get it over with." Dun opened the door, stepped into the rain, and then locked the SUV and set the alarm. This wasn't a neighborhood to leave an expensive vehicle sitting around unprotected.

They crossed the street and started up the block. The area was empty of people and vehicles; the rain did help in that regard. As they neared the end of the block, Knott signaled with his hand for Dun to go left, while Knott continued straight ahead.

Dun turned into a small alley behind the buildings, more of a drainage ditch than anything. It was so clogged with junk he was forced to pick his way through the 'minefield'—one careless step and tin cans, rusted hubcaps, or broken liquor bottles would sound alarms that would be heard for several blocks. Without any moon or streetlights, it was slow going.

Finally, he stopped and took his bearings. The apartment house was on his right, with what was left of a wooden fence surrounding the rear yard. He looked up at the badly deteriorated porch on the second floor. One end sloped at an alarming angle—it didn't look like it would support an anemic cat.

The soaking rain continued, but Dun's nervousness blocked it out of his mind. He surveyed his surroundings, looking for a place to set himself and wait. A small roof would help.

As his eyes became even more accustomed to the dark, he noticed an old wooden lean-to in the corner of the yard. That must be the 'building' Knott referred to. The run down structure was situated caddy-corner to the house and the back fence, with the opening providing a perfect panoramic view of the back of the house and the whole yard. It also had the advantage of some protection from the rain.

Dun stooped and climbed through a hole in the fence and worked toward the corner of the yard. The grass was almost knee high, so again he had to put one foot forward and test for any hidden obstacles. He reminded himself to bill Knott for his ruined leather shoes.

As he neared the lean-to, he reached around to the holster nestled in the small of his back and unleashed his Beretta. While he was a lefty, he had forced himself to master the use of a weapon that was designed for a right-handed person. Left-handed models were available, but way beyond the price limit Dun was willing to pay.

Dun moved under the overhang and leaned against the unpainted wall made from scraps of plywood. He loosely crossed his arms in front of him and rested the Beretta in his right hand. Just as he was clicking off the safety, he heard a noise to his right.

His heart stopped, and his ears strained to identify the source of the noise. Someone, or thing, was moving down the alley in his direction. Whatever it was, it was progressing at a slow pace, just as he had done, to avoid making any noise.

His muscles tensed, and he raised the Beretta as he caught the glimpse of something moving just beyond the corner of the structure. Holding perfectly still, he watched the figure come into full view. His heart was racing like a quarter horse with a full bladder, and he could feel the thumping in his temples.

It was a man! As he looked closer, the man appeared to be elderly. He was bent over, carrying an old gunnysack on his shoulder. The man stopped, looked around, and then stooped down to pick up an empty bottle. He held it up above his head, trying to see if there was any liquid left. He obviously couldn't tell, for he then lowered the bottle to his lips and tipped the bottom up until it the bottle was nearly vertical.

After a moment, the man wiped his lips with his sleeve, and carefully placed the bottle in his sack. Dun was amazed that he had accomplished all this with hardly a noise. The man then continued on his slow journey, he eyes glued to the ground, oblivious to the pouring rain.

He let out a soft sigh of relief. Was he having fun yet? The answer was definitely 'no.' It was still pouring, an old man almost caused him to have to change his underwear, and someone might just try to kill him tonight.

He swept the yard and the back of the apartment building with his eyes. In spite of the rain, he could see fairly well. The only noise he heard was the vanishing sound of the old man moving away, and the constant rain.

Knott had wanted him in the rear of the building in case whoever came to take the bait tried to escape through the rear. There was no rear door on the bottom floor, and the door to the second floor porch was an invitation to disaster. Anyone trying to exit that way would land on rotted wood that wouldn't hold a small dog. Even if it did hold, the outside staircase had long ago collapsed. It would be a two-story jump for anyone trying to use that route to escape.

Besides, Knott was waiting in the inside hallway. Anyone coming in through the front would have to pass in front of him. No way was someone going to reach the second floor.

The rain was beginning to let up, and he used the opportunity to check out the apartment building again. Was there another way out of the building, perhaps a bottom-floor door on either side? He couldn't see anything, and wasn't about to go poking around. He reminded himself that Knott and his agents had checked out the building earlier, and if he said the only out was by the second floor porch, that was it. Anyone coming out that way would have a hard time being quiet as he broke through the porch flooring. Dun almost laughed at the vision of that happening.

His best bet was to stay where he was and be alert for any movement. He tried to stop thinking about it, realizing that his nervousness was behind all those questions. However, had Knott told him everything? Up to now, the answer to that was always 'no.'

Just as the answer to that was forming in his mind, he heard Knott yell, "Stop, or I'll shoot!" The warning was immediately followed by two closely spaced shots that pierced the stillness like twin lightning bolts.

Dun ducked under the lean-to roof and ran toward the front of the apartment. About halfway across the yard, he came to a skidding stop. He was supposed to guard the rear exit point. How did he know whose gun those shots had come from?

He crouched on his heels and slowly started moving back a little, looking up at the porch as he did. Nothing. No movement anywhere. While his butt was getting soaked from the tall wet grass, he stayed on his haunches until his muscles couldn't hold that position any longer. If those shots had been fired from Knott's gun, he would have called the 'all clear' by now.

Dun stood up and started running toward the front again. Rounding the front corner of the apartment, he came to an abrupt stop. There was no one in sight.

He crept up the front stairs to the dilapidated porch, his Beretta sweeping in a small arc in front of him. The streetlights had been broken long ago, but even in the dark he could make out the body of a man laying half-in the front doorway. Behind it stood Knott, his pistol still held in front of him.

As he walked closer, he sucked in air as he recognized the lifeless form.

CHAPTER 57

"JESUS! What happened?" Dun looked at Knott, who was holstering his pistol. It was obvious from the look on his face that he was in mild shock.

"Shit! I wanted to avoid this. He didn't give me any choice." Knott walked over to the front steps and sat down.

Dun was in shock himself, but he looked down at the body. It was laying face down, one arm tucked underneath, the other extended away from the body, loosely covering a snub-nosed pistol. A pool of blood was slowly spreading from under the body.

He reached down, and using a handkerchief started to pick up the pistol. Just in case. Then he stopped, thinking of his PI training, and left the pistol in place. It was obvious that Cob was dead. No doubt about that, but he searched for a pulse just to make sure.

Looking at Knott, he holstered his Beretta, walked to the steps, and sat down. "What happened?"

"Tell you later. I happened so fast my mind is still catching up." Knott reached for his cell phone and made a call. When he was through, he turned toward Dun. "My guys will be here in a few minutes to collect Cob and examine the scene. I'll catch a ride with them. Better for you if they don't find you here, unless you want to spend the next two weeks answering questions."

"Whatever you say, Knott. Are you sure I can't help?" Dun could almost feel the pain Knott must be going through. To have to kill one of your own is every lawman's nightmare.

"No. Thanks for backing me up. Better go. I'll call you later."

Dun stood up and put a hand on his friend's shoulder, then turned and walked toward his SUV.

As he rounded the corner and headed down the street to where he had parked his SUV, he noticed two older teens angling across the street towards him. They were swaggering, hitting each other on the shoulder, and muttering in some language Dun couldn't understand. As they came closer, they spread apart a little and stopped to block his way. They just stood there, all cocky with broad smiles.

Each was wearing a bright bandana wrapped around his forehead, an oversized Hawaiian-type shirt, and baggy jeans slung so low on the hips that the boxer underwear showed. This ensemble was capped off with a pair of sneakers that contained more rubber than a tractor tire—they looked like little tug boats with huge rubber bumpers.

Dun kept walking right at them.

"Hey, mon. Whatcha' doin' in dis neybahood? Eh? Lookin' fa' trouble?"

Dun didn't hesitate or change his direction.

"Hey, mon. Maybe ya got somethin' ta share wid' us?"

Dun was only a few feet away when he casually reached behind him, pulled his Beretta, and walked into the guy on the right. Before the hood could move, Dun grabbed him behind his neck and smashed his head forward into the barrel of the gun, leaving a nice red circular welt on his forehead.

"This what you looking for, gentlemen?"

The punk froze, while the other turned and fled into the shadows. Dun unclicked the safety and pushed the weapon harder into the youth's forehead. He was tempted.

A good man, just around the corner, had to shoot one of his own tonight. And these punks were trying to be funny. He'd give them something to laugh about.

"Why don't you go home, sonny, before I blow your freakin' brains out."

Dun stepped back, reholstered his Beretta, and stared at the youth. He almost wished the boy would take a swing. Then, disgusted with the boy—and himself—he shoved the boy aside and continued down the street.

CHAPTER 58

HE didn't know whether to cry, scream, or throw up. Thoughts were cursing through his mind like miniature shock waves, all of them hitting the back of his eyes. He knew he should pull over and calm down, but he needed to get back.

As Dun drove back toward Alexandria, he glanced at the clock on the dash. Too late to stop by and see Sally Olivia. God, he wanted to. But she'd had enough of her own problems, she didn't need to hear more of his.

Tonight was unreal. He'd seen one federal agent who had gone bad killed by another—the other being his friend. The vision of Cob laying face-down in a pool of blood was one he would not soon forget—if ever.

Agreeing to work with Knott had been stupid from the beginning, but he knew why he'd done it. They'd been close high school buddies. He also hoped it would develop into a relationship and a source at the FBI.

As he thought about it, he realized that Knott had changed. Still the same in some ways, completely different in others. Knott had seen a lot of action, in a lot of different countries, and must have worked with all kinds of people, most of whom Dun wouldn't care to know. All this secret stuff, clandestine operations, and other hocus-pocus wasn't for him. Tonight showed him that.

He pulled into his apartment parking lot and set the alarm on the SUV. As he walked toward the stairs that led up to his apartment on the third floor, he promised that in his next life he'd find a place with an elevator.

He couldn't decide which was more weary, his mind or his body. The first two flights of stairs seemed to take forever. As he neared the third landing, he saw someone sitting on the top step. His heart skipped a beat.

"Dun, are you all right? I've been worried sick."

All his fears and tension flushed out of his body. He hopped up the last two steps and sat next to Sally Olivia.

"Hi," was all he could manage to say, as he wrapped his arms around her and pulled her close.

She stayed there in the comfort of his arms. "You're all wet, and trembling. What happened?" she whispered.

After a moment, he gently released her and sat back. "I guess I'm not cut out to be a PI. Let's go inside. I need a hot shower."

Dun stood up, helped Sally Olivia to her feet, and they walked to the door of his apartment. As he reached for his key, Sally Olivia took it from him and opened the door. Inside, she unbuttoned his shirt and helped him off with his slacks. He threw them in a damp heap in the hallway and started toward the shower.

"I won't be long," he said over his shoulder. "Then we can talk."

The shower wasn't much. But the antique tub with the day-glow tennis balls and the two shower curtains was his. This was home and he was thankful to be there.

He turned on the shower and didn't bother to wait for the hot water to arrive. Some days it never did. He stood there with the water splashing off the top of his head and smiled with simple pleasure as the water temperature began to rise. Soon the bathroom filled with steam, swirling around him in clouds and billowing over the top of the shower curtains. He didn't move, and vowed not to until the hot water ran out. Which it would. Soon.

He closed his eyes and tried to will all the unleashed thoughts out of his mind. It didn't work. The scenes from earlier that evening came rushing in like kids running through the entrance gates at Disney, with each one screaming for his attention.

The sound of the shower curtains parting snapped his eyes open. Sally Olivia stepped in, closed the curtain behind her, and walked into his embrace. "Can I share some of that hot water with you? I thought this might be as good a time as any to start that vacation we talked about."

"We'd better hurry," he murmured, kissing her neck. "This will be the shortest vacation ever if it depends on hot water." Sure enough, just as he said that, the hot water ended and the cold began.

Sally Olivia screamed, jumped out of the tub, and laughed as she grabbed a bath towel. Dun followed right behind. He scooped her up in his arms, and, dripping wet, walked toward the bedroom.

"Aren't you going to dry off?" Her laughter almost brought tears to his eyes. He hadn't heard her do that for a long, long while.

"Nope, we'll pretend we're making love on the beach in Hawaii."

"Oh, is there sand in your bed?" She was still laughing, in a rich throaty tone that made his heart sing.

Now he was laughing with her. He pulled back the top sheet and dropped her unceremoniously onto the bed. "You're about to find out."

As she landed on the bed, her bath towel unwrapped and draped open. He stood there, looking at her beauty, remembering their lovemaking in Florida. Suddenly all thoughts of earlier events washed away as she reached up for him and he joined her on the beach.

* * *

"Happy vacation," she murmured, her head resting on his chest. "This beach is really nice. I want to stay here forever."

Dun smiled and wrapped his arms around her even tighter.

"Easy there. You don't have to hold onto me for dear life; the waves won't wash me away." She smiled as Dun relaxed his arms. "And, thanks for getting rid of the sand before I got here. That might have been a little uncomfortable."

Dun laughed. Her sense of humor, along with her laughter, was back. "Yeah, you're lucky. I just shoveled it out yesterday. Two truck loads."

"You know, this is the first time I've been to your apartment. It's almost exactly as you described it."

"When I get my strength back, and you have a spare few hours, I'll give you the complete tour. Of course, you've already seen some of it, so probably it won't take the whole two hours."

"When you get your strength back, I've got something else in mind besides checking out your apartment."

"Well, we've got all week, so if you're lucky you'll get the tour before vacation is over."

"I'm not planning on it."

They both were silent for a few minutes. Dun hadn't felt this content in a long time. Or as happy. Having her there, in his arms, seemed to throw up an invisible barrier between them and the world.

"Do you want to talk about it?" Her voice was so low it took him a few seconds to register the meaning of her question.

"I don't know, Sally Olivia. I'd just as soon forget it all."

"I'm sure. But, you remember your advice to me in Florida? That I wouldn't be able to put it behind me unless I talked it out. Got it off my chest."

"I'm jealous."

"Jealous? Of what?"

"The only thing I want on your chest is me."

"Oh brother. Typical man." She swung her feet out of the bed, grabbed her towel, and walked toward the bathroom. "I'm getting dressed and putting on some coffee. Then we'll talk. Meet you in the kitchen."

"Oh, so now you want the tour?" He knew she was right, but still he wasn't ready to face what happened earlier. "It's late; the tour office is closed."

"Actually, if you don't mind. I'd like to just nose around on my own. This will be my first chance to see the real Dun Wheeling."

Dun paused for a moment before responding. "I haven't had a chance to clean it up since…ah…the agents and Alex were here."

Sally Olivia peeked her head through the open doorway to the bathroom. She was nearly dressed. "Don't worry. I understand. I'll only look with one eye." With a big smile, she turned back to the bathroom and hummed to herself as she finished dressing.

CHAPTER 59

"THIS place needs help."

They were sitting at the kitchen table. Dun had one hand wrapped around his coffee mug, the other covering Sally Olivia's hand.

"Hey, what'd you expect, House and Garden?"

"No, but I didn't expect Decorating for Oil Rigs Made Easy."

Dun laid back his head and roared. Wiping the tears from his eyes, he countered, "I *resemble* that remark. I've worked hard."

"Oh, yes. It shows. Those tennis balls on the bathtub are stunning. The non-matching shower curtains are quite in vogue. The window frames nailed to the brick are rather unique. And, the cardboard and screens in the windows might qualify for the Homeless Shelter of the Week Award."

"Well, you're wrong. This place doesn't need help; I do.'"

Sally laughed and leaned over the table to kiss him. "And, you're going to get it, whether you want it or not."

"Okay. Soon as I get paid by the FBI, I'll give you fifty bucks and you can go wild."

"Speaking of the FBI…"

"Ah, yes. Guess we should talk about it."

"We don't have to, if you're not ready."

Dun smiled at the look of concern on her face. God, he loved her.

Knowing it was now or never, he related everything that had happened. As it poured out of him, she sat there not saying a word. When he got to the part about Knott having to shoot Cob, her eyes moistened and she reached for his hand. But, still, she said nothing.

When he finished, he got up and walked over to the sink. He stood there, his back to the sink, looking at nothing, staring at everything.

Sally Olivia got up and walked over to him. She put her arms around him and nestled her head between his shoulder and neck. "I'm so sorry, Dun. That must have been awful for you. And for Knott as well."

Dun cleared his throat before attempting to speak. "Yeah, it was. I hope Knott is all right. He looked pretty down when I left him."

"From what you've described of him, he's been there before. He'll be okay."

"I suppose. I'll give him a call tomorrow and make sure."

"I'm not worried about Knott. It's you I'm worried about."

"Me? No problem. Ready to go."

"Come off it, Dun. I know better than that. But, you've made a good first step at recovery."

"Having you here sure helps. You don't know how much."

"Oh, yes I do. From Florida. Remember? You were there for me, right to the crazy end. If it weren't for you, I might have lost my sanity—not to mention my life."

He couldn't think of anything to say, so he just nodded and smiled.

Sally Olivia stepped back and looked up at him. "I love you, Dun Wheeling. Not for what you've done, but for who you are. I fell in love with you that first day we had lunch together at the resort, right after you rescued me from those horrible kidnappers. I've asked myself a thousand times over was it because you saved my life, many times, or was it really love? I know the answer now, and I've never felt happier in my life."

Dun looked into her eyes and could see the honesty there. "I knew the answer to how I feel about you a lot sooner than you did. But then, you had other things going on in your life."

Sally Olivia nestled back into his arms. "But that's over for me. And this is over for you. We'll face what comes next together." She paused for a split-second, then added, "Unless you're talking about a bad case of athlete's foot, that is."

CHAPTER 60

THE next morning Dun showed up at the office about an hour late, with Sally Olivia in tow. While the office was the last place he wanted to be right then, he needed to get some closure on this case. And, that included bringing Lucy up to speed.

"Lucy Cannon, I'd like you to meet Sally Olivia Sawgrass."

"Oh my God!" she exclaimed, jumping up from her desk and half-running over to Sally Olivia. "I feel like I've known you all my life." She gave Sally Olivia a big hug, then stood back. "And, you're more beautiful than Dun's led me to believe."

Sally Olivia laughed. "Nice to meet you, Lucy. And you're much younger than Dun has described you."

Lucy looked at Dun, initially with a scowl, but then laughed. "I think I'm going to like this gal. And you, young man, need to start taking better care of her."

It was Dun's turn to laugh. "Don't worry; you couldn't drag her away from me with ten Clydesdales."

After a few minutes of chitchat, where he could see the two of them had instantly hit it off, he interrupted. "I hate to barge in here, ladies, but why don't we go into my office and I'll bring you both up to date on everything."

Still talking, Lucy and Sally Olivia walked into Dun's office and sat down. He looked at them both, shrugged, and then asked, "Can I get you ladies anything? Coffee, soft drink, iced tea?"

Lucy started to get up. "I'm sorry, I was so engrossed with all this I forgot my manners."

Dun put his hand on Lucy's shoulder and gently pushed her back into the chair. "Nope, my turn. You've done enough of this, and it isn't your job. One of these days, when the business is rolling in, we'll hire someone to do these odd jobs. Until then, we'll split them."

"Don't spoil him please, Lucy. He's hard enough as it is."

He rolled his eyes. "Oh, brother. I'm outvoted. Okay, don't make this too complicated, so I don't have to write it down."

As he was getting the drinks, Lucy and Sally Olivia continued with their conversation as if he wasn't there. Dun was pleased. Sally Olivia didn't have any family now, and needed someone like Lucy—another woman—to talk with.

Dun delivered the drinks and sat down. Both women stopped talking and looked at him. He wasn't quite sure where to begin, so he started with the first day that Knott had called him and they had lunch.

It took him nearly an hour to go over every detail. A few times, either Lucy or Sally Olivia would ask a question, but mostly they just listened. Once, Sally Olivia looked away, tears in her eyes. At another point in the story, Lucy's face got red and he thought she might swear, but she got control of herself and remained quiet.

"After Knott discovered how the information was being leaked, he had a long fatherly talk with Sidney and got him to agree to take false information to Gloria. Of course, if he screwed it up, Sidney would be taking a long vacation in the Federal pen. However, I think he realized at that point that Gloria had only befriended him to pump him for information. A big blow to his ego, I'm sure. He felt like a real jerk for being sucked in like that, so he gladly cooperated."

"But, Dun," Lucy asked, "how did these guys find Alex before Sidney was involved?"

"Good question. Not sure, but we suspect that they followed him up to Maine once they discovered he was living in New Hampshire. I'm sure they've got his picture plastered all throughout the underground, with a healthy reward for anyone that spots him. Again, we're not sure how they tracked him to Annapolis, but they're grilling Gloria about that right now. She doesn't strike Knott as the type to have a high degree of loyalty, so he's hopeful she will provide a few answers."

Sally Olivia sat up. "After Sidney took the false information to Gloria, she took it to Cob Ferguson?"

Dun paused for a moment. "Yeah, Knott was staked out at her place, plus had her phone tapped. As he suspected, she made a quick call and then left to meet Cob."

"Why didn't they pick up Cob then?" Sally Olivia was having trouble staying up with all this intrigue.

"Because at that point they didn't have enough on him. He could have claimed that Gloria suspected a trap and falsely led the agents to him. Knott needed more evidence, plus he wanted to see if he could find out who Cob was working for."

"But, it's too late for that."

"Yes, Lucy, it is. Unfortunately."

After a few minutes of silence, Lucy spoke again. "I'm sorry it turned out this way. Tough on you, and Knott, I'm sure."

"Tougher on Cob. I need to call Knott, find out if he's learned anything new, and see how he's doing."

Lucy and Sally Olivia stood up. Sally Olivia leaned over and kissed Dun on the forehead. "Why don't you make that call? Lucy and I will sit outside and get better acquainted."

Dun stood up. "I've got a better idea. I'll make the call, and you two go out somewhere for lunch."

Lucy smiled. "You're kidding? You're actually going to buy us lunch?"

Dun tried to keep a straight face. "I didn't say that. But I did promise that when this was all over, you and I would go out and have dinner. Let's make it tonight, as long as it's some place peaceful. Of course, we'll have to drag Sally Olivia along, if you don't mind."

Before Sally Olivia could respond, Lucy jumped in. "Actually, I'll be glad to have her help. I think she and I will be dragging you."

* * *

After the women left for lunch, Dun poured himself another cup of coffee. He wasn't up for calling Knott and doubted that anything new had developed since last night. Knott was doing fine, he was sure, but he remembered the look on his friend's face last night as he sat on the front porch, Cob lying dead behind them.

Before he could procrastinate any further, Dun picked up his cell phone and called him. After three long rings, Knott's voice mail announcement came on and he left a message for Knott to call him.

He was surprised that Knott hadn't answered, but assumed he was busy tying up loose ends and pumping Gloria for what she knew.

As he placed the cell phone on his desk, it occurred to him that he would have to return it to Knott when he saw him. Also, he would need to find out what Knott wanted to do with the SUV and the credit card. He didn't want any part of them. They reminded him of things he'd just as soon forget.

CHAPTER 61

WHILE Sally Olivia and Lucy were having lunch, Dun tried to catch up on some paperwork. He needed to follow up with another invoice to the FBI outlining his out-of-pocket incidentals. As he put the list together, he was amazed as to how much it added up to. He should have kept better records, but everything had moved too fast. No excuse, he knew, and he vowed to do better in the future.

He heard the gals come back from lunch, but they never came to his office. Grateful for the peace and quiet, he placed another call to Knott on his cell phone. Same results. He left another message for him.

Was Knott out of reach of his cell phone, or not accepting calls because of what had happened last night? Then he remembered Knott telling him that those phones would work anywhere in the world. So, where was he?

He went back to work on the invoice, trying to remember each day since he'd started and any expenses that might apply to his work for Knott. Gas seemed to be the largest one. He was so averse to using a credit card that he mostly paid cash, even though Knott had provided him a card. That SUV sure didn't get the mileage his Miata did. He missed his little car, and he decided it was time to begin using it again—right after he took everyone one to dinner tonight, that is. Two in the Miata was a little tight; three was ridiculous.

After another hour of working on expenses, he gave up. Even with a calculator, he was having trouble with the numbers. His mind wasn't with it.

He placed one more call to Knott and got his answering message again. Disgusted, he put the cell phone in his desk drawer, stood up, and turned off the light to his office as he left.

* * *

"This is nice," Dun observed as the hostess seated them by a window with a view of the Potomac River. "Never been here before."

"Neither have I," Lucy admitted. "In fact, I've been to few fancy restaurants, thanks to my cheap ex-husband who is now in the Bahamas spending tons on his latest Barbie Doll look-alike."

Sally Olivia smiled. Her memories of this restaurant were not pleasant, but the food was good and the view outstanding. She used to come here often when her brother was trying to wine and dine all his phony socialite friends. The thought of those days made her shiver. However, she had recommended the restaurant for another reason; she had an account here and had already made arrangements for the bill to be put in her name. She knew Dun was nervous about the expense.

After their drinks arrived, Dun raised his glass in the air. "Here's to you, Lucy, for putting up with me. I really appreciate working with you. Thanks for trying out this crazy PI business with me."

"You are very welcome, Mr. Wheeling." She quickly gave up trying to be formal, and started to giggle. "If anyone is appreciative, it's gotta' be me. I love working with you, even if you are a little crusty at times. However, now that Sally Olivia is safe, maybe you can settle down and get some work done."

Dun laughed. "Me? Settle down? Why Luce, I can't believe you said that."

"And, Mr. Wheeling, sir," she continued, still giggling, "while you've been off traipsing around the country and saving the world, your worthy assistant has been working her fingers to the bone bringing in the bacon."

Dun sat up in his chair. "What bacon?"

"The bacon that's going to keep us going. Unbeknownst to you, and with no help from you I might add, I've been doing some skip tracing and other little tasks that has resulted in some significant invoicing already."

"You're kidding?"

"Nope." Lucy slid a piece of paper across to table to him. It showed the invoicing and collections she had accomplished to date. Lucy was beaming like a lighthouse.

"Wow! I'm impressed. Unbelievable. This may keep us going for a while. I knew I kept you around for some reason—I just couldn't remember what it was."

Lucy turned toward Sally Olivia. "See how forgetful he is?"

Sally Olivia had been laughing and enjoying this banter. This was a far cry from the dinners she'd remembered, with Aaron's so-called friends kissing up to him as he spread money around as if it was free wine. God, how she hated that crowd. She had been with them, but never one of them. She only did it because Aaron insisted the Sawgrass family name had to be honored. Bull. That was the reason she had walked away from all of it and went to Florida without telling anyone. That's when her troubles began, and Dun walked—or rather, crashed—into her life.

She looked across the table at Dun. He was real. Honest, sincere, loyal, and a lot of fun. No wonder she loved him so.

Suddenly, she realized that Lucy was talking to her. "Sorry, I slipped off there for a moment."

"I was saying, before you nodded off, that if it weren't for me, Mr. Wheeling here would be out on the street selling fireworks in November. Right?"

Dun objected, still laughing. "Whoa, wait a minute. It's the name, Wheeling, and the fine reputation it stands for, that's really bringing in the business."

"Bullcorn! The business name isn't even in the phone book yet."

"Okay, you two," Sally Olivia interrupted, wiping the tears of laughter from her eyes, "I think that's enough. You are both very special people, and I feel very fortunate to know you. More fortunate than you'll ever know." She raised her glass. "To Dun and Lucy, and the best PI agency that ever hit the D.C. area."

After they toasted, Lucy got serious for a moment. "Dun, I've been saving a little surprise for you, in spite of my teasing." She slipped another envelope across the table toward him. "I know this doesn't make up for all you've been through, but I hope it helps."

Sally Olivia could see by the expression on Dun's face that he didn't have a clue what was in the envelope. He almost seemed afraid to open it. As he did, and unfolded the paper inside, his eyes grew wide and a smile slowly spread across his face from ear to ear.

"Holy smoke! A check from the FBI for my services. Knott must have run that through the system by hand. I can't believe it." He turned toward Sally Olivia. "Look, our first major billing."

"Yeah, it came by messenger this afternoon, while you were in your office. Sally Olivia and I decided to give it to you tonight as a little surprise."

Lucy reached across the table, squeezed Dun's hand, and then took the check out of his other hand.

"Hey! What are you doing?"

She put the envelope and check into her pocketbook. "I'm going to make sure this gets deposited in the business account, so I can look forward to a paycheck for the next month or so."

Sally Olivia sat back and watched them spar and laugh at each other. They both needed this, for it had been a tough time. Lucy had admitted to her that Dun was the son she'd never had. She could also tell that Dun had developed a special affection for Lucy. They made a good team, and she hoped she could become a part of it.

Sally Olivia tapped her water glass with her spoon. "OK, you two. My turn. If you can both stop clowning around for a moment, I've got something serious I'd like to say."

That got their attention. Dun shifted his chair, and Lucy wiped the tears from her eyes with her napkin.

"You can't imagine how much I'm enjoying this evening with you two. You've both put up with a lot because of me. Dun, you running all around and putting your life and career on the line for me. And Lucy, you backing him up and keeping the business going while he was gone."

Sally Olivia paused for a moment, thinking she was going to start to cry. As Dun started to say something, she held up her hand.

"I don't know how to say this, but I've never had friends like you. Or family, for that matter. I felt like a figurine in a music box, expected to dance when anyone looked. My family was all appearances, everything for social gains. No one was real."

Now she did start to cry, but she was determined to continue.

"I almost didn't come to this restaurant tonight because of those types of memories. My brother never backed me up; he was too busy looking out for himself. My father only hugged me when there were people or cameras around. And my mother went along with all of it because of some silly pretense about a family name."

She paused to take a sip of her drink, then looked at them both again. "In a very short time, you both have made me feel loved and welcome. Not because of my family name, or some sizable trust fund I inherited, but because I'm a person, just like you. I want you to know how much this means to me. I feel like I'm starting my life over, and I can't think of anyone more than the both of you that I want to do that with."

She raised her glass. "Thank you for my new life."

As she wiped the tears from her eyes, she realized that Dun and Lucy were doing the same. Dun stood up and walked over to her, leaned down, and kissed her on the forehead. "I'd like to second that. Me too."

Before she could respond, Dun kneeled down, pulled a jewelry box from his coat jacket, and opened it. Inside was an antique diamond ring, the most beautiful one she had ever seen.

"Sally Olivia. Before everyone in this world, I love you and want to start that new life with you. Will you marry me?"

Her heat stopped. She hadn't expected this. Was he crazy? Right here in the restaurant, in front of everyone? Then she looked in his eyes and saw the love for her there. Everything and everyone around them vanished, as if they were all in a dream.

She knew he was the one. The one she had dreamed about when she had read fairy tales as a child. The one she fantasized about when she grew older. The one kneeling before her now.

With tears gushing from her eyes, and her nose starting to run, she made her decision. "You bet, Dun Wheeling. You bet."

Dun kissed her and slipped the ring on her finger. Lucy got up from her chair and rushed over. "I'll be dammed, Dun. You sure know how to surprise a gal. Congratulations to you both."

Suddenly, wild cheers and clapping rose in a loud crescendo, as everyone in the restaurant stood up and rejoiced in the engagement. The three of them looked up, the initial surprise on their faces slowly replaced with smiles. The ovation seemed to last forever, perhaps a prophecy of this union.

CHAPTER 62

AFTER the celebration stopped, Dun and Lucy returned to their chairs, although Dun shifted his chair closer to Sally Olivia. "So much for a quiet dinner," he quipped.

Sally Olivia and Lucy looked at him, their eyes red and streaked from crying. As if on cue, they all broke out in laughter.

They finally had their act together by the time the waiter approached the table for their order. Before they ordered, Dun spoke to the waiter. "Please bring the bill to me."

"I'm sorry sir, but that won't be possible. You see, the manager asked me to tell you both congratulations, and that this meal is on the house." The waiter turned toward Sally Olivia and winked, knowing she had already requested the bill be added to her account.

Sally Olivia nodded and said, "Why, thank you. Tell the manager how much I appreciate his generosity."

"That I will, Miss Sawgrass. In fact, here comes a bottle of champagne to help you celebrate."

Dun was amazed. Initially, he was concerned about paying the bill, then Lucy surprised him with the check from the FBI, and now the manager comped the meal. Things were looking up.

Dun smiled at the waiter. "Yes, thank you. That is extremely nice."

During the meal, while they tried to include Lucy in the conversation, Dun and Sally Olivia couldn't take their eyes off each other. As they talked, she kept touching Dun and holding up her hand with the new ring.

"You shouldn't have," she whispered. "It's quite beautiful."

"I didn't. It was my grandmother's. I can't afford a ring right now, but later when things improve I'll get you a new one."

"No way. This is the most gorgeous and unusual engagement ring I've ever seen. Just try to get it back." She laughed and squeezed his hand.

"As long as I have you, nothing else matters."

When they had finished the meal and were drinking their coffee, Lucy decided to liven up the conversation somewhat. "Sally Olivia, I had hoped to tell you this before you and Dun got engaged, but there's still time."

"Oh?"

Dun groaned inwardly. What was Luce up to now?

"Well, you should know some of Dun's shortcomings before you take the final plunge. For one, Dun can be quite devious."

"Really?" Sally Olivia looked at Dun with a pretend frown.

"I can't wait to hear this one. Remember, Luce, I pay your salary."

"And remember, I have the check in my handbag." Without pausing, she continued. "Yes, devious. An example might be the time he avoided a subpoena from the collection attorneys."

"Oh, a little behind on his payments, was he?" Sally Olivia was trying to suppress a laugh, and was having trouble.

"More than a little. He was about to kiss his Miata goodbye, and you know how much that would kill him." Lucy went on to relate the story of Dun climbing out the window of his office to avoid being served, clinging to the narrow ledge on the outside of the brick building in the pouring rain, and how the pigeon poop on the ledge got real slippery when it was mixed with water. "I didn't see it happen, but after the serving agent left, Dun shows up at the front door looking like something out of a Japanese horror movie. All cut, scratched, bleeding, and covered with wet mud." Lucy was finding it hard to continue, she was laughing so hard. After a minute, she caught her breath. "He fell off the ledge, landed in a prickly berry bush, and rolled down a muddy slope." That's as far as she got, as she covered her eyes with her napkin and shook all over with laughter.

Sally Olivia looked at him. "Is that true?"

Even he had to laugh. "Yes, I'm afraid it is."

"Serves you right for not paying your bills."

"Wait!" Lucy said, trying to compose herself. "There's more."

"Oh, God. This is going to be a long night." Dun leaned forward and covered his face with his hands.

Sally Olivia leaned toward him and gave him a hug. "Be a good sport. We all need a good laugh."

"Yeah, at my expense."

"Not really. The manager is picking up the bill." Sally Olivia laughed at her own joke, as Lucy prepared to continue with the roasting.

"Another trait of Dun's is he gets easily confused. Possibly a sign of old age."

"Oh goody." Sally Olivia clapped her hands. "Tell me what happened."

"Well, when he was in Jacksonville, looking for you, he discovered a pair of his pants had a split in the rear seam."

"Lucy, I swear I'll never tell you another thing about my trips." Dun's protests were in vain, and he knew it. However, he was secretly pleased to see Lucy and Sally Olivia hitting it off so well and Sally Olivia relaxing."

Lucy seemed to ignore his threat, for she went on as if he weren't even there. "So, he takes his pants to a Chinese tailor. Wong Tailors. And being the nice guy that he is, he informs the tailor that the huge clock outside the store had the wrong time."

Sally Olivia could see this coming and began to chuckle.

"So the tailor says something like, 'Ah, that Wong clock.' And Dun says, 'No, it's the right clock, but the wrong time.'" Lucy was having a hard time controlling herself. She took a deep breath and managed a few words here and there between bursts of laughter. "'Ah so…wong…time…on Wong…clock.' And Dun, relieved that he had communicated with the man, said 'Yes, that's right.' And the tailor said, 'Wong. This Wong tailor.'"

By this time, all three of them were almost out of control. Finally, Dun ended the story. "I found out the hard way that it *was* the wrong tailor. I'll explain the rest some day, when Lucy isn't around."

Sally Olivia sat back and looked at them. "Thank you. Both of you. I haven't laughed this hard in my whole life. I will cherish this special night forever."

"I think it's time to go, while I have any semblance of credibility and sanity left." Dun stood up, held the chairs for the ladies, and followed them out to the entrance.

As they passed the maitre-d', he wished them good night and thanked them for coming. Looking at Sally Olivia, he nodded his head and said, "Nice to have you with us again, Miss Sawgrass. And congratulations on your engagement."

"Thanks, Mike. See you again, soon I hope. It was a wonderful meal."

Dun stopped and observed the conversation. As Sally Olivia caught up, he touched her arm. "You must have come here a lot."

"Yes, I did, in my other life. That's over, and my new one is just beginning." She smiled, reached up and kissed him. "I love you, Mr. Wheeling."

"And I love you, Mrs. Wheeling-to-be."

Behind them, they heard a giggle. "And I love you both, Mr. and Mrs. Wheeling-to-be."

Dun grabbed Sally Olivia by the arm and steered her toward the front entrance. "Let's get out of here before that crazy woman decides to follow us."

Dun and Sally Olivia drove Lucy back to the office so she could pick up her car. They waited until she started it and got on her away.

"Well, the future Mrs. Wheeling, what now?"

"Let's just go back to your place. Much as I like Lucy, a little privacy would be nice right now."

"Amen. Yes, she's a sweet lady, but she tells too many stories."

"Gee, I thought that was the best part of the dinner…besides my ring of course." Sally Olivia held up her ring and rotated her hand so the diamond could catch the available light. "It's so beautiful. I'm honored to be wearing your grandmother's ring, Dun."

"And I'm sure she's smiling in her grave knowing that someone as beautiful and wonderful as you is wearing it. Just wish it were a little bigger stone."

"You can't measure love by the size of a diamond, Dun. It's symbolic of love, commitment, and faith in the future. No, I don't want a bigger one. Nothing larger or smaller could replace this one. It's more than you should have done."

"Nothing is more than I should have done when it comes to you."

"That's sweet, Dun, but what you've already done for me…oh, my God, this is beginning to sound like a Lucy story!"

"You mean the Dun done bit?"

"Yes. I didn't think I could laugh anymore tonight, but here I go."

"Don't ask her about it, please."

"You mean there is a story about this?"

"Oh, yeah. I'm surprised Lucy didn't bring it up during dinner, she covered damn near everything else."

"I can see I need to spend more time with that woman."

When they arrived at Dun's apartment, he parked the SUV and walked over to check his Miata. "Tomorrow, little one, we're back together."

"Oh, talking to cars now?" Sally Olivia was right behind him.

"Nope, only this one. She's my baby."

"Boy, Lucy mentions you getting confused, then I find you talking to cars. What else can I expect?"

"You can expect me to take you over my knee, as soon as I catch you."

"Not in this lifetime, Mr. Wheeling," she said over her shoulder, laughing and already running toward the apartment stairs.

CHAPTER 63

THE next morning Dun woke early and went to the office. Sally Olivia had been sleeping like a baby and he didn't have the heart to wake her. He left her a note and the keys to his Miata in case she needed to go anywhere. He suspected she might want to go back to her place and get a few changes of clothes.

As soon as he arrived, he went into his office and retrieved the cell phone from his desk. Pacing around the office, he waited for his call to go through. Damn! No answer again.

Stuffing the phone into his pocket, he sat down and tried to figure what might have happened. Surely, Knott was okay. Maybe the incident with Cob had affected him more than Dun realized. Maybe he decided to take a short leave of absence. Or, maybe he was forced to, given he had shot a fellow agent. He didn't know the procedures with the US Marshals or the FBI, but he seemed to remember something about an investigation after every shooting. So, what was going on with Gloria and Sidney? Were they in jail, being held for an indictment?

The 'maybes' were beginning to wear him down. He either had to get another brain or find another profession. The problem, he realized, was that he wasn't in control of the events and incidents in this case. He'd spent a lot of time in the dark, and was still there.

Again, he vowed to drop this crazy Federal stuff and get back to what he had planned to do with his new agency.

He felt better making that decision.

In the outer office, he heard Lucy arrive. He stood up and opened his door. "Good morning, Luce. Hope you had a good time last night."

To his surprise, Lucy came over and gave him a hug. "Dun, I had a wonderful time. Thank you. I haven't laughed that hard since my ex-husband found out one of his new girlfriends was a transvestite."

"Really?" Dun hadn't heard this one before.

"Oh yeah, for real. Serves him right."

"He really screwed up when he left you, Luce. I mean it."

"Why, thank you. That's the nicest compliment I've had in a long time. And, speaking of compliments, you've got a keeper there. Better hang onto her. And, I promise not to tell her any more stories like last night."

Dun chuckled. "Yeah, right. And I promise to trade in my Miata for a motor bike."

"Seriously. Congratulations on your engagement. You guys make a wonderful couple. I wish you both all the best."

"Thanks. I left her at the apartment with the keys to the Miata. I forgot to ask if she can drive a 5-speed."

"Well, if she can't, you'll find out about it soon enough."

They both turned as the phone rang. Lucy moved over and picked it up. "Wheeling Associates. Lucy Cannon speaking."

Dun watched as she scribbled some note on a pad. "Just a moment, sir. I'll see if he's available."

She put the call on hold. "Do you know a Mr. Leising?"

Dun shook his head. "Not that I can remember."

"Sounds like you should take this in your office."

Dun nodded, walked into his office and picked up the phone. "Dun Wheeling."

"Mr. Wheeling, this is Pete Leising calling."

"Good morning. How can I help you?"

"Obviously, you haven't connected my name. We need to talk."

"Sure, go ahead."

"Not on the phone, I'm afraid. This isn't a secure line."

"Fine, I'll be in most of the day, so please come by my office anytime."

"I don't think you understand. I'm at the White House. I need you to meet me here."

"Mr. Leising, please don't take this wrong, but I've just finished a job with the FBI and frankly I don't need any further involvement with the Federal Government right now."

"You're speaking of Knott Harrison?"

"Yes, do you know him?"

"I did."

"Did? What's that mean?"

"It means you'd better come here as soon as possible."

He agreed to be there within thirty minutes and hung up the phone. He grabbed his jacket off the antique clothes tree he'd found at a yard sale and didn't bother to turn off his lights as he left.

"Everything OK?" Lucy could obviously tell by the expression on his face that it wasn't.

"Dunno. I have to go to the White House for a meeting. Not sure how long I'll be. If Sally Olivia calls or shows up, tell her I'll call if I'm going to be late."

Without another word, he left the building and ran to the SUV.

* * *

As Dun pulled up to the guard gate at the White House, he realized he was carrying his gun. He was nervous enough without that. He'd never been to the White House before.

"Good morning, sir. Please state your name and business." The guard looked friendly enough, which helped Dun's nerves a little.

"Dun Wheeling. Mr. Leising is expecting me."

"Really?" The guard looked at his clipboard. "I'm sorry, Mr. Wheeling, but your name—"

The phone in the guard gate interrupted him. Dun watched him answer the phone and speak in low tones. Once he glanced up at Dun, then continued speaking. Dun began to sweat. He could feel the moisture starting to collect on his arms and chest. Just what he needed.

Finally, the guard hung up the phone and returned to Dun's SUV. "I'm sorry, Mr. Wheeling, that call was about you. Someone in Mr. Leising's office forgot to notify us about your arrival." The gate started to open and the guard instructed him to drive forward and park on the right.

Just as Dun started to pull forward, he stopped. He leaned his head out the window and spoke to the guard. "I apologize. I forgot to tell you I'm a Private Investigator and I'm carrying a weapon."

The guard smiled. "Don't worry, Mr. Wheeling. You won't get very far with it. Just pull up and park."

Dun drove forward and parked as instructed. As he got out of the SUV, two men came forward and stopped in front of him. Each was wearing a dark suit, a white shirt with a conservative tie, and a cord running up behind the left ear to an earplug.

"Mr. Wheeling?"

"Yes, that's me. I suppose you want to take my weapon?"

"No. You'll give that up inside. We're here to escort you to your meeting."

"Oh." He didn't know what else to say.

He followed the men to a side entrance. Inside was another guard station. This time there were two Marines holding automatic rifles backing up the guard. Now he was really getting nervous, but actually it went smoother than he expected. He was asked to show his PI license and hand over his Beretta. He almost dropped it as he unclipped it from his belt, but the guard didn't flinch and just smiled as he handed Dun a receipt.

His escorts then herded him toward an elevator and pushed a button for the floor they wanted. Dun was surprised to feel the elevator moving slowly downward.

CHAPTER 64

THE two escorts knocked on a door and opened it. "Dun Wheeling, sir," one of them announced. Dun was ushered into the office and settled in a chair. Then the escorts left, closing the door behind them.

Dun turned to face a large man, well over six feet and probably in the neighborhood of 250 pounds. He was wearing a dark pinstriped suit, a button-down blue Oxford shirt accented with a conservative striped tie, and fancy dress loafers.

The man's facial skin was coarse, with pockmarks that perhaps indicated a childhood disease. His hair was light brown without any traces of white, but Dun guessed he was late middle-aged and probably used some kind of hair coloring.

"Pete Leising, Mr. Wheeling." The man didn't offer to shake hands, but instead sat behind a desk that was considerably larger than he was.

"Nice to meet you, Mr. Leising. I think."

The man tilted his head back and laughed. "I like that. Just call me Pete."

"Okay, Pete. Why am I here?"

"Well, Mr. Wheeling—"

"Dun."

Sure. Dun. The reason you're here is that we have a little problem I'm hoping you can help with."

"Where's Knott? I haven't been able to reach him."

"That's the first question I was going to ask you."

"What? I just saw him two nights ago. I've called several times since then and left a message on his cell phone, but he hasn't returned my calls."

"I know."

"Jesus, you sound just like Knott. What's all this bureauspeak bullshit?"

"OK. Calm down, Dun. You're under no suspicion here."

"Frankly, I never even considered that. I'd like to know what happened to Knott?"

"So would we."

Dun was losing it. Never, ever, ever would he work with these clowns again. They all spoke like men with tissue-paper assholes. "Look, all I know is that Knott hired me to work with him on a WPP case. I thought it was all over, but now you tell me you don't know where he is?"

"Yes, I'm afraid that's it. Plus, a lot more. Maybe it'll help if I ask you some questions and we go from there. This bureauspeak, as you call it, is because this is a highly sensitive area and I don't know how much you know."

"Fair enough. Fire away and I'll do my best to give you a straight answer."

Pete rubbed his hand across his mouth before starting. "First, why did Knott hire you?"

"He wanted an outside PI, someone who wasn't known to anyone he worked with. He said he couldn't trust anyone internally."

"Good, I know that. What I meant is why did he hire you, specifically?"

"Knott and I go way back. We were close buddies in high school. After that, we lost track of each other until just recently. He discovered I was in the area when he was reviewing a case I was involved with in Jacksonville."

"I saw that file. Nice work."

Dun shifted in his chair. "Thanks, though I can't take any credit. I kinda' bumbled into the whole mess."

"I'd say you are a very modest man."

"No, truthful is more like it."

"OK. What did Knott tell you about what he was doing, who he was working for, that kind of thing?"

"He said he was working for someone high up—I think he said at a level he'd never reach. He told me there was a leak in the WPP program, and that he'd been assigned to find it and plug the hole. Something about it had more implications than just the WPP program, along the lines of national security. He never explained."

"He was working for me." Pete's face was molded like a brick.

"And your job is?" Dun didn't expect an answer, but it was worth a try.

"Let's just say I work for the President, as a sort of special advisor."

"Wow. I'm impressed." Dun sat up a little straighter in his chair.

"Don't be. It's a glorified whipping post. And right now I've got the welts to prove it."

"Sorry. What else can I tell you?"

"Tell me how it played out at the end, with Cob and all that."

"They found the leak—Sidney I think his name is, a programmer in the FBI office somewhere. Seems like he got sucked in—"

"That's an understatement." For the first time, Dun saw him smile.

"Yeah. Some gal named Gloria, who gave him a long sob-story about needing information on Alex because he had lied in his testimony. Something like that. Anyway, Knott planted phony information in the file, Sidney took it to Gloria, and she in turn gave it to Cob."

"That's what he told you?" Pete's face was no longer smiling.

"Yes. He said Cob was the culprit and he set a trap for him."

"Jesus!" Pete's face looked as if all the blood had drained out. He stood up and walked from behind his desk, taking a chair opposite Dun.

Dun was totally confused. "What? Talk to me. What's wrong?"

"Cob worked for me, also."

Dun's jaw almost hit the floor. He was speechless.

"You realize that everything said here has to be held in the highest confidence."

"Sure." Dun was afraid to ask why, other than the obvious concerns for the safety of Alex.

"They both worked for me. Knott from the FBI side, Cob with the US Marshals."

Dun couldn't believe where this was going. "Knott told me Cob reported to him, that he was a little squeamish about Cob and purposely kept him out of the loop until he was sure Cob was straight."

"Cob was a highly respected individual. So was Knott. Cob complained that Knott was running away with the case, not keeping him informed. Unfortunately, I wrote that off to intra-service rivalry."

"Are you saying that Knott was behind all this?"

Pete paused for a minute before responding. "Yes."

Dun stood up and walked around the room. "I can't believe that. Could he have been set up somehow? Someone making him the fall guy?"

"Dun, we have proof that Knott has been involved for some time."

"But when Sidney hacked the information from the computer—the false information about Alex that Knott planted there—he gave it to Gloria and she took it straight to Cob."

"No. He just told you that. She took it to Knott."

Dun's knees felt like they were going to fold. He went back and sat down. "I can't believe this. Not him. Can't be true."

"Gloria was working with Knott all along."

"But, that doesn't make sense. Knott knew where Alex was; he had him safely tucked away at Quantico. Knott had multiple chances to take him out if he wanted to. Why go through all that?"

"He hoped to cover it up, push the blame on Cob. He contacted Cob, told him he had moved Alex to another safe house, and needed his help. He gave Cob the address and asked him to meet him there after dark."

Dun filled in the blanks. "And Cob came, thinking he was there to help Knott. He didn't know Knott was waiting for him in the hallway." Dun scratched the tiny scar on his chin. This was too much.

Then Dun sat up. "Hey, wait a minute! How would you know that?"

"Gloria. She told us who she took the information to."

Dun took a deep breath. "Wouldn't Knott figure Gloria would squeal? You had her in custody."

"No. Knott had her in custody. He was the only one allowed to talk to her. By the time we found out, Knott had taken her before a judge for indictment and the judge let her loose on bail. We never got a chance to question her. Until later."

"Later?"

"Yes, we smelled something fishy. We picked her up as she was about to board a plane at Dulles. Under a little pressure she confessed everything."

"So, she and Knott were planning to go away together?"

"Looks that way. They almost made it."

"God. I still can't believe this. He was my friend."

"Yes—was."

Dun shook his head. "I guess he did it for the money. Must be it. No other reason. I would have thought with his job money wasn't a problem."

"It's always a problem if you don't think you have enough of it. I suspect the payout had to be considerable for Knott to be tempted."

"Damn! His parents will be devastated."

"His parents died last year. Killed in an auto accident."

"Jesus. He never told me that. So, he has no one."

"Well, he had Gloria."

"From what I hear, she's nothing special. Guess our friendship wasn't enough."

"Don't feel bad, Dun. He wasn't in this when he first contacted you— it happened sometime after, we're not sure when."

Dun took a moment to let that sink in. He still felt gut shot. "Now what happens? You move Alex to another location?"

"No, that's over. We never have to move him again."

Dun was puzzled. "Why? You still don't know who was behind all this, who paid Knott."

"He was killed, Dun. Knott went to Quantico, took personal delivery of Alex. We found his body in a ditch, about 15 miles away. Two bullet holes in his head."

Dun just stared. He didn't know what to say. His voice wasn't working, and his mind had achieved melt down. His body started shaking and he slumped in his chair.

Pete walked over to a credenza and poured a glass of ice water. He handed it to Dun and asked, "You okay?"

"Oh, sure. One of my best friends is a killer. Killed a US Marshall and some poor guy who was trying to be a good citizen. Sucked me in, thinking I was helping. Oh, yeah, I'm just great." Dun drank a huge gulp of ice water and started choking. When Pete started over toward him, he held up his hand. Finally, he got a few words out. "I'm fine. Thanks."

Dun sat there for a few more minutes before he spoke. "I feel like I've just been kicked in the stomach by an NFL place kicker."

"I know how you feel. I went through that earlier this morning."

"No word about Knott's whereabouts?"

"Nothing. With his experience, he'll be damn hard to find. We think he's already left the country."

"I hope he never comes back."

"So do I, Dun. So do I. For his sake."

They both sat there in silence. Dun wanted to get up, scream at the top of his lungs, and run out the door. But he forced himself to focus on the business at hand. "Ah, there are a couple of items we need to clear up."

"The SUV?"

Damn, this guy didn't miss a trick. "Yeah, and a cell phone and an American Express card."

"I'll send someone over tomorrow to pick them up. Just leave the vehicle open and everything in the glove compartment. We'll take care of it."

"OK. I'll be glad to get rid of them. One other thing, there is an outstanding invoice for out-of-pocket expenses Knott...ah, he asked me to send in."

"Send it to me, personally. I'll take care of it."

"Thanks. That's about it. Can't think of anything else. Ah...I can go?"

"Sure, Dun. Thanks for coming in. I'm sorry about what happened. I appreciate your cooperation."

"No problem. Just do me one favor."

"What's that?"

"Don't call me and ask if I can help out with a case."

Pete half-smiled as he shook Dun's hand. "I understand." He then pushed a button and the two escorts immediately walked into the room.

CHAPTER 65

DUN pulled out of the White House gate and made two right-hand turns to get back toward Route 1 south toward Alexandria. While he was proud of the city, its history, and magnificent monuments, he cursed the street planners for turning the original grid pattern layout into a labyrinth from Hell. It was impossible to get from one point to another without running into one-way streets, restricted lanes for commuters, and traffic lights that made the whole area look like a giant pinball machine. He suspected the street planners were former IRS forms designers.

He found he had to force himself to focus on his driving. His brain was mush. It had gone into a self-imposed coma right after he left the meeting. His body was trembling and his hands shaking as he tried to steer the huge SUV through city traffic. The only thing he knew for sure was that he needed to get away, go somewhere and get drunk, and lie in the sun and let it suck out all the conflicting emotions from his body.

At least he had Sally Olivia to lean on. Thank God for that.

As he rounded a rotary near the Tidal Basin, a man stepped out from behind a tree and walked toward the curb. Dun almost ran off the road in shock. It was Knott!

Dun cut across two lanes of traffic, incurring the wrath of shouts, threats, and blaring horns, to take the next left. He circled around to get back onto the street where he had seen Knott and pulled into the first parking spot he found. He was lucky, it was just large enough to park the SUV.

Knott wasn't in sight anywhere. He turned in his seat and looked out every window. No sign of him. Maybe he was seeing things. All the pressure and emotional strain was coming to a head. He rubbed his eyes and looked again. Still finding no trace of Knott, he opened the door and stepped out.

His heart was beating like a tom-tom, with the pulses in his forehead throbbing to the point he felt they would burst. He must have been mistaken. Knott was surely out of the country by now. Long gone. Why would he hang around and take the risk of being seen and arrested?

However, if that was Knott, why was he here? Did he want to talk to Dun, proclaim his innocence, protest that he had been framed, and ask for his help? He hoped so.

Then another thought occurred to him. What if Knott were trying to lure him into a trap? What if he felt Dun was a liability and could help the FBI track him down? What then? Would Knott try to kill him?

If he had killed Cob and Alex, and God knows who else, would an old friendship stand in his way? He didn't know. And he wasn't sure he wanted to find out.

Dun moved around the front of the SUV and walked across the grass to the sidewalk. This was a beautiful area of D.C., with thick rows of Cherry trees, park benches, and a rail around the Tidal Basin where you could look across to the Jefferson Memorial. At the right time of year, this whole area was packed with people tighter than a blocked intestine.

Dun looked to his left and right, but saw no sign of Knott. A little nervous now, he walked toward an old stone building that had been the gatehouse for the canal than had once run through here. It was surrounded by dense trees and a high spear-tipped iron fence. Dun came up on the backside of the building and peered around the corner to his left.

As he stepped around the corner, he felt someone tap him on the shoulder. He froze, his body going rigid.

"Excuse me, sir," a tiny voice behind him spoke, "can you help me?"

Dun whirled around, almost scaring the little old lady standing just behind him. She barely came up to his waist and couldn't have weighed fifty pounds if she was carrying two grocery bags full of can goods.

He felt the air escape from his lungs. "I'm sorry, ma'am. You startled me. What can I do to help?"

The woman smiled, reached into her handbag, and pulled out a one-pound bar of chocolate. Soon she would weigh only forty-nine pounds.

"I'm selling this to raise money for my granddaughter in Michigan, so she can come to D.C. next spring on a class trip."

Dun smiled at the tiny woman. "Of course, how much?"

"They are $1.00 each. Would you like more than one?"

"No." Dun reached into his wallet and almost smiled at the disappointment on her face. "I really don't eat much chocolate, but I'll donate $5.00 to the cause. You keep the bars and sell them to someone else."

"Why, thank you, sir. That's very generous of you."

"You're very welcome. I hope your granddaughter gets to take the trip. Everyone should see this fine city."

"And the nice people here, as well." She smiled her gratitude, took the money, nodded, and went on her way.

As Dun was placing his wallet back in his pants, another voice came from behind him. "Hi Dun. That was sweet of you." Dun recognized the voice and froze again.

He felt like he was playing musical chairs, freezing in place when the music stopped. Only in this case it was when the words began.

Without turning around, Dun responded. "Well, guess who's here? I'm hearing bad stories about you; I hope they're not true."

Without any apology in his voice, Knott confessed, "It's true, Dun. All of it."

Dun slowly turned around and faced the man he had once felt to be a close friend. Was it possible for someone like Knott to turn that way? Or, had it happened a long time ago, before Dun had run across him again? He'd probably never know.

Knott continued. "I wanted to talk to you personally, so you got it straight from me."

"How'd you know I'd be coming this way?"

"It's the only direct route back to Alexandria. I took a chance. I needed to talk to you before I go."

Dun was still frozen in place with his left hand on his wallet that was half-in his back pocket. "Aren't you afraid you'll be recognized and arrested?"

"Naw. Those guys are looking for me at all the airports and other transportation terminals. They'd never think I'd still be in the city. I know how they think, and most often they don't."

Dun eased his hand off his wallet, grabbed his Beretta, and brought it around pointing directly at Knott's chest. Knott didn't even flinch. He looked directly at Dun and smiled. "I don't think you'll use that. Not on me. You're not a killer."

"No, I'm not. But you are. The killer of two people that didn't have a chance, both of whom trusted you. Like I did."

"Did?"

"Yeah, Knott. Did, with a capital D."

"You have no need to be afraid of me, Dun. Unless, of course, you try to take me in."

The tone of Knott's voice left no doubt that Dun would have to shoot him, at least enough to temporarily cripple him if he were to try to take him in. "Why'd you do it?"

"I got in too deep. No excuses, I brought it all on myself. Before I knew it, there was no other way out."

"Oh, yes, there was. But that involved giving yourself up and you weren't man enough to do that. You chose to kill instead."

Knott's eyes narrowed and Dun tensed for an attack. But it never came. Knott's shoulders sagged a little and he looked away before he spoke.

"You're right. That was an option. But not for me. A Federal man in prison becomes a target for every psychopath and pervert in the place. A long, slow death. Trust me."

Dun thought about it and guessed Knott was right. A former FBI agent in any prison would be marked as surely as if he had a huge target painted on his chest . . . or some other part of his body.

"Maybe you could have worked a deal, bargained for some other place where you would have been safer."

"C'mon, Dun. Face it. I'd be publicly crucified, draped on a hook, and offered as a sacrifice by the FBI as proof that they run a tight ship with zero tolerance."

"Jesus, there must have been some other way. Must have been." Dun didn't want to admit even to himself that his high school friend had turned into a fiend. A killer.

"I'm sorry. I didn't see any other way out. You won't believe this, but it bothers me that I can kill so easily. A decision to be made and then do it. I've come a long way since high school, and all of it has been down hill."

"I'm gonna' have to take you in. You know that."

"No, I don't. You won't use that gun on me. Your conscience would tear you apart if you did. You and I are different now. You've turned into something I'd like to be, and never can be. I've turned into something that's far beyond your capability, thank God for that. At least one of us made it."

Dun's arm started to grow tired, and the Beretta wavered slightly. He struggled to keep it steady, but it was like holding a broom straight out in front by the end of the handle.

"I've got to go. But, before I do, I wanted you to know I never intended any harm to come to you. If I had ever thought that was a possibility, I would have given myself up, in spite of the consequences. All the best to you, buddy." Without a word, Knott turned and walked away.

Dun raised his pistol and placed the sight right in the center of Knott's back. But he didn't fire, and knew he couldn't. He lowered the Beretta and watched a part of his life walk away.

* * *

On the way back to his office, Dun started shaking again. He pulled over to the side of the road and sat there, staring out the windshield. He couldn't believe what he'd just done. He let a criminal, a killer, walk away. That he was a former friend didn't matter. He'd sworn an oath to uphold the law, and didn't. Sure, he could excuse it by rationalizing that Knott was a trained killer and probably would have overpowered him if he tried. Still, no excuse. No excuse. He laid his head back on the headrest and closed his eyes.

If it had been anyone else, he would have tried to take the person into custody, even if he thought his own safety would be in jeopardy. It was only because Knott had been his friend and he was still in shock over what he'd learned from Leising that he'd let him walk away. Was this the kind of conflict he would face being a PI? If so, he wanted no part of it. He'd find something else to do.

He kept his eyes closed and tried to flush everything from his mind. Damn guilt, it never goes away. He opened his eyes and was startled to see a face peering in the driver's side window at him.

"Hey, buddy, no parking here. Move it." The policeman stepped back and waited for him to move his vehicle. Dun waived, started the engine, and pulled out into the traffic.

"Buddy." He hoped he never heard that word again.

* * *

When he pulled up in front of his office, he realized he couldn't remember driving there. His mind felt like two hundred pounds of molten lead. He shut off the engine, placed the keys, credit card, and cell phone in the glove compartment, and closed the door behind him. It was like a part of his life flushed down the toilet, a bad dream that he was sure wouldn't go away for a long, long time.

He walked into the office to find Sally Olivia and Lucy staring at him. He guessed the look on his face was enough to shut off their words. He stood there, not knowing what to say, where to begin, how much he could tell them.

Finally, he sat in an empty chair facing them. "I've just come from a meeting at the White House. I can't tell you everything because some of it's classified. However, none of it is good news."

Sally Olivia got up and came over to him. "You don't have to tell us anything, Dun. Let's just go back to your place and you can lie down for a while."

Dun looked up at her. "Can't. I've got to get this off my chest."

Sally Olivia didn't say a word. She sat on the floor beside him and put her hand in his.

"Looks like my friend Knott was behind the whole thing. From almost the beginning." His voice started to crack, but he forced himself to go on. "He set up Cob as the fall guy...and I was there, part of it." He lowered his head and placed one hand over his eyes.

He started to go on, but Sally Olivia reached up and put her fingers over his lips. "We know all about it, Dun."

Dun lifted his head. "What? You know? How could you?"

"Knott sent you an email this morning, just after you left." Sally Olivia handed him a sheet of paper containing the printed message.

He picked it up and tried to read it, but his eyes were moist and blurry. He handed it back to Sally Olivia to read.

"Dun, by the time you get this you will have heard what happened. I know you must be in shock and feel one of your lifetime friends has betrayed you. Believe me, I didn't intend for it to end this way. I honestly wanted your help in the beginning, but then a temptation came along that could change my whole life.

"I'm sorry, but it was bigger than I could resist. My family was gone, and my former wife remarried with children. The children I never had. And probably never will. This was a chance to start over, and live comfortably for whatever time I've got left.

"Another killing didn't seem to matter, considering what I've done in the past. Too late to worry about final consequences.

"Somehow it all got out of hand and I had no other choice. It was the only way out at that point; I was in too deep. Thank God, you didn't get hurt in the process.

"I'm heading out of the country and won't ever be back. This may seem distasteful, but I wish you and Sally Olivia all the best and hope you are blessed with long lives and wonderful children.

"I will think of you often, and regret that you will be trying to forget all about me. But I've brought that on myself, and will have to live with it.

"Take care, buddy.

"Knott."

Sally Olivia handed the message back to Dun. "Where do you think he'll go?"

Dun couldn't look at her. "I've failed Alex…and you, Sally Olivia."

"Oh, Dun, don't go there—"

He held up his hand for her to stop. "I just saw him. In D.C. Standing on the side of the road. Like somehow he knew I'd be coming that way. I prayed it was all a mistake, that he'd been framed or something. No . . . he admitted everything."

Dun leaned over again and slowly shook his head from side to side. "I had my gun on him, but couldn't use it…I let him walk away."

He stared at the email message for a moment, then ripped it into small pieces and threw them on the floor.

Printed in the United States
19952LVS00002B/72

9 781589 612051